About the Author

Penny Deacon was born in Scotland, christened in Dorset and first went to school in Sri Lanka. Wandering has always been part of her life and, though she thinks she's now settled in the West Country, she wouldn't be surprised to find herself on the move again.

It may have been the long sea voyages to and from Sri Lanka which triggered her love of sailing and the sea – a love which led to spending ten years following her graduation from Oxford living aboard a yacht. During this time she and Sebastian The Cat sailed twice to the West Indies.

To earn a living Penny has taught sailing and English and dredged for oysters. More recently she has been a school librarian as well as a writer.

Penny has always written – journals and diaries, short stories and romantic novels, and even a couple of management workbooks – but *A Kind of Puritan* is her first venture into crime. She hopes to become involved with Humility's adventures again very soon.

1

Beneath the oily scum of the water's surface the jointed neck bent and stretched. The mouth gaped. Teeth closed on ooze and debris and decaying matter and tore it free from the clinging river bed. Messages from the weighted jaw told the neck to lift and swivel until it could spit its load on to the waste ground opposite the harbour.

Each mouthful brought up junk thrown or dropped into the water and too heavy for the tide to swirl away. Old oildrums and outdated machinery; a sunken raft not worth the salvage; something which might have been anything, long past identifying; and a cable, still new enough to be tough for the teeth to sever.

It took three bites before one end of the cable broke and the thing it held slithered free. It had almost slipped from between the jaws before it caught and hung, white and bloated and flaccid, half out of the teeth which lifted it from the water.

2

"*Shit.*"

No one except a one-legged gull took any notice but I hadn't been speaking for anyone else's benefit. It's just that a stubbed toe inspires comment. I sat down clutching my foot and tried not to remember Jack's voice telling me, yet again, how dumb it was to go barefoot on a boat.

"Where else? I'm not fool enough to try it on shore."

He'd shrug and grin and pretend to light the foul thing he called a pipe. Why he couldn't chew or sniff or shoot his drugs like everyone else I never did find out. Never asked. But if I'd listened to him perhaps I wouldn't have half-broken my toe on a cleat and wouldn't have been sitting on a coil of wet rope staring down river at just that moment.

No one would have cared. Not the Net or Eurogov or the Corps, not even the God my mother still believes in. Certainly not Jack's long-dead bones. You can't change things. However hard you try.

I never learn. Jack said that, too.

The dredge was on a flat yellow barge between me and the sunset. Somewhere on shore an operator had long since been bored into stupor by mindless repetition, the surveillance of this and thirty other identical machine-beasts which needed no watching. It stopped when it had to, when proximity alarms told it of passing traffic, and then went obediently on with its work. On the whole, the machine's job was more interesting than its operator's.

I watched the monotonous programme: the precisely timed passes as it dipped beneath the water and rose again with the same weight of dripping silt to be dropped in neat alignment with the oozing heap from the previous pass. Two passes. Three. There was something hypnotic about the way the black silhouette moved against the low sun. It was only when it swung aside from that glare to dump each load that I could see any details. My head was swinging with the crane arm, the throbbing in my toe easing to dullness, as I watched the end of the fourth pass.

Then I was shouting at the phone. It heard the three numbers and dialled me into the Port alarm. Everything stopped: the crane gantries halted mid-swing, the grumble of the recyclers ceased, even the plodding thud of the pumps clearing mud and water from the newly dredged marina went silent. The phone squawked back at me as I watched the dredge's contents dribble out from half-opened jaws. The last bit of rubbish caught briefly between the iron teeth before it flopped on to the wet muck beneath. It was too far off to hear but I knew what sound it made.

And the sea gave up the dead which were in it.

"Humility? That you?"

Daisy's face was a bluish blur in the small screen but I didn't need hi-definition to know about its expression.

"Me."

"What the fuck are you up to? Do you want to put the Port into penalty time?"

"Depends. What's the penalty for dredging up dead bodies?"

Silence. Then, cautious, "Say again?"

I grinned. "You heard. The dredge downstream from me just snagged itself a corpse."

3

She swore again. Then I heard her muffled shout down another line: "Number seven dredge. Take it off-line then get the rest of the system back up." Daisy was always practical. "I'll send someone out. *You*," she added, back on my line, with an emphasis holding little friendship, "can transfer over here. Right now."

I'd need shoes after all. Even as I pulled them on, the bored operator in the room back in the grey Port building would have been startled alert – by alarm or light or minor shock – and I didn't suppose he or she would be any more grateful for my interference than Daisy.

I'd only been back in the Midway Port a day. Once I'd persuaded the Harbour Master he had a cheap niche for *The Flying Pig*, there had only been a couple of reasons to go ashore. I hadn't been into the city yet. It could wait. Cities are good at waiting.

3

There was a new tekkie on security at the main entry.

"ID?"

I let the scanner's eye swing level with mine. Stared at it. Scanner communication is strictly one-way. It told me nothing about itself.

The tekkie was bored. Then he read his printer and looked at me, really *looked*, for the first time. I knew what was coming.

"New Puritan, eh?"

"No." My turn to be bored.

"With a name like that?"

"I didn't choose my name. My parents christened me."

"Christened?" The heavy frown cleared. "You mean Named."

I didn't. I meant christened. Children are Named when they get their IDs, within hours of birth these days when you're still wet and helpless. That's when they put in the chip that lets the state know you're alive and will one day be able to pay their taxes. Where I come from, they reserve judgement on you as someone worth calling a person for at least six months. *Then* you're christened. The non-Persons? Don't ask.

Anyway, I wasn't going to explain any of that to this tekkie who was labouring his way through the rest of my ID display, comparing my image with its reality. I slung my weight solidly on my left hip and returned the survey levelly enough to remind him that my 180 centimetres gave me a four centimetre advantage. I might not have been up to his weight - most of which he carried around the straining belt displaying his credit status as well as his paunch – but working a boat keeps you fit. And perhaps the red hair should have given him a warning about temperament. What the grey eyes and freckles did for him I didn't want to know.

He looked up, small eyes saying he was willing to show a primitive the delights of civilisation

"Where's Jon?" I asked before he had time to put in his bid.

"What Jon?"

"The one who was doing your job last time I was here."

The display would have told him when that was, even if it didn't say Jon had been a lot better company. The tekkie shrugged, bored again.

"Who cares? Must've been another drifter."

Whose drifting had opened up a hole for this bonehead. Jon's file had been cleared. Happens all the time.

"*Are you going to spend all night out there?*"

Daisy's voice from the second screen, the one which gave her access to the entry, and this one did have hi-def. The irritation was more marked than ever. It worried the tekkie more than me, but at least he cleared me through with no more comment than another snigger over my name. I ignored it and went on through the grey door swinging open into the grey lobby. The Company didn't waste imagination or paint on functional decor.

Daisy's office was grey, too. She was sitting on the grey swivel chair, booted feet on the grey worksurface. Around her the dull grey luminescence of screens which could be brought to life with a brush of her palm and, always within view, the single masterscreen with its constantly changing display of figures. She might seem to ignore it, but I knew she'd spot it instantly if anything unusual entered the matrix.

I never knew where to sit in that place. I didn't like watching the screen but I didn't quite trust my back to it either. I don't like interactive systems.

In the end I hitched one hip on a corner and waited.

"They've got the body." Daisy never bothered with polite noises, but it was more than three months since we'd met and I had expected at least a greeting. Except she wasn't pleased to see me. "I thought you were joking."

I wasn't clear if it was my sense of humour or the fact that I hadn't been exercising it after all which was getting to her. Best to say nothing. That didn't go down well either. She swung her feet to the floor and stood up. She was taller and broader than me, and there wasn't room in the office for her to take more than one stride across the floor, but I got the picture. Exasperation.

"OK. So you weren't joking. I wish you had been. Then I could just have emptied your credit account."

"It's already empty."

She wouldn't be doing her job if she didn't know that, and Daisy was always on top of the job.

"Then I could have kicked you out of the Port. Let you and that antiquated rustheap sail off to wherever it was you were last thrown out of."

"France. Bordeaux."

A brief flicker of interest. Daisy knew what cargo I carried. But not even the thought of several litres of something drinkable was going to distract her from today's crime.

"Why did it have to be *you*? Anyone with any sense would have ignored it. Hell, they wouldn't even have *seen* it. Another line of loads and it would have been buried under two hundred tonnes of sludge and no one would have had to open any sort of file. Now what have I got?"

"What?"

"A dead male. Unidentified. No match with any Missing file and peeps crawling all over the place. *And* a dredge I can't use till the mess is sorted."

That hurt most. One dredge out and the plans for the new dock were set back by a time I'd guess any one of the terminals in here could calculate down to the last nano-second, with penalty clauses for late completion no doubt queuing up. The Corps didn't like delays and were quick to find someone to blame. I saw her point.

"Why the peeps?" No one brought the police into official business if they could avoid it.

"Because they've got the contract for first go at any sudden deaths. If it's murder they'll be on a bonus – and probably getting payback from some entrepreneur dealing in Company shares who wants to hear of any trouble we might have. *When* I can persuade them it's an accident, no doubt they'll let Port security in to do the job they're paid for and tidy it all up. Meanwhile, time's wasting."

I could see that hurt. She glared at me. Seeing the peeps she couldn't control.

"Damn them. This is *Company* business." She had too much sense of propriety to use the slang term for any of the Companies controlled by Europe's major Families.

"A Corps corpse?"

She didn't laugh. I didn't blame her. But she was taking it harder than I'd expected. When I was last here in late Feb she'd been eating little problems like this for breakfast and then looking round for more. Sometime since then she'd lost her appetite.

"Daisy?"

"What?"

"What's up?"

She hadn't looked at me since I'd walked in. Now she sat down again, slumped even, and stared hard.

"Haven't you heard? I thought the Port was full of it."

"I only got in this morning. Besides, I don't have your advantages."

Daisy has thought me deprived and abused ever since she found out I wasn't fully Netlinked. I had a basic ID, of course, but no one from my community had any of the upgrades which could link you to anything from the stock market to permanent porn or on-line shopping. We'd argued about what constituted a proper upbringing, and the propriety of regularly augmenting implants, since we first met and were never likely to agree. Jack and I had sailed *The Flying Pig* into Midway in late summer six years back. Daisy had just been brought in as Port Officer and was determined to learn all she could about the misfits who floated on to her territory. We'd been even more broke than usual, the epitome of all Daisy despised – feckless and irresponsible. Against odds that even Jack wouldn't have taken on, we'd become friends. She'd even found me some paying work, though when she'd heard about my upbringing she'd come as near as I've ever seen her to giving up.

A healthy, happy childhood free from techno-input and full of clean air and natural food is a great idea. It is also worse than useless when you leave home and look for a job. Of course, I hadn't been expected to leave home. Home was the Wessex New Puritan Community and the return for all that healthy growing was my adult input into the Community. But after one look at my chosen Life Partner, I'd decided to default on my debt. I ran away to sea.

It's a little old-fashioned, but what do you expect from a New Puritan?

"So," I persisted, "since I don't have a chip in my skull keeping me on line with all the gossip, are you going to tell me what's wrong?"

"Apart from the odd body in a dredge?"

"As well as."

"Someone's trying to wreck me or the Port, that's what. Or else I'm off my head. Same bottom line, however you balance it, and my job's on it. Hell, Humility, I shouldn't even still *be* here."

I knew what she meant. I'd been surprised to get a mooring as easily as I had done because I'd assumed she'd already bought her way out. She'd been well in line for it last year and Daisy wasn't easily put off from a chosen course.

"So what did you do wrong? Bed the wrong woman or foul up with the Corps?"

I knew she hadn't done the former. Daisy would make a better Puritan than my mother. Her partnership with Sheba had been solid for five years. Fouling up at work was even less likely. Like I said: a good Puritan.

"I *don't* foul up!"

"So who has?"

"If I knew do you think I'd be sitting here worrying about it?"

No. Solutions to little matters like incompetence or industrial sabotage were both quick and permanent. Daisy might be a Company woman but she'd been running the Midway Port long enough to have tapped into the local net. She could easily arrange to delete that sort of virus without troubling even the Company peeps. The Feds didn't bother with provincial problems, nor did the Corps – unless revenue was affected. If it was they'd be looking for the source soon. And Company investigations weren't noted for delicacy or concern for the individual. No wonder Daisy was worried: she could see herself being wiped.

"So tell me what you do know."

"I don't even *know* if there's anything to tell. All I am sure of is that there've been so many minor 'incidents' in the past two months that revenue's down twenty points and falling. If I can't block the hole – if there *is* a hole – I'm going to find myself transferred to checking out the Channel Tunnel for unwanted pets and vagrants with communicable diseases."

Few jobs were more dead-end. In every way. Since the bombing after the twenties food riots, the Chunnel was almost derelict, certainly not a place to venture near on your own. I'd heard it was still possible to get a ride through, but whether you or your credits would still be whole at the other end was debatable: it depended on who you knew and where you scattered the bribes. You certainly didn't travel alone, and only people who had nowhere else to go and nothing to lose lived round the Mouth. I'm glad I've my own way of crossing.

I stared at Daisy. She was always neat: coveralls sharp-edged, hair clipped short, the single flamboyant earring the only non-Company note about her. Alert, wired to everything around her. Today the earring was a plain stud and the control looked more like hi-tension. She really was worried and I didn't like it.

"You want help?"

It was a cautious offer. She was more touchy than a cit about privacy and, besides, you didn't let outsiders in on Company business. But there'd been something in her voice I couldn't ignore. Desperation. I knew how it felt. And it had been Daisy who'd picked up the pieces four years ago.

She'd found a berth for me when I'd sailed in with Jack's body in the hold and no credit in my account. She'd paid for the berth, found me temporary work and put me in touch with the people who dealt in the sort of freight the *Pig* could carry. The sort who were more concerned with security and discretion than with the time the transfer took. Nothing very illegal. Strictly borderline. Jack would have hated it: "*You're* trading, *girl! Where's your sense of adventure?*"

"*Buried, Jack.*"

I could never repay her. Didn't try. From time to time I brought her souvenirs of my travels – in addition to the regular free samples of the cargo. Last year I'd found a bundle of old lace down on the western Iberian coast. Daisy had given it to Sheba, her partner. Perhaps that was why I'd got the berth here this time, despite the hollow bleat from my credit chip and the known feelings of the Harbour Master. But I still owed her.

Unfortunately her current problem didn't sound the sort of thing I could help with. Not if it was Company business and certainly not if it involved anything techno.

I was on the Net to the extent that everyone was. It read my ID and knew I existed and noticed if I failed to pay taxes – but beyond that we ignored each other. Daisy knew that as well as I did.

It showed in the twist of her mouth and the shrug she gave, thumbs tucked in the belt of her coverall. A gesture which had once been bold but today looked helpless. The uncharacteristic speed with which her anger had drained away alarmed me.

"I don't suppose you can help. But I am glad you're here, despite the corpse. It's good to talk to someone who doesn't want my job."

I laughed. The Port would shut down in a week if I ran it. And I wouldn't care. Daisy's mouth smiled but she wasn't finding it funny. *She* cared.

"So tell me about it."

Whatever she was about to tell me was lost. A buzzer sounded and she glanced across at the screen which had flickered into life. She sighed.

"Come on. I'll introduce you to my other problem."

He was waiting in the outer lobby where the vids screened visitors and assessed their status. I wondered whether Daisy would have let this one into the office if I hadn't been there. That she chose to go out to him rather than talk over the screen told me something. I wasn't sure what.

I disliked him on sight. He had that sleek look of someone who'd never had to discover what life was like on the streets, cruising an empty credit chip. Besides, technocrats always annoy me and he was techno from the smooth soles of his New View boots to the elegant circuitry traced in gleaming white against the black of his hairless skull.

13

He'd change it next week just when someone had begun to think it meant something. I knew his type: the ones who can afford every possible implant and who get more kicks from long, intimate conversations with obscure subsets of Net life than from any human interchange. I was surprised he bothered with anything as slow as regular speech.

Daisy knew how I felt. It showed in the wariness in her voice when she introduced us.

"Humility. Meet Byron."

"Byron Cody," the soft voice amended as he bowed slightly, ironically. I got a closer view of the circuitry which still meant nothing at all. Typical 'crat: the almost insulting addition of his formal name which said he had no need to conceal his Net address. Or that it was so well hidden he could afford to be open. "Pleased to meet you, Humility."

I wasn't going to give him another name even if he was free with his. I wasn't even sure I could claim another. I'd never shared Jack's and hadn't yet found a need to choose one. The one I was born with had gone when I left the Community and they Shunned me.

I waited for the 'crat to make the same comment as the tekkie. Was infuriated when it didn't come.

"Byron." I nodded.

I'd take bets he didn't know a thing about his namesake. Technocrats don't *read*. Not that Puritans are meant to read Old Romantic poetry, but Jack had been a man of many interests. As long as they didn't interfere with the gambling.

Daisy glared at me as though she'd added telepathy to her skills. She didn't want this man upset. I'd ask about that later.

"Byron's here for an audit."

That explained a lot. Routine audits didn't demand the presence of anyone with the sort of capacity I'd guess this man possessed. So this was anything but routine. Whether it was because of Daisy's recent problems or just one more to add to them, it spelt trouble.

Whatever Daisy had wanted to tell me would have to wait. She wasn't going to discuss work problems in front of someone who was obviously here to find out how serious they were.

Nor was I. "Come over to the *Pig* when you've finished here. I've some stuff you might like."

Let Byron make what he wanted of that. If he'd scanned her file he'd know Daisy was clean. More important to me, no one was going to overhear any conversation we might have on the boat. Not unless he had an ear against the hull.

Daisy nodded. Understanding. "If I can."

"I'll call Sheba. Say hello and warn her you might be late."

Daisy gave the first real grin since I'd walked into her office. "She'll want to kill you."

She always does.

4

The Flying Pig is an old rig. Fifteen metres long, steel-built at the end of the last century more than fifty years ago, still capable of carrying sail if you aren't in any hurry. She also has a drive which is mercifully free of circuitry and which I can usually repair myself. I live in the after deckhouse and the small cabin below. There's one other cabin and a washroom. The rest is hold space. It's taken up at the moment by the spare tank I'd put in two years ago with the credits I'd earned from an earlier cargo, which hadn't been as risky as the man offering the contract had assumed. Though I'd come out well ahead on the deal, I'd decided you don't get that lucky twice. Besides, I'd already planned what cargo I'd carry if I could choose. So I had the tank put in. It had finished paying for itself on the last run. Which left me broke but out of debt. Better than Jack could ever have claimed. I wondered if he was disappointed in how I'd turned out.

I had plenty of time before Daisy arrived. Not only time for the pale orange glow which passes for darkness round the city to settle in well, but time to cook and set out a bottle and glasses. Time to pour myself a drink and watch the vid. The usual gameshows and lotteries. I surfed channels. A newscast showed a funeral. *News?* It's only news when it's Family. The dozens who die in the streets don't even get listed on the statistics. But when it's someone who's part of one of those great groups who run Eurogov, own all the major Companies, and call themselves by the misleadingly cosy name of Families, then it's News.

I only kept this one on while they showed the usual obit highlights of her life because she was a minor Vinci. Same Family as owned the Port. She'd been beautiful, of course. If she hadn't been born that way the Family's body-sculptor would have put that right. She'd also been young: didn't look much over twenty. Death that early was common enough on the streets. In a Family it was unusual.

"Humility?"

Daisy calling from the dockside. Wise. The *Pig* may not have many of the refinements which most people consider essential, but she did not welcome unannounced callers.

I told the vid to shut itself off and disarmed the *Pig*'s systems. "Come aboard."

She walked warily. She'd been tipped into the harbour once before and, as she'd told me when I'd hauled her out and left her coughing over the rails, swallowing that water could seriously damage your health.

I didn't ask any questions until she was sitting in her usual place, body slumped deep in the too-soft chair bolted to the deck under the starboard window, feet up on my chart table, a glass of red in her hand. Even then I waited until she'd drained it and wordlessly accepted a refill.

"Taste it this time," I recommended.

Her hand tightened on the glass. Good that it wasn't crystal. Then she relaxed, sighed, took a sip.

"This," she decided at last, "is the best thing that's happened in weeks. How much have you got for me?"

I thought of the full tank. "Enough."

"Good. Perhaps Sheba will forgive you after all when I

return home drunk."

"Who said anything about getting drunk?" I didn't bother to ask why it was me, not Daisy, who'd be blamed.

"I did."

I switched off the micro. I wasn't hungry anyway. "So. Are you going to tell me what's been happening round here?"

It was a long story. More than one bottle long. But I understood why it was driving Daisy mad. Too many small things had gone wrong: the files wiped because no one had backed them up and the power had gone out; the delayed arrival of urgent freight; the unexpected arrival of perishables when storage was unusually full; the usual minor breakdowns just when things *had* to run smoothly.

"Sabotage?"

She added one more scar to the chart-table's chipped surface as she dropped her feet to the deck. "How the hell do I know? Nothing's happened that can't be shrugged off as 'one of those things'."

"Until you add them all together."

"That's it. And I don't even know if I'm still looking at a total that doesn't exist. I could just be having a lousy year to make up for the past few good ones."

"I didn't know you were superstitious."

"I'm not. Perhaps I'm just not coping too well with this damn development."

I looked through the darkened porthole. I could see the unmoving lights of number seven dredge. Further downstream the sweep of lights showed where the other dredges went on with their work. I wouldn't have been sorry to see them all stopped.

I'd always liked Midway best of the three Solent Ports.

Sutton and Pompey are overcrowded warrens, but here at the heart of the haphazard sprawl of city there are still a few places where a river or creek flows sluggishly through saltings which no one thinks worth developing. This harbour had been one of them till the Family which owns it, after ignoring it for years, had come up with the unlikely idea that recreational boating could become fashionable again here – if the scenery and facilities were suitably adjusted, of course. The development had been going on for over a year now, the substantial investment – in prestige as much as credit – meaning rapid advancement for Daisy. If she was beginning to doubt her own abilities she was even more worried than I'd guessed.

"And I'm a software specialist."

She laughed. "All right. So I don't really think I'm imagining things. But I still don't understand *why*. And your find this afternoon hasn't helped anything," she added, remembering the grudge she had against me.

The body. I refilled her glass. "Another 'accident'? Do you know who he is, *was*, yet?"

She shook her head, staring down into the glass as though it might offer some answers.

"The ID'll show up in the postmortem, won't it? Or was he so badly damaged that..?" I didn't like to think of the sort of injuries which would make someone's ID unreadable.

Daisy wasn't squeamish.

"I suppose they'll salvage it. But I still wish you hadn't seen him. I could have dealt with a casual body but the minute you slammed on the port's alarms it made everything official. The postmortem's only going to add to that."

"Perhaps it'll confirm he just fell in and drowned,"

I offered. Although I'd known since I saw the legs flopping from the dredge that it wasn't true.

"You don't 'just fall in' stark naked. Not unless the parties round here are wilder than they're reported. Particularly not when you've been hit on the back of your head."

Events must have moved on since I left her with Byron, the techno. I understood her mood now. Drownings were routine in a Port and wouldn't cut much into anyone's schedule. Casual killings in the city's backstreets were common. But murder on Company turf? That was different. That was the sort of thing the Family would want to know nothing or everything about, and it had become too late for them to know nothing the moment I phoned it in.

"Investigator coming?"

Someone more ruthless than the irritating but ineffectual peeps or the Company's regular security staff, I meant.

Her mouth tightened and she reached for the bottle I'd left handy between us as though that might rinse away the bad taste. "Already here."

It took me a minute. Then I realised who she meant.

"*Him?*"

She nodded.

"I thought he was meant to be an auditor?"

"I don't know what he is. I can't find out. He's been through every program in the place and now he wants to know about this body! That's why he'd arrived when you met him. I tell him it's restricted and he inputs a code I didn't even know existed and I'm told to co-operate."

I wasn't sure if alarm or indignation were dominant in her disgust.

"And you think he's out to blame you for whatever's wrong?"

"With reason. I'm meant to be running this Port. If it's falling apart, I either find out who's doing it or pay the price myself."

Daisy's sense of responsibility has always seemed overdeveloped to me. I didn't like her logic either. Losing her job was the least that might happen to her if the Company's project was seriously delayed.

"Why would he think you were behind the problems? He's got to see that you've plenty to lose."

"I doubt if he cares. If they or I can't track down what's going wrong, they'll sack me and bring in someone who can."

"Byron?"

"No. I think he's wired into too many other circuits already. But he's probably got friends or relatives who'd like the job."

That's how the system works.

"What does he think's going on?"

"Who the hell knows what goes on in a brain like his? Perhaps he thinks I've been bought out by another Family."

I laughed. Apart from the fact that that sort of double-cross has a very high mortality rate, the idea of Daisy turning traitor was crazy. I sometimes think she has loyalty circuits programmed in.

Her smile wasn't quite even. "Thanks. I think."

"No sweat. So, you want my help?"

"What can you do?"

I wasn't sure. Any help I could give would be strictly street-level. And it sounded as though her trouble – if there really *was* trouble – was a combination of politics and technofraud. I've spent over twenty-five years avoiding understanding either.

I shrugged. "I'll keep my ears open."

"Thanks."

No blame to her if the gratitude was a little feeble. So was what I was offering. I topped up her glass and mine, surprised to discover that this bottle was almost empty, too.

"So, tell me. Is there any *good* news around?"

She looked into the glass. Drank. "Depends. Sheba's pregnant."

"She's what? That's great! It's what you were hoping for! Let's drink to her - even if she did hold out on me when I called."

It seemed a good enough reason to reach down for another bottle from the rack I'd built under the berth I was stretched out on. Daisy held out her glass.

"She knew I'd tell you. Besides, it's not looking so great now, is it? We hadn't planned to bring up a kid here."

They had an apartment in Pompey. It was well-guarded but I knew what she meant. A year ago they'd both thought they could bank on her promotion so she could buy herself out to somewhere healthier.

"I'm sorry. But we'll get this mess sorted somehow. We'll have to, or Sheba'll never invite me round again."

Sheba and I are never quite easy together but I value her cooking. Besides, the alarm in my voice made Daisy laugh. And hiccup.

"You're right, of course. And now I'd better get back to her."

She was surprisingly steady on her feet, carrying the

five-litre can I sent her off with up the ladder and on to the dockside as though it weighed nothing. I was the one who wasn't focusing quite right as I watched her walk away towards the transport shed.

I wasn't tired. Two cups of caf and my sight wasn't blurred any more either. My mind hadn't cleared much. I reached into the drawer under the chart table, pulled out a battered pack of cards and started to lay them out.

It had been Jack who'd taught me to play cards, though patience had never been his game. Before I'd joined him and the *Pig*, the only cards I'd seen had been my grandmother's tarots. Now when people wonder why I don't get rid of the old-fashioned, over-large table, since no one has paper charts any more, I usually show them my well-used collection. It shuts them up. I don't explain that the table is the only piece of furniture on the boat big enough to hold a spread of Blue Moon patience.

I looked at the unpromising array of cards. All fifty-two face up and in the open and it was up to me to find a way to rearrange them into a pattern which made sense. It would take a lot of work.

5

My head was thick next morning and the cards still made no sense. Nor did Daisy's problem. I couldn't even think of a good reason to involve myself since she clearly expected nothing from me. But I *had* found the body. And I was curious.

Be not curious in unnecessary matters. My mother would have said it with a frown. Grandmother would laugh and answer my question if she could, or tell me a story which was usually better than an answer. It was years before I realised the stories often *were* the answer. I wished I could ask her now, but she'd been gone for a dozen years and anyway I knew where she'd tell me to start.

The beginning. The body's ID.

Because my stomach didn't fancy another conversation with the overweight tekkie on the door to the Port offices, I stayed where I was and put in a personal call to Daisy. I was half-surprised when she took it.

"Humility? What's up now?"

She probably felt as rough as me so I didn't take offence at her tone. It was my fault.

"I was just wondering if they'd ID'd the body yet."

Her face shut down. Blank. I half-expected her to say, What body? "Why?"

"Curiosity."

"Sure." She hesitated, realising I would find out anyway or would keep on pestering her. "Come over."

Something in her voice stopped the obvious questions.

I made my way to the main building wondering just what she was up to, not liking any of my answers.

The man on the gate was another stranger. He didn't even look at me as he passed me through. Daisy came out to meet me.

"Come on. This way."

I'd never been through this part of the building, out the back and down a covered walkway to a long hut. I stopped when I saw the red cross on the door.

Daisy nodded. "Medical facility. Still curious?"

No. Never that curious. Was this Daisy's way of getting even for my interference? I could have turned back. *Should* have done. Instead, I took the step which made the door cycle open for me and walked through. "Let's get it over with."

It was cold in there. Not the cold which went with the drizzle outside but something far deeper, tasting of death. Never mind that this was a place where people came for cures: I knew what was behind the door where Daisy had stopped.

She must have signalled our arrival. The door swung open and a man in a white coverall stepped aside for us.

"He's in there."

It was a small empty room. The air in it was stale. Perhaps because the only other person in there had no need of air any more.

"Go on." Daisy's voice was hard, the anger barely suppressed. I couldn't tell if it was meant for me or for whatever I was going to see if I lifted the cloth over the shape on the table.

I don't handle death well. I prefer not to deal with it at all but that isn't always possible. What I'd done yesterday had led me directly here and I couldn't step back from it. If my hand was unsteady, trying to snatch itself back from what I was making it do, then that was between it and me.

Then I looked at what I had uncovered.

We were outside the too-clean building before either of us said anything. I had left it to the man in white to clean up the mess I'd made over his scrubbed floor and he hadn't protested.

"You knew him."

It wasn't a question. I nodded, still dealing with the knowledge that the thing I'd seen dangling from the dredge had been someone I'd known and liked. It took me three attempts to find my voice, and then it wasn't one I recognised.

"Jon. Used to work for you. In security. But you knew that, didn't you?"

That was making me angry. She hadn't needed to put me through this, hadn't even known I'd recognise him. Just because she was pissed with everyone else didn't give her the right to do that to *anyone*. Especially not to someone who'd thought she was a friend.

"No."

"*No*? You said they'd salvage his ID."

She was shaking her head. "I'd assumed they would. The chips are buried deep enough…" She must have seen me change colour because she stopped and began again more carefully. "You saw the damage. The important bit was missing."

I'd not looked closely. Only close enough to see that swollen face: lead-white, with the stains of corruption just showing. Close enough to know him and to wonder how it was possible to know anyone who looked like that. Close enough to see that the shape of the back of the skull was wrong.

"Did you guess I'd recognise him?"

She shook her head. Breathed out heavily in exasperation at herself and me as she pressed the heels of her hands against her eyes.

"Not really. I didn't recognise him, though you say he was staff. I just thought there was a chance, if he came from round here, you might know him. You're better at faces than most people."

Most people look at screens, not faces.

"Then *why?*" My anger was beginning to show now.

"I guess I wanted you to share the trouble you started. I was sick when I saw it, too."

I hadn't expected that. Daisy was too efficient for me to think of her stomach being turned by any part of her job. It was an apology of a kind. Suddenly I was too tired to stay angry. Too tired to deal with problems.

"OK. Now I've ID'd the corpse do you mind if I go? I've still got a hangover to sort out."

"Go."

6

I knew what drove Daisy. Our friendship would survive. Right now, however, I wanted a bit of distance. I left without another word and she didn't try to stop me.

Back on the *Pig* I took several deep breaths and tried to remember what Jon had been like, alive. Medium height. Dark hair. A beard which grew quickly so he always looked rough by the end of the day. Brown eyes turning down slightly at the outer edges, giving him a sad look which was misleading. He laughed easily at jokes which weren't that funny and liked puzzles as long as they weren't too complicated. He snored. I only knew that because I'd seen him pass out at a party we'd both been to. Boredom keeps me sober and I'd left early but not before I'd heard him snore. I smiled, remembering someone who had been easy to like. Not that white *thing* on the table.

And now that I'd remembered, I had to make up my mind what I was going to do next. Doing nothing would be simplest, but last night I hadn't been able to shake the sound of the body hitting the wet mud from my dreams. Now I had a face to put on it, I doubted if I'd sleep well tonight either. And, despite what she'd just done, I still owed Daisy something and she was still in trouble.

I thought of the lout who'd taken the job on security and thought perhaps I owed Jon something, too. I don't like debts.

7

Gus, the Harbour Master, was waiting outside the small office from which he ruled. Gus was a sturdy, square man who wore his uniform as though the Port were a military camp. He liked to be addressed by his job's title – if he'd been able to find a rank he'd have used that – and he liked the power he had over the people who visited here. So he didn't like me. I didn't have any proper appreciation of the value of hierarchies and systems and I don't give a shit about rank. He hadn't liked finding a berth for me yesterday and I'd guessed that if I hadn't had a friend who was also the Port Officer and therefore senior to him he might not have found one at all.

Not that the mooring was a place anyone else would fight for. The *Pig* was tied up to a rickety wooden jetty which would probably disappear on the next spring tide, and the ladder which went from it up the harbour wall was made of rust which stabbed my palms. It was also pulling away from the stonework in places.

"You staying long?"

"Is that the warm and friendly welcome they're training you to offer the idle rich when they come down here to waste time?"

He sneered. He would have spat if it hadn't been inappropriate to the uniform. I wondered if they'd keep him on when the new development opened. Wondered if he wondered. Was *he* interested in making sure it never did open?

"Well?"

I shrugged. I wouldn't have told him even if I'd known the answer. "Why? I'm paid up, aren't I?"

That was bugging him. "Only for ten days. After that we'll see. I might not be so keen to do you any favours then."

Another sneer. A limited vocabulary, but I got his meaning. If even people like him expected Daisy to be out of a job that soon, she hadn't been imagining any of her problems.

I had hoisted my sack on my shoulder and walked past him towards the barrier when he shouted after me: "You'd better check in with your river-trash friends. While you still can!"

He wanted me to stop and ask what he meant, which was enough to ensure I didn't. At least the dock barrier wasn't upset by my return, lifting meekly when I stared into its scanner. Perhaps it knew as well as I did just how many other ways there were of getting in and out of the Port.

Except for official traffic – which meant deliveries, maintenance and whichever members of the Company's main Family wanted entrance – no powered vehicles were allowed in the Port. Not even public transports. No one cared if the workers got wet in the steady drizzle which blurred the angles of offices and stores into something softer, a landscape. They had to walk up the steep hill to the public road just as I did, though the Company did run a privilege bus service.

The road gleamed with reflected wetness: dark grey and slick with the oil which creeps to the surface in hot weather to become a trap in the first smear of rain. I was staring down at it because I didn't even want to admit to myself that I was involved, that I had made a decision back there on the *Pig*, or that I was headed for Sutton to do anything more than sell on a cargo of wine.

8

The bus was crowded and slow and smelt foul. EuroGov keeps claiming it will meet pollution targets – sometime – and meanwhile congratulates itself on taxing autos out of legal reach of anyone but the Families. It didn't seem worth their while to invest in improvements to the public system. There are plenty of buses, aren't there? Who cares what they smell like?

It's always worse after being away. At sea you discover how clean the air can taste. You can see stars at night and listen to silence. After a while it drives me crazy but it's still hard to adjust to the city. The smell is the most direct assault, scorching your throat and leaving a coating on your tongue so that even food tastes of burnt fuel. Before long it begins to seem as though that's the way food should taste. It's the other things I don't adapt to, if only because I can get away from them on the *Pig*. The constant hum of electronics, just below the hearing threshold, sensation as much as sound. The flicker of terminal displays on the edge of your vision. I sometimes wondered if the constant background muzak was the cits' defence against the unheard noise, the VR holos their fight-back against the screens' unremitting displays.

My first day back in Sutton always makes me wonder why I'm not on tranks. A hangover and the memory of that sheeted body made today worse.

I clung tightly as the bus failed to slow when it swung past the barricade of the old dock gate on its programmed route, before it turned right to thread its way up through the maze of alleys to the Old Town. Here there were still shopfronts spilling goods on to the streets, though the shops themselves were mostly half-ruined. What had once been a multi-storeyed auto-park loomed skeletally over one block. Not a place to go near even in daylight. We passed the old civic buildings. Still intact, still overstaffed, still defending themselves from responsibility and bleating that they only followed orders. I was surprised no one had yet bombed them.

I swung down when the bus slowed. The place I wanted was on a corner across from what had been a park, between a shuttered but undamaged store and a building which only opened at night and which I didn't want to know about.

Tom Lee's wasn't crowded. Most of his legit business went on in the evenings or at the turn of a shift, when you couldn't get near the counter without being crushed close up against someone, and when the caf was either too weak because one of the new staff had made it or full of grounds from a jug which should have been declared empty two mugs ago. No one complained, either about the caf or the crowds. At this time of day the caf would be fresh and worth the journey.

Despite the rain there were tables set up outside. The awning dripped over those near its edges but the others were dry enough if you didn't mind the cold. I do, so I went in. Outside tables were a kind of boasting, telling anyone who passed that the place had more powerful protection than steel grilles or sonic blasters. Hell, the entry wasn't even wired.

That didn't mean I hadn't been noticed the minute I

walked on to his territory. I picked up a caf from the counter, paying with the local coins they still use for small deals in most parts of the city, and looked around. There was a table against the wall where I could see the street as well as the rest of the room. The contrast between them was another comment on Tom Lee's status.

Outside, the rain had turned the gutters to gritty mud and the drains were blocked with cast-offs which not even the derelicts could use. Water, or worse, belched upwards through a broken cover. No one's yet found a way to cope with a city's waste. It's not worth the trouble, since no one with the money to do anything would choose to live anywhere near a city, and who cares about those who must? If they're thinned occasionally by crime or disease, it doesn't matter – as long as neither becomes epidemic and threatens to touch someone's Family.

Inside, the place was unnaturally clean. Polished chrome gleamed and there wasn't a crack in the black plasteel of the tables or counters. Another sign of status. No damage said two things: money to replace whatever was broken, power to defend it. There was even a mirror behind the counter, though that almost certainly had a practical purpose. The only mark on the table in front of me was the smeared circle I had made when I'd let the caf slop over the rim of the mug. Careless. The table would be cleaned in seconds if I moved. Employing more staff than he needed was not just another form of display: it gave Tom Lee valuable tax concessions. I grinned at the thought of Tom Lee gravely submitting a tax return.

I didn't ask to see him. It's not the sort of thing you ask. I just waited and watched. You can tell a lot about a person from the way he or she walks and I prefer watching people to watching screens.

Most of those passing by outside took care to walk around the empty tables beyond the territory staked out by the awning, accepting the rain. They were huddled in shapeless clothes, looking down at the slick paving beneath their feet, seeming to know without looking when they risked brushing too close to another walker. Some instinct seems to be born in the cit to know without question who is dominant, who must step aside. Though I'm more comfortable here now than I ever was in the Community, it's still an instinct I'm unsure of. More than once I've read it wrong and been lucky to walk away with no more than the odd bruise or a curse sounding in my ears. I guessed that most of those out there had some-where to go to – or to escape from. They moved with purpose. I watched them. After a while it was easy to guess who was hurrying *to*, who running *from*. There's a difference in the turn of the head to look behind, the hunch of the shoulders, the hesitation on a street corner.

There were others out there, too. I'd seen them hanging round the dock barrier, hoping for handouts, or shivering against a wall. Sometimes they squatted on the broken paving, hugging their knees and staring down, seeing whatever dreams their drug gave them. They were luckier than those who just drifted with the same irrational impulses which tugged a broken carton this way and that in the sluggish stream of the gutter.

"Heard you were back."

Tom Lee nodded and pulled out the chair opposite while a girl put a fresh mug down in front of me, wiping the table as she did so, and scuttled off without looking at me.

He was tall and thin to the point of gauntness, dressed

in black as always with a white silk handkerchief knotted at his throat. His hair was slicked back into a pigtail which seemed to pull the skin even tighter across the flat planes of his face, tugging the corners of his eyes so that they were always narrowed, smoothing out the lines which might tell you what he was thinking. His mouth was thin. Close. Tom Lee wasn't his real name, of course. The place had been called Tom Lee's long before I first came to this city and it had changed hands at least twice since then.

I nodded back at him, thanks for the caf. "Surprised if you didn't."

And he wouldn't have admitted it anyway. Besides, he had more wires into the Net than anyone else I knew. *Except Byron Cody?* The thought startled me but I shrugged it off. I needed to concentrate.

"Good trip?"

"All right." Enthusiasm tended to drive the price down.

"Bordeaux?" Something else he already knew.

"Yes. Got a full tank for sale."

I didn't see the gesture which summoned the girl back, this time with a glass for him. I took the bottle from my sack and poured. He sipped, his movements precise, fastidious. The fact that his nails were always black with dirt never failed to turn my stomach. I wouldn't have minded in one of the drifters outside, but here… I swallowed, watching his impassive face.

"Who you dealing with?"

"Your choice first."

I knew better than to offer him competition. Besides, this was more ritual than real bargaining. I'd been selling my wine through him ever since my first trip when I'd realised that it was a cargo I could make a profit on. Most bulk-imported wine was denatured or blended so messily it wasn't worth drinking. I wasn't a big dealer in the market, didn't want to be, but it kept my credit open when there was no other work around.

He'd take a while to consider, I knew that. Knew, too, that he didn't want to talk.

I let my attention stray to his other customers. A few were alone. Most were in close groups of two or three, discussing in low voices something too private to be trusted to the Net. No one showed any interest in any of the other tables.

That lack of interest had been one of the things I found hardest to adjust to when I first came to Sutton. I was sixteen and without Jack I wouldn't have survived. Knowing that you didn't invite any except close friends home, didn't offer a last name unless you must, didn't look directly at anyone you passed, wasn't the same as living it. It was years before I accepted that for most cits the lack of interest was real, not simply discretion.

You could tell Tom Lee's customers were the types who wouldn't have avoided walking under his awning, even if they hadn't been coming in. It showed in their imported clothes made from sleek fabrics which the rain would never touch. It showed in the elaborate haircuts and the complex body-paints. A black-haired woman sitting alone and tapping into the table's screen had a snake curling round her upper arm, its scales pulsing iridescent green and blue, its forked tongue flickering.

Tonight's clientele would be different, noisier. Eager to boast they'd bought a drink in Tom Lee's before moving on to try out whatever new show was on at one of the VR places in the next street.

"Same price again?"

The colourless voice drew my attention back. He didn't like wandering eyes.

"Plus twenty."

His laugh was as colourless as his voice. "The little lady likes her joke."

"Plus twenty. The weather was rough."

"So the wine's going to need to settle. I should charge you for that."

"Except you won't be putting it out for another six months anyway. A year if you're wise. It'll have plenty of time to settle. Besides," I looked around, "how many people here would notice if it hadn't?"

He didn't turn to look "I'd notice."

"So would I. And I still think it's worth plus twenty."

He poured another glass. Sipped. Put the glass down. When he lifted it again I noticed it didn't leave a wet rim mark on the table. He was too careful. He set it down again. Tapped on the table with dirty fingernails. Straightened.

"Plus fifteen."

I made myself wait, seem to consider. I'd been prepared to drop to plus ten. "Deal. You'll pick it up tonight?"

"Tomorrow. High water."

Good idea. Off-loading that much wine, even with his equipment, would be a whole lot easier when the boat was the same height as the harbour wall.

I unlocked my bracelet. Passed it across. I was sure he didn't need it but it amused him to observe the forms, although I noticed he didn't look at it as he tapped a number into his handset. When I took the bracelet back the credit mark had lost its pinkish tinge.

Wine maketh merry but money answereth all things.

"Deal done." He raised a hand and the girl, who had been expecting it, came over with a plate. "You're my guest."

A flaky pastry, honey oozing from both ends. Tom Lee employed only the best cooks, and I couldn't afford his prices, so this traditional bonus to the deal was a treat.

He was already part way to his feet before he saw I wasn't eating. "Something else?"

My stomach wouldn't let me eat. I should just shake my head, stay quiet. *Keep out of trouble.* Jack never took his own advice, either.

"Perhaps. There was a dead man down at Midway yesterday."

"Heard." He hadn't sat down again.

"Heard why?"

"What's it to you?"

"Liked him."

It wasn't a reason by his reckoning but perhaps it made him curious.

"What's he called?"

"Jon."

A frown. Jon isn't an uncommon name, even when it's genuine. Then he tapped something else into the handset and frowned some more.

"In security?"

I nodded. "He was harmless."

"Can't have been."

In streetcode harmless also meant unharmed. You didn't get hurt if you weren't in anyone's way. That was the theory. I thought of the naked body and the fact that the back of his head had been missing.

Tom Lee waited another moment, to show he wasn't being pushed into anything, then sat down again. He knew

I was right and I knew he didn't have an answer. Dislike of the gap in his own knowledge more than any concern for a dead man made him interested.

"I listen for you, what's there for me?"

I'd known he'd bargain. That's why I'd sealed the wine deal before opening this one. Besides, I hadn't been sure I'd go through with it.

"What d'you want?"

A pause. Considering. He knew my limits. Knew I had little of market value. "What's the word on the new development? They settled the concessions yet?"

So. He wanted an outlet in the Port. If it attracted the sort of customers it wanted, it made sense for Tom Lee to branch out there.

I shrugged. "Doubt it. Work on that side's not complete. I might be able to get you in with the Port Officer. She'll get word to you."

Whatever else Tom Lee was involved in, his reputation meant that Daisy would at least have to consider any offer from him. The Company might even like the idea. His stuff *was* good.

Tom Lee came as near laughing as I'd yet seen him." What's that worth? Word is, she's out of there."

"Word can be wrong."

I kept my voice even. No credit in running scared with Tom Lee. He'd wipe me without a thought. The silence was sceptical. Then he pushed his chair out and stood up. I'd blown it.

"I'll open a file."

Relief after certain defeat ended whatever appetite I'd had. I waited till he was out of sight, then picked up my sack and left. Wondering if I'd just killed myself.

9

I had a choice. Go back to the Port, exchange a few more pleasantries with Gus, see whether the spread of cards had improved in my absence, or pay another visit.

I didn't want to. I'd done enough when I'd asked Tom Lee for help, for which he'd probably make me pay on every cargo from here to the next millennium.

The trouble was a bit of information I had which I wasn't sure even he had access to.

I'd last talked to Jon the day before I'd sailed out of Midway. With the weather clear for the first time in six weeks, I'd been thinking only of getting away from the smell and the crowds of shore life. I'd said goodbye to Daisy, bumped into Jon as I was leaving her office.

"You're away then?"

"Unless Met's trying to establish new records for inaccuracy I should have three clear days. Time enough to make some southing. Find a warm spot for the rest of winter."

"Not going home for Easter?"

We hadn't shared much personal data but he'd heard about my background. Was fascinated by the idea of a theocratic society. I didn't bother explaining it was like every other: those who had the power gave orders to the rest.

"No."

Nor had I gone there for Christmas. I wouldn't have gone even if they would have been willing to let me in. I do my best to ignore all the festivals. The Community can't just treat them as public holidays. They have to go in for the full mid-winter or equinox rites with an overlay of Christian smugness and a little Armageddon-anticipating. Despite the fact that the food riots of 2020 were almost thirty years ago now, they never quite stopped looking forward to the end of the world. Here in the city I sometimes wondered if it had ended and no one had noticed.

Jon had stood there, as though he had something to say and was unsure how to start. Uncharacteristic.

"You going away?" I asked him. We'd shared a drink from time to time, not personal data.

"Perhaps. If I ever get off-duty here."

A thread of something I couldn't read in his voice. Not quite excitement. Anticipation? Frustration, too.

I answered that: "Extra shift?"

"And no notice."

"It's a problem?"

"It clashes with another plan."

I didn't ask what. Most tekkies had a second job if they could find one. I was about to sympathise, shrug and walk off to finish getting the *Pig* ready for sea. Something stopped me. I waited.

He hesitated, took a breath. Decided. "Ask a favour?"

"Ask."

"Need to drop something off. Packet."

It didn't sound difficult. "Far?"

"No. Down at the northshore flats. I've a room there."

"You want me to leave a packet in your room?" I was startled. The occasional drink didn't make us that close.

He shook his head. "In my mail slot. It's in the lobby. You could be in and out in a minute. Bus runs right past."

The buses ran once an hour if you were lucky and that

route had more power failures than most. I didn't remind him. I owed him a drink and I really didn't have much left to do on the *Pig*. I'm always ready too early, and the day before I leave drags while I fidget around trying to remember what I've forgotten. It was still daylight. No harm in taking a run out to the northshore.

"I'll take it."

"Saved my life!"

I'd assumed he was exaggerating.

And now he was dead I might be the only one who knew where he'd lived when he was alive. And it was just possible that somewhere there was something which might give me a reason to stop fretting about his death.

Perhaps I was high from too much caf on top of a hangover. Whatever the reason, I found myself taking the bus which led towards the shore between Sutton and Midway. It's bleak. There had been a shipyard there once but nothing else. No freight terminal, no ferries. Certainly not the recreational sailing they were hoping to bring back to Midway. The military weren't interested in this place and even the bridge from Sutton straddled it, leaving it cut off and shadowed. The blocks of utility housing here should have been pulled down fifty years ago. Now the authorities were just waiting until they fell down.

Two of the three blocks were more or less intact. The third was a skeleton; a fire last year had finished what neglect and decay had started.

When he handed over the packet Jon seemed unable to stop giving me details I didn't need. All I wanted was the box code. Instead I learned about the wretched state of his over-priced room on the north side of the fifth floor of the taller block. He eventually gave me the code. I hadn't been up to his room. Hadn't wanted to. The place smelled as much of defeat and death as it did of drains.

It hadn't changed. There was still no one guarding the lobby. Not much to guard and no one to pay for it if there had been. Two of the mail boxes were smashed open. Jon's still looked intact. No name on any of them, of course. I looked towards the steel coffin which was the elevator and read a few of the comments sprayed inside it. Smelled it. Headed for the stairs.

I was glad he'd lived no higher than the fifth floor. Sailing keeps me fit but doesn't give me much practice on stairs. I stopped at the third to breathe and stare out of the barred window. In some places I hear people pay for a sea view. Not here. Not when the only view is across the water to the smoke of the industries on the other side. They say you can sail this branch of the Solent blind and know where you are by the different stinks. All toxic, of course. The rain had more or less stopped and the sea was flat and grey, absorbing rather than reflecting light. Only the ripples round a buoy betrayed just how fast the tide was running.

Jon's door was no different from the others on this level: bare of paint, peeling. Blocked by a metal grille. The door itself was certainly lined with steel. I looked up. No light from the small lens set out of reach near the ceiling. Out of reach just means a challenge to some people. It probably hadn't worked since the day after it was installed. I rang the bell, then hammered on the door through the grill-work.

Nothing. What had I expected? That Jon would open the door and prove Daisy wrong? The place was empty. Sealed until Jon's death was confirmed by the Net.

"What do you want?"

There'd been no build-up of trash in front of the door-sill. That should have told me someone had been in and out recently. I took a deep breath, trying to convince myself my quickened heart-rate was the fault of the stairs.

"Looking for Jon."

There was an eye behind the small square grille which had been slid open. Bloodshot, pale blue. Light eyelashes. The voice was male. If I passed him in the street I wouldn't recognise him.

"No Jon here."

He was going to slam the grille.

"Wait!"

I felt his hesitation. Guessed his hand was still raised to shut the little hatchway.

"Jon used to live here," I tried to explain.

"Not now. No one here when I moved in. Two days ago."

He added the last three words reluctantly, unwilling to give away personal information, suspecting I would go on pestering him. It was more than I'd hoped to get.

"Thanks."

I turned to go, then, because he had answered the door to a stranger, advised, "I'd get the vid fixed if I were you. Or a remote scanner. You can get shot through a grille."

It had slammed shut before I finished. Inside he would be stepping back fast, wiping damp palms against his trews, probably wondering just what my threat meant. No point explaining there was no threat, more important he took the advice.

Especially since he'd been able to move into an empty room two days before it could possibly have been listed as vacant.

10

By the time I walked back through the Port barrier it was raining again and I was tired, hungry, wet and puzzled. I wanted to get back on board the *Pig* and settle down to some serious thinking. Instead I saw Byron Cody walking towards me.

"Humility. Hoped I might see you."

He'd probably had a circuit rigged so that he was told the moment the barrier read my ID. He wasn't the type to walk anywhere just for the exercise. And he was about as comfortable in the rain as a cat.

"Byron." I nodded and kept moving.

"Heard you were interested in the body that was dredged up?"

"I found it." I was certain he needed no reminder.

"The dredge found it. You noticed it. From a distance."

Pedant. Was my interest meant to diminish with distance? I tried not to remember that it wasn't until I knew who the body had once been that I'd become involved.

"It was close enough."

Too close. It would be some time before that particular memory was far enough off to suit me.

"So, you're curious?"

He should meet my mother. Clearly curiosity was not a virtue in his eyes either, even though he was soft-voiced and I could hear no threat in his words. Warning? Maybe.

"Curious about a lot of things. Such as what you're

doing here."

He hadn't expected the challenge. Blinked. Checked his databanks and decided I didn't need a real answer.

"An audit. As the Port Officer told you." Total recall. Of course.

"An audit." I hoped my lack of expression conveyed my disbelief. Couldn't tell. I also hoped the rain would drive him away so that I could go home. But it seemed he still had some questions.

"Heard you ID'd the body?"

I wasn't surprised. For all I knew he'd watched my reaction to it.

"Heard right."

"You sure of it? Can't have been easy."

So he *had* seen. I swallowed the bile which that memory produced and managed an adequate answer. "Sure."

"Port Officer didn't recognise him and he worked here."

I couldn't tell if it was question, comment or criticism. "I'm good at faces."

Even faces which were white and bloated, features almost lost.

He nodded. Didn't push it.

We were passing Gus's office. I saw the square silhouette with its self-consciously straight back sitting at a table inside and was glad the weather had put him off coming down to goad me some more. Byron had at last had enough rain. He nodded towards the plexi-walled hut.

"I'm going in there. I'll see you around."

Not if I saw him first.

The tide was in, so the climb down to the *Pig's* jetty was no problem. I thumbed the remote for the alarm and stepped on board, slamming the deckhouse door behind me with more force than its slight warping usually demanded.

Food. There was some soup left. I heated that, warmed the last of the bread and remembered I should have shopped while I was out. That way I could have used up some local coin – there was no way of guessing how much it would be worth next time I docked. Too bad. Thanks to Tom Lee, I had enough credit to take the easy way. I called up the inventory of the nearest store and put in an order which would keep me stocked for the next three weeks.

After that I was left to wonder about Byron "hearing" of my interest in Jon's body. I remembered my call this morning but couldn't see Daisy discussing me with him. Which meant he had an intercept on my phone. Or on Daisy's.

I glared down at the cards. I had run through the spread twice already and it still made no sense. With a comment which would have made grandmother laugh and earned me a mouthful of soap from my mother, I heaped the cards together, shuffled and stacked them, and dropped them into the drawer.

The trouble was I didn't know what to do. This business with Jon had thrown everything out of line. I had come back to the Port to sell the wine, restock, get back in touch with some old friends. Perhaps even take on some casual work and settle till boredom or lack of credit or a spell of fair weather shifted me on again. I'd sold the wine and restocked but it obviously wasn't a good time to touch Daisy for work. And if someone with the capacity of Byron was tapping into my circuits as well as "auditing" Daisy, perhaps I'd be better off setting sail again.

Gus would be delighted. That thought was enough to

make me want to stay. Then I thought of his gibe about "river trash", recalled that I had other friends here besides Daisy and decided to call up Em.

"Humility! You back at last? Come right on over. I'll give Rusty and Clim a shout."

Em and the others lived upstream. I could take the small dinghy but walking was no problem. I had almost shut the door behind me when I remembered and went back in to retrieve another couple of bottles from the supply I'd set aside for my own use. At this rate I'd *have* to leave by the end of the month or stop drinking.

11

Em lives on the *Wild Goose*, once a cruising yacht, designed by some rich Family man with a nostalgia for a time only old books recalled. Now she lay aground in a mud-berth, stripped of mast and rigging. An empty hulk, neither ship nor house. Though there was a kind of pathos about the old vessel, I had to admit that the furnishings were of a quality I'd never be able to aspire to on the *Pig*. Wood from trees which didn't grow anywhere any more – with names like teak and mahogany summoning up images of ancient romance and adventure – gleamed in the light of the oil lamps Em insisted on using though power is cheap enough. The berths were upholstered in deep blue velvet, rubbed and faded now, the nap balding, but still breathing wealth and idle comfort. Em keeps the brass polished, so that it was like stepping back into the early days of the 20th century to climb down the companionway into the crowded saloon.

It was crowded because she'd asked round a dozen or more, not just Rusty and Clim. It was going to be impossible to find a seat which didn't crush me close up against someone I hardly knew. Em's cheerful invitation had depths I hadn't seen.

Em herself was at least seventy. Her partner, Mike, had died three years ago. Until she smashed her arm trying to do work on the boat which two men would have found heavy, she'd worn her hair in long white plaits coiled crownlike on her head. Finding she couldn't cope with an arm out of commission, she'd made me cut her hair with her own shears and kept it short even when the arm was healed. I wanted her to keep the two thick braids. She laughed at my sentimentality and told me to burn the bloody things. Now the white fluff was a deceptive halo round her wrinkled face. She grinned when she saw me, reaching out one hand for the bottles and offering me a full glass with the other. Fair exchange. I looked around for somewhere to sit among the crowd.

They were all around her age and I knew them all by sight at least. It was a close community. They lived on barges and hulks and the wrecks of yachts and landing craft. One small group had set up home on a decommissioned ferry. None of the other hulks had quite the class of *Wild Goose* but they were all prized in their way. Their owners were survivors from a system which had broken down when they were younger than I am now, but something of the old spirit clung to them when they got together like this.

Once the greetings had been exchanged I told them a little of my last trip and they all told me for the hundredth time how fortunate I was to be on a boat which still *went* places. I wondered how many would accept if I offered to take a couple of them on my next trip. Then I looked from Em to the others and sensed the preliminaries were done.

"What's up?"

It's funny how quickly a friendly noise can quieten into uncomfortable silence. No one was looking at anyone else. In the end it was Clim, thin and small and weather-beaten, who spoke. "You tell her, Em."

She needed prompting. "Em?"

"Have you spoken to Gus?"

She knew I had to have done to get a berth. She also knew he wasn't someone I'd choose for casual conversation. "As little as I can. What's he done now?"

"It's not *him*."

A muttered chorus agreed with her. So this was more than the man's usual irritating enforcement of petty restrictions.

"Then who?"

"The Company, I guess. The Family. I thought you might have heard about the development."

"The development's been going on for a year now. I could hardly avoid knowing about it."

"And about the fact that they're going to have the hulks towed away?"

Rusty's voice. Cracked from too many years and too much alcohol but explosive with outrage. I registered it automatically as the meaning of what he was saying sank in.

"Where to?"

Em shrugged. "Out of here. After that Gus says it's up to us where we go. They won't even charge us for the tow."

Her voice dripped ironic gratitude. Most of these hulks would sink if they were pulled out of the mud. Those that didn't would turn over when the first wave hit them. None of them had functioning drives.

"But *why*?"

"We don't suit the new image."

Clim's voice. Dry. Clipped. Telling me what I should have seen much earlier. Of course there was no room for old wrecks like these, both human and marine, where rich Family members might have to look at them. Not in a recreation Port where nothing unsightly was left unreconstructed. The plans for dredging out the mud-berths to extend the harbour were probably already drawn.

"I doubt if the *Pig* does either."

"But you can sail out of here. And your friend Daisy will help you."

I was close enough against the hip of the man beside me to feel its bony weight but I was suddenly on the far side of a gorge I hadn't known existed. They were all watching me.

Choose sides. They wanted an answer. Now. "Have you talked to her?"

"We thought you might do that." Em. Neutral. I saw that she'd set the bottles I'd brought aside unopened.

Why did they think I could do anything? I didn't want the responsibility. Didn't like the way they were all watching me. Waiting. I sighed. Gave in.

"For what it's worth, for myself as well as you lot, I'll do what I can."

I didn't add that there seemed little chance of my debatable influence with Daisy being of any use, since she could well be unemployed by the end of next week. I couldn't stomach the cheer which would go up.

Em was watching me narrowly and looking only half-satisfied but she reached for the bottle. "Let us know what happens."

They seemed cheerful enough for the rest of the evening, used to the idea they were living on the edge of disaster and willing to forget it for the moment. But I couldn't find an echo of their mood. I left early, just as they were on the third chorus of an old song with lyrics suitably adjusted to express their opinion of the Company.

I agreed with every word.

It wasn't raining. The yellow ceiling of night was over the city again and the path back to the dock was deserted.

I kept telling myself that it was deserted for the half hour it took me to walk. Only the certainty that I would be making a fool of myself stopped me running it in twenty minutes. Thoughts of Jon's death, and the gloomy bitterness of people who were as close to friends as I had, were making me imaginative. The shadows were only shadows. No one was watching me.

I was still repeating it when I slammed the deckhouse door behind me and leaned back against it with all my weight.

Yesterday morning my life had been uncomplicated. Now it looked as though one friend was being sabotaged out of a job and other friends were likely to be made homeless before the season ended.

I wished I was back at sea.

12

I was up late next day. Not because I had slept well, more because the world was a warmer, simpler, more comfortable place viewed from inside my bunk than whatever awaited me outside. I stared at the deckhead above me. It needed repainting. So did most of the *Pig*. It was one of the jobs I'd planned to get on with while I was in the Port. For the first time it even seemed appealing.

I tried to order my thoughts. Too much had been crammed into yesterday: Daisy's sabotage; Jon's death; the threat to evict Em and her friends. Just how far were they all connected? And could I do anything about any of them? Or should I?

I shook my head. Despite yesterday, Daisy was the one I'd like to help, but I couldn't see how. I remembered Byron's comment about Daisy not recognising Jon and wondered again how much suspicion there had been in it. Impossible to tell what had gone on behind a face as bland as a blank screen. But if he was determined to pin the blame for some or all of the trouble on her, there was little I could do about it.

So, talk to him again. Find out if that's what he's after.

Simple solutions always sound plausible when you're in a comfortable bunk and the fog of sleep hasn't quite lifted from your brain.

I'd done what I could about Jon, for the moment at least. As for Em, helping Daisy might yet be the best way of helping the others. A little bit of gratitude can be useful currency.

Which brought me back to Byron.

Closing my eyes didn't work. I could still see him. I would have to face the day after all.

There were no access codes for him. He had no listing I could find and the Net had no information to give. It was more annoying than surprising. If my other guess was right and he was running an intercept – illegal, but who cares? – then he was likely to call me back when he saw I'd been chasing him. I contemplated waiting for his call but it seemed like abandoning the initiative. There are other ways of looking for someone.

Gus was in his office. Early arrival and late departure were standard for him. A matter of pride – which he made sure others noticed. When I knocked on his door he sneered at me through the plex but pressed the button which gave me entry. Around him were screens displaying harbour movements and tidal flow, a bank of switches in case there was a need for manual override on any systems, a secondary display series which I couldn't read but which probably had something to do with the developers' progress. It didn't leave much space for anyone except Gus and that was how he liked it.

"You leaving?"

It was an economical way of telling me how he felt, even though he knew I'd never leave a berth I'd already paid for.

"Not yet. I went over to see Em last night."

Something like a smile stretched his mouth. Em and the others offended his sense of what was proper.

Even more than I did. "Told you they were going, did they?"

"Told me they'd had notice," I corrected.

He didn't like the implication. The hint there might be trouble when it came right down to eviction. His imagination had problems with the idea that people might resist Company instructions. It would be worse if he was the one who had to enforce them – for all his bluster and military precision I knew, and he might have suspected, there wasn't much behind the polished badge. He'd be terrified the Corps would blame him for any trouble.

That was what I was banking on.

"You stirring things up?"

I spread my hands. "Me? I came to give you something to say thanks for finding me a berth at short notice."

He was frowning. I could read the emotions chasing across his face: surprise, suspicion, curiosity. Greed.

I produced the bottle from my sack. Its contents were from a thin batch I'd sampled and rejected. No loss to me and Gus would never know the difference. I held it out. He hesitated, took it, looked at the hand-written label I'd stuck on as though it meant something.

"Thanks." It sounded as though the word hurt him. Perhaps it was just rusty from disuse.

"No sweat." I turned to go and then, casually, turned back. "What's the data on this techno who's hanging around? I haven't seen him here before."

Gus looked as sour as the wine he was holding.

"*Him*. Doesn't know one end of a boat from another and thinks he can tap into any system he likes without asking leave."

He probably could.

"Family?"

I needed to know. If he was tight in with the very top of the Company, the inner circle for whose benefit the whole system was run, then I had real problems. It was logical but I wasn't convinced it was that simple.

Gus was. He frowned. Considered. Shrugged. "What else would he be?"

Stupid to have expected imagination from Gus. The Company and, at its heart, the Family were all that mattered to him. His ambitions were all on promotion, moving up the hierarchy. Gaining favourable notice. He didn't understand anyone who operated outside the system. Byron had status: he must be high-ranking. The logic was simple.

"He staying long?"

"Hope not. He's been here a week."

"Where've they got him stashed? I don't suppose he's finding it comfortable."

I watched him consider crushing me by saying the information was classified. The bottle and the urge to show off his knowledge of Port movements won. He gave a knowing laugh.

"Wherever it is, it's certainly not HQ standard."

He liked the thought of the techno having to survive without the luxuries of a home estate. Then he looked concerned in case I thought he was envious of Byron's access. I kept my expression appropriately serious.

"They haven't told you where he is? He's not in the Company block, then?"

The Company kept a block of apartments on the edge of the Port. Far enough out to avoid any noise and disturbance, near enough for its presence to be felt. Especially when the suites were occupied by someone on the Board. Most of the time the block was empty – a flaunting of wealth which did not endear itself to most of the

Company's employees but which the Company claimed gave them something to aspire to.

Gus hated my knowing there was something he hadn't been told. Had to flaunt what he did know. "They've given him an office in the main building."

They must have thrown someone out to do it. Space in that block was limited. Daisy's office was twice the size of most. I should have been relieved she wasn't the one to be displaced.

I had as much information as I was going to get and the smell of envy was becoming rank. I straightened from where I'd been leaning against the wall.

"Enjoy the wine. I'll talk to you later about extending my berth for another week."

I left before he could find a quick way of saying No. A glance back showed him staring at the bottle on the table in front of him and wondering whether he'd just accepted a bribe. It would be interesting to know if he'd be able to bring himself to open the bottle. I didn't think he'd find the willpower to give it back.

I headed over towards the main building. No point in wasting time. Besides, I didn't want to lose my nerve.

The thug was back on the job. "Humility. Can't stay away, then?"

I had a very unPuritan impulse to kick him just below the sagging belly. Smiling was one of the more difficult things I'd done that morning. "I always enjoy company."

"Pity I'm not off-duty for another four hours."

Someone somewhere was on my side. "Pity I shan't be around then."

He managed to look disappointed and relieved at the same time. "So. Patch you through to the Port Officer?"

I shook my head. "Byron Cody."

I said it as though I knew he was in there. As if he might even have been the one who'd asked me over. The tekkie was standing closer to me than I liked but he was suddenly very still.

"You sure? There's no record of any appointment in the log."

He paged through the screen and showed it to me as though he had to prove his point.

"That's because I haven't got an appointment."

"Then I'm not sure I can…"

"Just try. Or shall I do it myself?"

He didn't believe I had the codes but he wasn't certain enough to call my bluff. He'd never make a card player. Jack would have loved an evening with him.

"If he goes into overload I'll say it was you who insisted," he warned.

"You can say I threatened to show you just how a primitive like me gets her kicks if you like." I smiled. Differently this time.

I didn't see what code he input or whether he received a command through whatever augment went with his job. The important thing was that he stepped back and the flicker which was the barrier going down.

"Corridor to the left. Third door on the right."

He stepped back. I'd a feeling I'd lost an admirer.

The corridor wasn't long enough to need a walkway. It had one, of course, just in case someone suggested the Family couldn't afford it. I stepped on to the moving grid and off again at the featureless door. I wasn't surprised when it swung open before I raised my hand to knock.

13

"Humility."

He had risen to greet me.

"Byron."

I can be polite too. I was trying to meet his eyes while taking in everything I could about the room. It was as small as I'd expected. The only reason for my first impression of size was that it was almost empty. There was a small table. There was one screen. Just *one*. I thought of the banks of monitors in Daisy's office. Their constant movement. This screen was blank. I didn't make the mistake of taking the lack of obvious circuitry for its absence. Not when he had a table like that. Its matt surface was a dark not-quite-black and I could almost feel the cyberlife which pulsed through it. I guessed it had more capacity than the combined power of all the other terminals in the Port. He'd brushed a palm against one edge when he stood up. Calling up data to his implants? Recording? Wiping something?

There were also two chairs in the room. He waved me to one as he sat back again into the other. Mine was comfortable and seemed uncomplicated. I didn't ask what was built into the elegant structure of his.

He was sleek. There was no other word for the slick fit of coveralls which were not Company issue, the smooth gleam of his skin, the lack of any of the signs which betrayed an upbringing in the streets. When he smiled his teeth were even, white. There was no expression at all in his dark eyes.

"You wanted to see me?"

In person? The query about such unnecessary and unusual behaviour was unspoken. Then I remembered that I'd tried to get him on the phone and that he probably knew. And that I'd failed.

"Yes. I'm curious."

"So you told me yesterday. Has your curiosity taken you far?"

If I could have answered I wouldn't. I didn't look forward to discovering just how far it might take me.

"I'm not talking about Jon. Not this time. It's Daisy I'm concerned for."

I'd thought about subtler approaches but decided that subtlety was something he probably specialised in. I had enough handicaps without trying to confront him on his own territory. Besides, bluntness might startle results out of him.

He didn't seem startled. "Daisy? Oh yes, the Port Officer is a friend of yours."

I didn't for one nanosecond believe he had forgotten.

"Yes. And I wanted to find out how much you're blaming her for this sabotage."

He didn't blink. "There's four assumptions in there."

"Four?" I'd only counted three.

"That there's been any sabotage. That the Port Officer is its target. That she is being blamed for it. That I have any concern in the matter."

He listed them with precision as though reading them from some inner screen. Perhaps he was. He certainly saw no need to tick them off on his fingers as I would have done.

"An audit doesn't concern itself with sudden, unexplained Company losses?"

"It might." It was as much of an admission as I was likely to receive. I was about to seize on it when he went on. "An auditor would need a good reason to discuss business with someone outside the Company. Especially someone who is still listed as Missing from her home, and who would appear to be living on a vessel to which she has no clear title."

I'd known I was still Missing. It went with being Shunned. Though I contacted my mother every year on her birthday, I would remain Missing until I came to my senses and returned home. It was the bit about the *Pig* which had me gasping.

"What do you mean? I inherited the boat!"

"The ownership's still registered to Jack Fane. Deceased. There's an argument which says unclaimed property reverts to the state after a certain length of time."

I didn't ask how long. Didn't want to know. My instinct was to get back to *The Flying Pig* and take her out of harbour as fast as the tide allowed. Only the suspicion that that would exactly suit this 'crat made me sit fast.

"The state," I said deliberately, "can plug both ends into the same socket and go sit in a puddle for all I care. And if you don't want to talk about Daisy then perhaps you'll listen."

His voice hadn't changed from its polite blandness when he'd threatened the *Pig*. It didn't change now. "Of course."

"I just wanted to be sure you factored into your calculations the certainty that hurting the Port is *not* in her interest: its success is her ticket to further promotion. Out of the city. She'd be a fool if she undermined that.

So, unless you think the Corps regularly appoints fools to senior jobs, that must mean someone else is behind what's happening."

"If I accept that there *is* anything, she could be after a bigger prize than promotion. There are more influential Families than the Vincis. If one of them is interested in this site, they might well prefer its development to fail. They might even offer an incentive to someone in a position to assist that failure."

I'd laughed when Daisy had suggested it. I didn't feel like laughing now.

As a child I'd played games of chase, of make-believe, of Them and Us. They had always involved the Families. When I'd been even younger there'd been chants, too. The Family names, chosen years ago from sentiment or whim by people whose own names meant little. *Gates,* Bismark, Nelson, Short. *Vin*-ci and *Tal*-ley-*rand.* I couldn't even remember them without hearing the rhythmic repetitions. Of course the order sometimes changed, though Gates always came first.

Of the six Families which ran the Companies – which were, in effect, EuroGov – the one which owned Midway Port was the second smallest. Vinci. I don't know much about business or politics, except that there's little difference, but I did know that much. Byron had spoken as though he had as few feelings on the subject of Family rivalries as one of his computers, but I couldn't take it so calmly. I pushed my chair back and stood up.

"If you believe that, your logic circuits have been screwing your common sense. Unless it's cheaper to look for a scapegoat and never mind the truth."

He didn't react to insult or challenge. He didn't react at

all. I wondered just how deep that circuitry on his skull ran.

I headed for the door, conscious that I'd not only failed to learn anything but that I'd also probably made a fool of myself.

"In case you need to know, I'm going to speak to Daisy now. And don't try to bug the *Pig* while I'm away!"

I don't know why I said it, he'd already had opportunities enough, but it did get a reaction from him.

He laughed.

"Bug that boat? I doubt if I could. I've never seen anything with less to plug into. I don't know how you survive on it even when it's in harbour. At sea..." He shuddered.

In a way that cheered me up, even though it said he'd already looked into the subject. I didn't believe he couldn't do it, of course, but I liked the idea he might find it difficult. A challenge? I dismissed the thought before it could take root and left the room without troubling about how hard the door swung shut. I wondered as I left just how he'd managed my ladder in those smooth-soled boots.

14

Daisy let me in without argument and even switched the screen she was using to Hold.

"Find a perch."

I propped myself on the usual corner. Looked hard at her. She seemed calmer. "How's it going?"

She moved a hand in a see-saw motion. "Better. Nothing's gone wrong in three days and I've managed to make up a week of lost time and save fifty credits on a shipment. It may not last but it's an improvement."

A long earring dangled, clicking softly as its bright beaded tassels swung against each other. This was the Daisy I was used to.

"And the body?"

She grimaced. "Him. He left yesterday evening. The Company agreed to cough for the cremation."

It wasn't what I'd meant and she knew it, though I was unreasonably annoyed to find I'd lost the chance to say a decent goodbye to Jon. I didn't like my last memory of him to be of vomiting on the floor beside his body.

"What about the investigation?"

Her answer had the cynical edge which working for a Company can produce even in someone as straight as her.

"What investigation? Byron went over it with me and we decided that he could as easily have fallen in upriver as on Company property, which means it's not our problem any more. Even the peeps have agreed to file it as an accident. Unless someone files a complaint."

Now they had an ID they must have been able to discover he had no kin. It seemed no one else cared either. He was a problem only if someone wanted him to be and no one here did.

"That's it? You don't want to know who stripped him and smashed his head in and threw him into the river?"

She shifted but didn't look away. "Perhaps he hit his head when he fell in."

"After having taken off his clothes?"

"He might have been going for a swim." She looked aside as she said it. The message was clear enough.

"You mean you don't mind what happened as long as you're not going to be blamed?"

She didn't avoid my eyes this time. She knew what she was doing and accepted what she heard in my voice.

"I know how it sounds, and if I could see anything useful I could do I would do it. But right now I'm concerned with keeping this job and making sure there are no other 'accidents' to prevent this development going through. It's due to open in two months and at this rate we might, just might, bring it in on schedule."

I knew the pressures she was under, especially with Sheba pregnant. I couldn't argue with them. And if she and Byron were working together – although he'd taken care to give me precisely the opposite impression – then I had to be pleased she was more secure. It took an effort, but I smiled.

"I'm sorry. And I'm glad things seem to have turned round for you."

She relaxed, leaning back in her chair, relieved I was being sensible. "So's Sheba. She says I've been impossible lately."

"How's the pregnancy coming on?"

I'd never seen her face soften quite like that, as though she were thinking of something she'd dreamed of but never believed would happen. Her voice was softer, too, sort of blurred.

"It's great. There's another scan next week and after that we just have to sit back and wait."

"Some things even technology hasn't speeded up."

She laughed. Herself again. "Why don't you come over for a meal? Tomorrow? Sheba would like to see you."

I wasn't convinced of that, but it wasn't an invitation she offered lightly and I couldn't find it in me to refuse. I accepted and then left her so that she could turn back to the waiting screen.

Then I walked back to the *Pig* swearing under my breath all the way. Was I the only one left who was angry that a man had been killed and thrown out with as much ceremony as a dead cat?

15

Tom Lee's loaders arrived just before midday. I don't ask how they got a permit to bring a tanker in or who they had to pay: details like that are just business. Daisy has a bribes budget and the Company expects her to show a profit on it. Business. Even Gus ignored the men who ran the hose down to the *Pig's* hold.

Transfer didn't take long. They didn't need me there, either, but I preferred to be around when someone's collecting stuff from my boat, even when it's paid for. I listened to the low hum of the hose sucking the tank dry, convinced myself I could feel the *Pig* lighten, and hoped Tom Lee would give the wine rather more than six months to recover from what we'd put it through.

The silent types who'd done the work were ready to leave when one of them recalled he had a message. He was the sort Tom Lee usually employed: muscled and close-mouthed and able to take care of himself as long as he didn't have to think much about it. Remembering a message was more than he usually had to do and the effort was costing him.

"You the owner?"

I'd been sitting on deck while they transferred the load from my boat. Tom Lee must have described me and I was probably the only tall, thin red-head in the Port. It wasn't much of a guess.

"Me."

"Tom Lee said to tell you your man doesn't show up

dead on his files."

My turn to look dumb. "What do you mean?"

The question was beyond him. He'd delivered the message, that didn't mean he understood it. A shrug and a spit covered his answer.

I watched them drive off as I tried to work it out. The hatch cover I was sitting on was steel and neither warm nor soft but a move to somewhere more comfortable would mean asking arms and legs to work. I wasn't sure they would. I wasn't sure of anything. I couldn't have imagined what I'd seen in the mortuary. I'd have given every credit on my chip to have been able to believe it was a bad dream but not even the worst of my nightmares are that convincing.

So had I been wrong about the identification?

I don't like being wrong. I wasn't going to like admitting it to Tom Lee or, worse, Daisy. But the face *had* been bloated and disfigured and I hadn't seen Jon in months. Nor had we been that close. Could I be sure I'd even have thought of him if it hadn't been for the bonehead tekkie who'd taken his place?

Now I understood Byron's questions. He wasn't sure if the ID I'd made was ignorance or if I'd been covering. He had more and faster access than Tom Lee and he *knew* Jon was alive: his files said so.

If Jon was alive I should be pleased, even if that meant a bit of embarrassment and an anonymous corpse on the table in the white room. Except that I was still certain it was Jon's corpse.

And there was still a stranger living in the room Jon had called home.

I uncoiled myself from the hatch cover, creaking, and

went below. The saloon was a mess. I picked a couple of cushions off the floor and tossed them on to the worn settee which doubled as a sea-berth, moved an empty plate from the chart table to the sink, and went down the companionway to my cabin.

There's not room on a boat to hoard much. If I haven't used something in six months I throw it away. It's a system meant to stop me getting sentimental about old things and clinging on to pointless memories. Though it had taken me over a year to clean out Jack's cabin.

I hadn't done anything about a clear-out since I'd returned to Midway, so perhaps what I was looking for would still be here.

The lockers beneath the bunk were overfull. I had to empty them to discover that what I wanted wasn't in either of them. I pushed everything back, including two remotes which I'd been given in trade on the promise they would give me control over all the ship's functions from anywhere on board or off-shore up to thirty metres. Neither had ever worked. A second's thought had me pulling them out again and throwing them to one side: they could be the first to go if I ever got round to the clear-out. Somewhere there was a malfunctioning autopad which could join them. Then I kicked the locker doors shut. The automatic catches failed but a turnbuckle held them just as well. I sat on the bunk, considering.

Where would I have stashed something unimportant which I didn't yet want to throw out? Under the bed. Except that it wasn't there. I thought back to the day Jon had given me the packet, wishing I'd thought it important at the time. I'd just thought I was doing a favour at little cost to myself.

But when I'd got back to the Port I'd found the small square object waiting in my mail chute. No message, unless you count "Thanx. Jon." coming up on the screen when I put in a query. No comeback call number.

I'd dropped the thing into my sack without a thought. I hadn't even looked at it closely. I'd assumed he wanted to pay a debt. I'd also known he had nothing of value to trade. I might have been wrong. At least if I found the square object it might give me a clue. At the moment I could barely recall what it looked like.

It had been solid, made of some sort of metal. I remembered now that I'd emptied out that sack because the shoulder straps were working loose. If you don't want your sack snatched from your shoulders you keep the straps tight. I know plenty of people who deliberately keep them loose because they'd rather lose a bag than get into a struggle but I've never been able to think like that. So. I'd been mending.

I don't use autobonding, though it's fast and, whatever Jack said, the seals are strong. But he'd made me learn the old way – sail needle and waxed thread – and since he'd been gone I'd found I preferred it.

The mending things were buried deep in a box beneath the hold workbench. I had to go back on deck and down the hatch I'd been sitting on before I could squeeze my way through to the forward end of the hold, past the now-empty storage tank. The air was heavy with the sweetness of spilled wine. The muscle had managed to siphon a little side-benefit. I shrugged. Tom Lee's problem, not mine.

The box was a mess. Tangles of thread of varying sizes. An autobond iron in case I got lazy. I tried the switch: it didn't work. Two knives, both sharp. Needles. There was even an old leather sailor's palm for pushing the needle through thicknesses of sailcloth. Real leather.

I swallowed. It was one of Jack's more grotesque leftovers and I'd meant to throw it out years ago. Trouble was I could barely bring myself to touch it. I found an old rag and used that to lift it, trying not to think of skinned animals. Jon's token was underneath.

I dropped the palm into the tide and the rag with it before I took a good look at what I'd found. It didn't tell me anything. I was holding a cube of some pale, lightweight metal I didn't recognise. I'd thought it was solid, now I wasn't sure. Each face had a symbol on it but none of them meant anything to me: a circle with a line through it, a series of concentric squares, a diagonal cross. No way of knowing if the marks meant something or were someone's idea of ornament.

There was some damage or wear which made three of the faces unreadable. The cube had probably been thrown out before it came to Jon but what it had meant or whether it had ever had a purpose I couldn't tell. I couldn't ask Jon. I could only hope it might mean something to someone else. It would probably turn out to be some sort of puzzle toy that Jon had given up on.

I laced on my boots, put the thing in my sack and set the *Pig's* alarms behind me.

16

I left the Port without an encounter with Gus. I hoped he was avoiding me while deciding what to do with the wine and wished I'd thought of it earlier. I didn't see Byron, either.

It was shift-change. Company workers in Company grey crowded round the barriers, jostling their way towards waiting transports. I heard some swearing and saw a bent elbow shove a woman aside but few looked at each other. They probably didn't know each other. Looking at the blank faces I understood why some chose to stay on the streets. The Company might offer a way out but it cost too much.

I walked past the transports which had already unloaded the incoming shift. Daisy would have got me a Company pass but I preferred the public system even though it was slow and its fumes would poison me. I'd choke faster if I had to take anything from the Corps.

The bus was a long time coming. When it did I stood, ignoring the thirty other bodies beside me, while it jerked and swayed along the pot-holed shore road. Whatever sensors controlled its route were outworn and slipping. Jumping on and off was hazardous: you could never be sure it would slow at the scheduled pull-ins. Once as it sped past a would-be passenger fell heavily as he tried to board. We'd rounded a corner before I could see if he regained his feet. If anyone else saw him they kept quiet. No one tried to slow the bus or help. That included me.

The girl I was pushed up against was in her own world. VR glasses let her believe she was in some more glamorous transport, perhaps her own auto, and her dreams didn't have room for passengers. She swayed aside with reflex ease when I moved past her as I glimpsed the shore towers.

I jarred my ankles jumping off. I always do. I swore, then hitched my sack more securely and headed across the barren ground to the tower.

The stairs to the fifth floor smelled of urine, and trash piled in an almost orderly heap told of more than one body finding shelter here overnight. I stepped over the rags and old containers, hoping they held nothing more dangerous than roaches, and made my way up. I still had no wish to try the elevator.

The fifth floor had the advantage of being high enough to discourage the worst of the derelicts. Its filth was the responsibility of those who lived here. Which said little for their cleanliness. I knocked on the barred door again. The vid was still out of action.

I was prepared to wait. I was also prepared to keep hammering on the door until I had an answer. Assuming, of course, that the new tenant was inside. I was beginning to doubt it when the grille slid aside. The pale blue eye stared.

"Can we talk?"

"Why?"

Unpromising. I fumbled in my sack. "This?"

The eye blinked. It's a lie to say you can read expression in an eye. You need the surrounding territory.

"Where did you get that?"

He wanted to slam the grille. I could feel it. The small cube was stopping him. So it was a key of some sort. I wished I knew what.

"A friend."

The truth is useful sometimes. Even when it conceals a lie. If Blue Eyes believed I had a powerful friend, not one lying dead on a slab, it might give me a lever. Silence stretched out while he stared, then he stepped back and I heard the rattle of a heavy bolt being drawn, a chain freed. The tumblers of a lock fell into place, then the grid in front of the door slid back into its casing. The door edged open, just enough for me to slip in sideways.

He had a knife. It was wide in the blade and tapered to a wicked point. The handle was black, dimpled for a better grip. A professional's knife. It also trembled in his hand as if the sweat on his palms wouldn't let him take a firm hold. It might have been his own weapon but I doubted it. That didn't make it less dangerous, just less predictable.

I stepped clear of him, leaving as much distance between us as the narrow hall allowed. "You need that?"

He looked down at the knife, then back at me. Almost embarrassed. He set it down on the scarred table which was the hall's only furniture. The small clatter seemed to make him even more nervous. He wiped his palms down greasy coveralls.

He was my height or a little shorter – the way he hunched his shoulders made him seem small. His frame was wiry, brittle-looking. I could feel the tension, the uncertainty, and was glad he'd put down the knife. He smelled sour. His coverall was grey beneath the grime with one knee torn, the other badly mended. His autobond must work almost as badly as mine. The clothes hung on him as though he'd lately lost weight. Or they'd been bought for someone bigger. He was fair, bleached-looking, with an ugly UV scar marring one side of his thin face.

Left out in the sun as a kid? Left unconscious in it more recently? I didn't want to know.

His head jerked towards the inner doorway. "Go in."

The room was not quite square. Worn plastic covered the floor, its pattern long since faded until it was mottled and unreadable. There were holes in it where someone might have dropped something which burned, others where long-standing furniture had worn its own places in the room. Except that that furniture wasn't there any more. Instead there was a couch with spindly legs which doubled as a bed. A pillow and a couple of blankets still lay across it as though Blue Eyes had not long left them. There were another two chairs, one with a ripped cover, a low table and a big monitor in the corner which would get all the entertainment channels. It was the only new thing in the room. I guessed there would be a sink and a micro behind the screen, perhaps a shower cubicle. I didn't want to look at either.

I walked across to the single window. Blue Eyes didn't get a sea view. He looked across at the skeleton of the burned tower and down to the broken concrete of what had been a kids' play area. There were kids down there now, hanging round the broken frame which had once held swings and throwing stones at sacks of trash. At least I hoped that was what was in the sacks. I turned away from the view but not before I'd registered that someone had replaced the old glass with plex. It hadn't been Blue Eyes or even Jon - the plex was scarred and weathered with age and starred in one corner where something had hit it. A stone? A bullet? Plex doesn't fracture easily.

"You goin' to say why you here?"

He was trying for defiance but he'd need to straighten

out the quaver in his voice before he got successful.

"Told you. Looking for Jon."

"And I told you I don't know the man. He ain't here."

That much I'd guessed myself. Jon had gone and, from what I could see, so had all his possessions. Though I hadn't been inside this place when Jon had lived here, I was certain none of these things were his. They belonged to someone who needed some furniture, any, and had neither time nor credit for choice. They came from one of the sales held on the waste ground most weeks when people traded the little they had for enough to keep them going for another week, another fix.

"How'd you hear the place was empty?"

A shrug. But he'd sat down on the bed now, his hands clenched between his thighs. Still tense, but I had the feeling it wasn't me he was afraid of. Now I was in I'd crossed a boundary.

I'd found the same thing before, though this was the first time I'd invaded privacy so brutally. It was as though once they'd let you into their territory, even unwillingly, you'd passed some barrier which separated stranger from - what? Not friend, not colleague or even acquaintance, nothing that intimate. Perhaps it was just an acknowledgement of identity. A willingness to *see* the other person, not just to let your eyes slide away and your feet step aside in the queue and the crush.

I walked over and sat in the chair with a torn cover. "You going to tell me?"

I kept my voice soft, casual, though we both knew there was nothing casual about my presence here.

He was looking down at the indecipherable pattern on the floor. "Man told me."

I waited.

He looked up. "Just a man. Didn't give his name, didn't ask questions. Just told me there was a place here."

Had Jon even been dead then? The man, whoever he was, had known Jon wouldn't be going home. I wished I didn't believe Blue Eyes, but I did. There was more, of course – no one gives away roomspace – but Blue Eyes wouldn't have a name to give me.

"What happened to Jon's things?"

"How the fuck I know? Place was empty. Man didn't even leave a bed."

I couldn't tell if he meant Jon or the man who'd offered him the room but the resentment was genuine. The faint hope Jon might have left some clue here faded. I stood up. Wondered just what I'd hoped to find.

"So. What you paying the man?"

"I never see him again. And who says I pay?"

"You don't get a room, even junk like this, for nothing. And I know it didn't get offered on the regular list."

The Net listed vacant properties and made deals about rent or benefit. But Jon hadn't been officially dead when Blue Eyes moved in. If Tom Lee was right, he wasn't officially dead now. Whoever offered the room had his own way of knowing Jon wouldn't be back. Had also known, I now realised, that the Net wouldn't advertise the place as empty because Jon wasn't Missing. I was getting more and more curious about this man. Unfortunately Blue Eyes was having second thoughts about the wisdom of letting me into his prized room.

"Seems like you know nothing. You think I got credit to pay rent?"

Nothing about him or the room suggested any sort of

credit, but rent can be paid in all types of coin. I didn't think it was his body he was selling and he didn't have the look of one who sold secrets or drugs: people like that tend to affluence and he still smelled of the streets. His question only made me curious about just what he had to offer in exchange for the luxury of one squalid room.

"I think you're running scared. Or have you forgotten this?"

I tossed the meaningless cube high and caught it again. His eyes followed it, the lump in his thin neck bobbing as he swallowed.

"Where you get it?" he asked again.

I took a risk. "From a dead man."

It worked too well. More colour than I'd thought he had to lose drained from his face. He took a step back, staring at me now, shaking his head. I was glad the knife was out in the hall: he looked as though he wanted to defend himself.

"You kill him?"

"Kill who?"

He still looked as though he did not believe what he saw but all he wanted now was to get rid of me.

"You out of you mind. They gonna *delete* you! Get outta here – I don't know how you got that thing but I don't want no part in the virus it give you. When he shut you down I'm gonna say I never see you!"

He thought he was doing me a favour. Or himself. If I didn't go he would try to make me and though I was probably the stronger I wasn't desperate and he was. It made a difference. I lifted both hands.

"OK. I'm away."

I was backing out of the room because I didn't want to

turn my back on him. Especially not once I was out into the hall and he was almost within hand's reach of the knife.

"You've got the door codes," I reminded him.

I couldn't open the locks and, with luck, nor could he unless he put down the knife he was reaching for. I could see him weighing up the chance of wasting me against the problem of dealing with the mess afterwards and was relieved to see his fingers slide away from the black hilt.

Nudging me aside, he worked on the door, a thin shoulder hunched to hide the key and the codes from me. At last the outer door jerked its way back into the wall.

"Out."

I walked past him. I'd never thought I'd find the air of that landing fresh but now I drew a deep breath as though I'd not used my lungs for some time. Behind me the familiar clatter of the locks had begun. He was in a hurry but I just had time to turn and smile.

"See you again," I promised as he slammed the last grille.

He didn't need to say it: Not if he saw me first.

I had started down the first flight of stairs when I heard a grille slide shut. Not Blue Eyes'. He wouldn't be opening to anyone just yet. This was from one of the other four doors on that landing. I couldn't be certain but had the feeling it had been the one diagonally opposite the door I'd used. The red light glowed on its vid.

Someone there was curious. I wondered if it was me or Blue Eyes who was under surveillance. No way of knowing, but I was thoughtful as I went on down the five flights.

17

It was the middle of the afternoon. There was work to be done on the *Pig* and I needed to talk to Daisy about Em's problem with finding a new berth. But I was hungry and I had to think about what to do next and I wasn't quite ready to leave the shore area. I began to walk up the road.

When I'd been in the Community I'd thought of cities as massive single-celled entities of enormous power. I'd been wrong. They're multi-celled, loosely organised. A series of territories whose boundaries are liable to shift in the time it takes for someone to die or get rich or discover a source of drugs or goods which someone else wants. Tom Lee was at the heart of one territory. I wasn't sure its boundaries reached this far; if they did they were breaking down. Perhaps there wasn't enough here to show a profit. A little smuggling, perhaps: the remains of the old slipway was still sometimes used to launch rafts and boats small enough to manhandle. Small enough that no one asked what cargo they carried or what they fished for in the slimy water.

The tide was low now, the broken stonework of the slip-way ending in mud which glistened, an oily film covering its smoothness. I shivered and turned away. That mud is so fine you sink into it almost as easily as into water. Getting out again is a different matter.

One of the bridge's main supports was a blunt concrete shaft down through the centre of the huddle of buildings. Some had been pulled down to build it and the rest of the place had been forced into new routes, splitting and dividing around the monolith. The broad carriageway ran indifferently overhead, darkening the huddle of buildings beneath.

I found my way to an open-fronted stall which was frying something nameless but which smelled OK. In exchange for a couple of coins I accepted two coarse sausages wrapped in thick bread. The grease and the heavy dough were comforting, a physical satisfaction which eased the mental discomfort as I reviewed what had happened. I didn't ask the nature of the protein in the tough skins.

I felt as though I had picked up a handful of wires with no way of understanding any of them or telling how they were connected. *If* they were connected. The encounter with Blue Eyes had only raised more questions. He knew more than he was saying, but perhaps not much more.

What I needed to know was just what he did in exchange for the room. And who he did it for. Whether Jon had done the same thing was another question – and whether it had led to his death.

How, *if*, all that tied in with the sabotage at the Port and who that had been aimed at was still obscure. As was the fact that Tom Lee did not think Jon was dead.

I wiped my mouth on my sleeve. There were too many questions and I wasn't the person to answer them. I wasn't an investigator. The Company guards and the peeps all had their resources, so had the other private operators who ran their own territories and traded safety for a price. Byron probably had more than all of them. None of them would help me. Some might try to stop me. If I went on asking questions Blue Eyes' forecast of my future just might come true. I should go back to my boat and start the painting or the clearout and plan my next trip. Perhaps lay out another spread of Blue Moon.

But I wasn't fooling myself. I didn't want to walk away. Jon was dead. Whatever Tom Lee claimed, I hadn't been wrong when I identified him. And I couldn't let his death be meaningless. No one else wanted to ask questions, so it was left to me to make a nuisance of myself.

The last chunk of bread and sausage had become indigestible. I threw it away and began a slow walk back towards the shore towers. Behind me something scrabbled out of the rubbish and snatched the discarded food.

There were fewer people around once I was beyond the bridge. I had been pestered once for coin and had the usual comments shouted after me, but I don't look rich and I didn't answer the comments. I also know better than to show an interest in whatever's going on when I see a group of girls watching silently from a corner. I shifted my sack on my shoulders and tried not to hurry.

I still had a couple of hours before dusk. Time to explore. The towers stood up from the flat emptiness around them like stumps. The rest of the shore was wasteland. At high water the tide must nearly flood the lobby of the nearest tower. The road split it from the other two: the ruined one and the one where Blue Eyes lived. I made my way down to the shore.

Above the tide line the mud yielded reluctantly to oily sand. Broken ends of metal and glass ensured no one came here to paddle. If the Company ever wanted to turn this bit of real estate into a recreation area, it would take more than a face-lift: the place needed a total peel. The whole shore was a health hazard. I shivered as I looked across to the ugly buildings on the far side, half-smothered in their own fumes. Then I went inside.

The lobby *did* flood. You could tell that from the rim of grime half a metre up the wall. Like standing in a bath tub which hadn't been cleaned in years. I went up as far as the first half-landing to take a look at the inshore view.

Nothing unexpected. A bleary sun was setting behind me and a few glints reflected from scratched plex in the nearer tower. One or two windows were shuttered and some had lights on inside.

Around the block was nothing but broken concrete and scrubby grass. Little else. It was the place's peculiarity: in the middle of the Solent sprawl – a city overrun with people fighting to hold on to their own niches, elbows crooked against intrusion, defences high – was this space. A desert a couple of kilometres square in the middle of a jungle. Only some sort of contamination could have stopped the city overrunning it.

A shadow moved behind a blind on the fifth floor opposite. Not Blue Eyes. His room was on the far side. I frowned, concentrating, working out that the movement belonged to whoever had been watching me when I left earlier. No matter: I had enough problems without worrying about some over-cautious neighbour's curiosity and whoever was there was staring into the sun. It wouldn't be easy to see me. I went back down to the scummy entrance.

The lobby's wide entry might once have had automatic doors, now it gaped emptily. Security started at your own entry and was in your own hands, the building itself was open to all. The post boxes had mostly been torn from the wall though a few still looked sound. The same pattern as

Blue Eyes' building. There was no obvious rear exit. I went outside, my feet crunching on grit and sand. There. On the same side of the tower but half-hidden by a short, low wall from which bricks had fallen or been taken – for throwing? – was the second door.

I'd known it must be there, though it might be sealed. There had to be more than one way out of somewhere like this. It might once have been a service exit, even a fire escape. All I cared was that it existed and I knew where. And that these were the only two exits from the block.

They had all been built alike. Not much of an assumption, once I'd seen the lack of imagination which had designed everything else about them. Now all I had to do was find somewhere to wait.

It wasn't easy. The desert operated against me, offering little cover, and I wasn't dressed to pass for a drifter. Just loitering would be to ask for attention from whatever security the place possessed. There would be some, though I'd seen no sign of it. Wherever people live there's someone offering protection and prepared to make it very clear what will happen to those who think they don't need it.

I needed not to be visible. I wanted a bunker.

It took me twenty minutes to find one. There was no way of telling what the concrete shelter had been built for or what had been stored in it since then. I was only glad a recent fire had removed most of the traces. The important detail was that from here I could watch both entrances to Blue Eyes' tower without being seen. I could live with the lingering taint of smoke. I leaned against the blackened wall and then slid to the ground hugging my knees to my chest. It might be a long wait.

I was waiting for Blue Eyes. He'd been at home both

times I'd called. Unless he never went out that meant he was a night crawler. Whatever business he did in exchange for his filthy room must take him out at night. If I could follow him ... the plan faded a bit at that point. I hadn't realised just how open these surroundings would prove. Nor, if I were honest with myself, was I sure what I hoped to learn if he did come out. The identity of the man he'd spoken of?

I was still trying to work out how best to follow anyone and thanking providence that I'd chosen dark clothes – wishing the same providence had encouraged me to add another, warmer, layer - when the kid bladed past me.

It was almost fully dark, hard to see any details. He or she was thin with the wiriness of someone who'd grown up on the streets with never quite enough to eat, never an uninterrupted night's sleep. Dark hair cropped close. A long muffler wound close around neck and mouth. Impossible to say whether it was for warmth or disguise or display. All three perhaps. The blader was showing off.

It was a solitary dance, performed for no one's pleasure but his/her own. Watching, I suddenly felt I was spying. I'd felt no such guilt when I'd chosen to crouch here against the smoke-blackened concrete and wait for Blue Eyes. This was different. Unexpected. The blader was using the open spaces of the towers' desert to celebrate freedom from crowds and narrow streets. Breaks in the concrete paving, slopes and steps and scattered junk – all were opportunities, not obstacles, as the lithe body twisted and crouched and momentarily defied gravity in the exhilaration of flight.

It lasted only a few minutes before the figure skidded to a stop and took a last slow circle of the forecourt, accepting unheard applause. And then he/she swung up to the tower's entrance, sliding across the hall straight over to the line of personal post boxes.

My view of the boxes was uncluttered. There was even a dim bulb glowing in the lobby. By its light I saw the figure check something on a digital readout strapped to one thin wrist, then a code was punched in. A pause. A box door swung open and shut and then the blader was away.

I didn't move. There was no chance of catching someone travelling on blades. Besides, I was working out what I'd seen and cursing my earlier stupidity. I had seen which box the blader had opened. Knew it because I'd checked on my last visit that it was still intact. Still in the same state as when I'd dropped a package into it all those months ago. Jon's box.

Of course whoever employed him would not meet Blue Eyes. If they'd ever had more than one direct encounter I'd be surprised: they'd have worked through at least one cut-off and probably done everything through the Net. That big monitor was more than an entertainment centre: it was bribe and communications in one. And the key to it all was still the mailbox. That was probably all Blue Eyes had to offer in exchange for his room. All he had to do was ignore whoever used his box.

Like Jon? No. He'd paid rent. But he'd also been paid for his box. And it was beginning to look as though he hadn't played by the rules.

At a guess the package he'd wanted me to put in his box had been something he'd wanted put *back* but didn't want to risk putting back himself. Because he always had been too curious for his own good and he'd taken it out to have a look at. And realised that this time he just might have done something that might mean trouble. Thanks, Jon.

The forecourt was empty now. The wind was blowing litter fitfully across it before letting it pile up in shadowy corners where scavengers would later root through it. Though there were lives going on in all those rooms not thirty paces away from me, it was a desolate place. The desolation crept inside me and I shivered. Something about the solitary blader reminded me of my own isolation.

There would still be buses running towards Midway. I decided to start walking and hop the first transport back to the *Pig*. Home. Blue Eyes would not come out now, and if he did he would not lead me where I needed to go.

18

I dreamed of Jack. Jack rescuing a runaway boy who turned out to be a girl and hiding his disappointment so well that we'd been sailing together for a month before I realised why he didn't try to seduce me. Jack who had taught me I could survive outside the Community. Jack who had shared his love of the sea with me. Jack who had gambled and lost and stayed an optimist. Jack who I'd brought home time and again from the young men who took him for all he had. Jack who held me and let me cry when my own first love proved as reliable as all of his young men.

Jack who was dead and whose drowned white face was spongy with decay when I reached out to it and felt the flesh shred beneath my fingers.

I woke sweating. My throat was sore. I didn't know if I'd been shouting or crying in my sleep. It felt like both.

The shower was hard and cold and I was angry. Angry with myself, with friends who died, with questions without answers. In the end I stopped punishing myself and adjusted the temperature control to hot. In a shower no one can tell if the water on your face is tears.

Two cups of caf improved my outlook. Dreams of the past were no use now, whatever set them off. It didn't take a psych to tell me I'd imposed Jon's death on Jack's because it was Jack's which filled me with the greater sense of injustice. Jon's I just might get the chance to do something about. Though I wasn't yet awake enough to think what that might be.

Perhaps my visit to Blue Eyes would panic him enough to provoke some action. But I couldn't spend all day out at the shore watching for him to emerge. And I didn't have the facilities to access his calls.

Byron undoubtedly did, but I wasn't going to ask.

Tom Lee might. There were new questions I needed to ask him, too. But you don't go empty-handed to the biggest Changer in the Solent. He'd only deal if he could use whatever you had to sell. I needed a bargaining chip.

He'd been interested in the concessions here. I decided to spend the morning seeing how far the development had progressed in the months I'd been away.

19

Further than I'd realised. The continued presence of the dredges when I'd arrived back here had made me assume the infrastructure was still unfinished. Now I saw that the work I had halted must have been almost finished even then. The dredges were gone. The piles of spoil on the far bank were already drying out, the black mud bleaching grey and beginning to crack. In the two months left before the scheduled opening I had no doubt a gardening team would make the muddy heaps flower. That the flowering would be entirely synthetic, the plants rooted in nothing and replaced overnight by automated attendants when they wilted, would cause no one to lose sleep.

The pontoons for the expected craft were already in place: pale and mostly empty. They'd used some sort of material which looked like wood but which would never splinter or provide any other sort of discomfort for the men and women who could afford the exotic delights of pleasure boats. The hookups for vids and VR and comsets were all ready. No one would need to lose contact with Family or business. They wouldn't even need to leave the Port. Virtual sailing was safer and more comfortable and who could tell the difference? I compared the marina with my own dock-side berth: the lock which meant they would never see the mud even when the tide dropped with the rusted ladder which led from the *Pig's* pontoon at low water. Jack would have snorted and said he preferred reality but I understand the appeal of comfort, artificial or not.

"Keep out of there!"

I didn't need to turn to recognise Gus warning me off.

"Fraid I'll contaminate the water?"

"You're not cleared for the marina. Security's tight and it doesn't cover deadbeats like you."

He was proud of his foolproof and brand-new system.

"You mean I'll get dumped in the river like poor Jon if I take a step over the line?"

His face went from red to purple. For a moment I thought he might have a fit and waited with some eagerness, but he drew a deep breath and the colour ebbed.

"Just get away!"

I shrugged. Though I was interested in the marina and had fantastic visions of the *Pig* wallowing in all that luxury, it wasn't what I'd come over here for. I thought I heard Gus shouting something more, when I strolled in the direction of the land-based section of the development, but I ignored him. He couldn't keep me off something that was part of the Port for whose facilities I had actually paid. Though I had no illusions about what would happen the nanosecond my credit ran dry. All the more reason to make certain Daisy stayed in her job. And to do my exploring while I still could.

They had built on the site of a disused boatshed and some old stores. A pity: I had been in the habit of using the old shed when I'd had to work on the dinghy or on fittings from the *Pig* which needed more space than one rickety wooden jetty allowed.

Someone had decided that the new facilities would look more authentic if they pretended to be old ships. I'd have thought boatsheds would have been more appropriate but that didn't offer the same scope for imaginative design –

flaring shapes and curved walls simulating ships' sides, a sharply pointed bow looming over an entrance way – did they know *nothing* about ships? They had even simulated the planking of a laid deck in the flooring. No doubt the ropes and a mast – complete with Company flag – would arrive soon. All the automated building work was complete, leaving some human agency to decide questions of taste. At a price.

Beneath the absurd architecture and the designer's trappings, the concessions were about what I'd expected. There were the usual VR booths – both solo and group – though they were furnished with far more luxury than any I'd ever seen. There was a clothes shop: there's something about searching through racks of clothes with real live assistants fawning around which apparently has a powerful appeal for the mega-rich.

I don't like shopping. Families do. For people like me and most cits or streetpeople shops are alien – if they mean places to browse through a choice of goods, where attendants try to coax you into buying. If you have credit you do the respectable thing and stay at home and call up what you want from the Net.

I found my way to the open space where it looked like the food stalls would be. Eating in public was currently fashionable – as long as you were selective about your public – so there was room for a number of tables where people could watch and be watched. This side of things looked almost complete. I wondered if I was too late.

"Hey, you! Nothing's open yet."

I looked around the empty shelves and half-built kitchens where mechanical and human workers were doing noisy things with drills and saws. "You don't say."

The big man who had shouted grinned and wiped his hands on a cloth that looked substantial enough to cover one of the tables. "Don't worry. It'll all be fixed in time for the opening." He frowned. "Unless the Port jinx hits us." So Daisy's saboteur was no secret here, either. "You're not one of the contractors."

Half question, half statement. Meaning: what was I doing here and would he be within his rights to throw me out? I hoped he didn't have the same mind-set as Gus.

"No. I live on one of the boats moored here and I thought I'd look round. Are all the concessions sold off yet?"

The frown didn't quite lift. "Not all. You thinking of buying into one?"

I couldn't blame him for the suspicion. Even at my best I don't look like I have the sort of money that buys concessions in premium malls. And my manner probably doesn't suggest someone aching to serve the public. I trusted in my open and honest smile instead. "Not on my credit balance. Just interested. Might know someone who could afford it, though."

He seemed willing to suspend judgement and offered to show me round. Introduced himself as Steven and admitted to being superintendent of the concessions, so my luck was in.

"What's that over there?" I pointed at something that looked like a primitive flame pit.

"Barbecue." I'd been right. "Customers can pick their own raw food and watch it cooked."

"The sophisticated version of roughing it?"

The wide grin was back. "You got it."

He walked me round the rest of the space, which was

apparently going to be called The Piazza. Then looked at me with shrewdness beneath the amiable surface. "So you don't want to buy, you don't want a job and you're just curious? Doesn't seem like your sort of place."

"It isn't," I admitted. "But I told you, I know someone who could be interested in the food side. He's good," I added when the guy still looked sceptical.

"Would I know him?" Implying that he already knew anyone round here who was any good.

I decided to take the risk. "Tom Lee."

He stared. "*Tom Lee?* You've got some weird friends."

"He's not exactly a friend."

"Glad to hear it. Just what makes you think there's room here for the biggest fence on the south coast?" At least he knew who Tom Lee was.

"He prefers to be called a Changer. More class."

"I don't care what he calls himself these days. How popular am I going to be if I invite organised crime on to Company property?"

I didn't point out that it was probably already here. "You ever eaten at his place?"

The silence stretched, told me what I'd guessed. Thought the guy was remembering. At last he said, "You trust him?" as though it was an alien idea.

"If he's made a deal, yes. Otherwise no."

"And you think he wants to make a deal here?"

"Could be."

He thought about it. Shrugged massive shoulders. "OK. He calls, I'll talk to him."

So. I had my trading token. If Tom Lee's interest was genuine, I could give him a contact which didn't rely on Daisy's influence. It might be enough.

I took a few minutes more to look at the rest of the place: there were bars and a caf-house conveniently between the gym and the bath house. Someone had given the layout some thought after all. The bath house, I guessed, was meant to resemble ancient Rome: conspicuous decadence was the main design criterion.

It was in my mouth sweet as honey: and as soon as I had eaten it my belly was bitter.

I had a sudden image of the shoreside flats and the contrast with this place was more than I could stomach. Gus wouldn't need to find a way of banning me from the place once it opened: it would take something more urgent than I was willing to imagine to drag me back inside.

I needed to go back to the *Pig* or find a public terminal to put in a call to Tom Lee.

20

My progress back through what little was left of the old dockyard was interrupted. Clim was scavenging.

"Humility." He nodded at me.

I gestured at the sack he carried. "Clim. Picked up all the useful stuff?"

"Still a few bits lying around."

"The contractors are a messy lot."

As I looked I could see what he'd been poking around in: heaps of discarded metal, broken tools, off-cuts, the unwanted ends of rolls of material The waste-recycler wouldn't be here until the contractors were gone, no point calling it in before the mess was complete. Which gave people like Clim enough time to sort out the useful stuff. People like me, too. Under normal circumstances I'd have been through this waste heap once already.

Clim bent to pick up a half-used spool of tape, straightened, looked at me.

"Contractors have been messy since before even I was born. It's what gives people like you and me a head start."

"Meaning?"

My voice must have been sharper than I'd intended. His eyes narrowed.

"Only that their leavings cost us no credit. What you think I meant?"

I wasn't sure. I was just remembering that he knew more about boats and dockyards than most people I knew. I shook my head. I was being paranoid.

"Nothing. Guess I'm just pissed that the boatyard's finished and that there won't be pickings like this left much longer."

A good part of the *Pig* was fitted out with what Jack or I had found discarded around old workshops and places like this.

Clim chuckled. "Don't you believe it. Those overdressed bits of plascrete may not look like any boat you or I would be seen dead on, but that doesn't mean they won't need maintenance. Give it a year and there'll be all the gear you could want lying around. More, perhaps: folk who own boats like them don't bother much with repairs – they just throw things out and order new."

"And you'll be standing around ready to catch what's thrown?"

"Why not? If Gus knew what was good for him he'd get himself an easy cut. As it is…"

As it was, Clim enjoyed running rings round the Harbour Master and didn't have to pay anyone for what he salvaged. Then the mischief left his face and I was reminded how old he must be, remembered that a moment ago he hadn't straightened quite as fast as he'd used to.

"Course, way things are, we're not likely to get much chance to profit."

It wasn't quite a question. I didn't have any easy answers.

"I'm seeing Daisy this evening, when she's off-site."

It wasn't much but he nodded, his face brightening as though I'd offered something of real value. "Good idea. That way it's unofficial."

"I can't promise she'll help."

I had to add it. He was hoping for too much, expecting too much from me. I hadn't wanted to get involved in the first place; now I felt the drag of his expectations, and Em's and all the others', and wanted to struggle free. If I could have taken the *Pig* out that moment, I would have gone.

"Something'll work itself out, you'll see. You just talk to that woman. She's Company but she's always been fair in the past, no reason for things to be different now."

I couldn't tell if it was himself he was reassuring or me. I didn't believe in miracles any more. But still I hoped that Daisy's rigid honesty could survive the pressures of a threatened job and Sheba's pregnancy. Hoped that Daisy still had influence here.

"No reason at all."

"Smile when you say that, girl. Here, take this. Your boat's looking a mess."

He handed me an almost unused can of paint. I took it. No point in asking him where he found it when none of the new boats used oil-based paints. Besides, my own stocks were low and I'd been wondering where I'd get more. And he was right about the *Pig*.

"Thanks. I'll do my best with Daisy."

"Know you will."

He stumped off, the sack on his shoulder making him list like a ship in a gale. I knew better than to offer help.

21

I was seeing Daisy that night. Before then there was something else I had to do. I had to talk to Byron again. I didn't want to but, whatever else he was, he was official. He had authority and could deal better than I could with what I'd learned. It went against the grain to seek help, especially from someone like him, but even though I might be stiff-necked I can recognise the point where pride risks harming someone apart from me. Daisy deserved better than that. So did Jon.

The tekkie thug was on the gate again.

"Byron."

He let me pass without a word and with none of the greedy speculation in his eyes there'd been earlier. The hostility which had replaced it was only marginally less unpleasant. There was something else there, too, as though he knew something about me that I didn't. I put it down to my access to someone with Byron's weight, and went quickly into the building trying not to hurry, not to feel the way his eyes followed me. As though I was prey. I was glad when the door slid shut behind me.

Byron's door was open.

It crossed my mind to wonder just *why* I had such easy access to him and then I was back in the chair I'd sat in before, hoping I looked confident.

"Thanks for seeing me."

He nodded. Waited. I wished he'd give me an opening but couldn't blame him. I'd made my feelings clear enough on our last meeting.

"It's about Jon."

A frown, pretending not to recall. "The tekkie who used to work here? The one you identified as the body?"

Wrongly identified. He didn't quite say it. I kept my voice even but my hands tried to tighten into fists.

"That's the one. I didn't tell you I knew where he lived. Went over to the northshore flats to check it out. Someone else is living there."

"You sure it was the right place?"

Fair enough. The Net doesn't offer addresses and casual acquaintances certainly don't hand them out. For a moment I wondered if Blue Eyes' presence was as easily explained as that: I'd got the wrong room. After all, I'd never actually seen Jon there. No. It smelled wrong. I nodded.

"Sure."

"Just confirms what the files say, then. He's moved on, didn't want anyone to know. Sub-let the room to realise whatever assets he had."

Perhaps he was an auditor after all. It was the first time he'd sounded like one.

"I don't think so. Man in there was frightened." I swallowed, forced myself to go on, ask the favour. "Thought you could check it out."

He leaned back in his chair. "Nothing to check."

It was no news to him that someone living in the city was frightened. I fished in my sack. Took out the cube which had scared Blue Eyes. Held it up.

"What about this?"

He did look at it. Didn't reach for it. Certainly didn't look scared. I looked at the battered cube and wasn't surprised – it was such a trivial object that I was embarrassed to be waving it at him. I closed my hand on it, let the hand retreat to my lap. Waited.

"Interesting." He didn't sound interested. "Damaged, too. If you had it from your friend, I'd guess he scavenged it somewhere."

It was only what I'd thought when I first received it. And if Byron Cody knew what it was, he wasn't telling.

"So you're not going to do anything about Jon."

A shift of one shoulder which might have been a shrug. "What should I do? No crime to leave a job."

"Even if he's been murdered?"

"No proof he's dead."

My word wasn't proof, not against what his files told him.

"No. Even the body's been burned."

He ignored the edge of bitterness I couldn't quite control. "Not my business."

"So what is?"

I didn't expect an answer. He looked straight at me, lifted both hands and let them fall. Surprised me.

"I'm in security."

"A *peep*?"

I nearly laughed at the twitch of distaste.

"No. Private. Independent."

He had to be very good. Independent meant no Family ties and yet he was good enough for a Family to consult. And Families don't ask outsiders in without being certain there's profit in it.

"Technofraud?"

Not that I needed to ask. He wore his speciality with arrogance.

"Of course." One hand moved on the table in front of

him. Idly? I couldn't see any answering response from the matt surface but who knew what his fingertips read? "The Vincis called me in to trace the origin of the delays here."

I mistrusted the apparent frankness. Wondered what it hid. "Why tell me?"

Another half-shrug. "Two reasons. One: you're not going to keep out of it, are you?"

No point in lying. "No."

"Thought not."

"The other reason?"

"I've had a look round. I don't think this is techno. Not entirely. I can't find any signs of deliberate interference, just a few messy mistakes. No more than usual."

For people not as gifted as him, he meant. And the same arrogance had convinced him that if he couldn't trace deliberate interference, there wasn't any. Which, I reluctantly conceded, was probably right. It didn't lessen my resentment of him.

"You're saying Daisy's incompetent?" For her that would be almost as disastrous a verdict as finding her culpable.

Byron shook his head. "No. No worse than some. Better than most. And if she is involved in the delays, she's been very clever."

"She's too clever to be involved in anything crooked."

Flat statement. I wouldn't accept anything else. Byron didn't work like that.

"Proof?"

"I know her."

It didn't make sense to him. Didn't *compute*. But he had insight enough not to argue.

"Perhaps we can bargain?"

He had settled back into his chair. He hadn't looked

tense earlier but suddenly I knew we had reached the point he wanted. The one he'd been waiting for since he'd agreed to see me. It made me very cautious.

"What bargain?"

"I look a little deeper into the disappearance of this Jon. See if I can access the housing records. You watch for real-time interference in the Port's business."

He meant *human* interference, not machine. I didn't trust him even though he was offering what I'd wanted. I did know what was making me uncomfortable.

"I won't spy on Daisy."

I'd been going to say I wouldn't *spy* at all, but what had I been doing last night down at the northshore flats? And I had already promised Daisy I'd look into the sabotage and would have gone on poking around with or without Byron's help. He was watching me. Nodded.

"OK. If she's the source I'll deal with it. Agreed?"

I didn't like it. Felt as though I was conspiring against my friends. Saw little choice – except that I'd make my own decisions about what I shared with him. Hoped he wasn't making the same reservation.

"Agreed."

A sudden grin. Unexpected. Almost tempting me to share amusement at what was little more than an armed truce. Daisy thinks I'm good at reading people. I couldn't read this man at all.

What worried me more as I left his too-empty office was why someone who didn't believe in Jon's death was so willing to investigate it.

22

Daisy lived east of the Port. She and Sheba had an apartment in a block set back from the sea, part way up the steep hillside where the suburbs of Pompey crawled. Better than Sutton, light years away from the shore flats, but I couldn't have lived there. In return for reasonable security and clean air they had three rooms in a grey, Company-owned building with a lobby staffed by grim-faced guards I'd never seen smile. If I hadn't travelled in with Daisy they'd have done everything but strip me to check my identity. Given any provocation they'd have done that, too.

The journey in the Company car had been faster and more comfortable than any public bus. I'd just felt an uneasy sense of guilt. I'd said I wouldn't spy on her, I *knew* she had nothing to do with the trouble at the Port, but that didn't make me any easier. I had a nagging sense of things left undone. Unlike me, Daisy grew more relaxed with every metre we travelled from the Port. Perhaps it was the right time to keep my promise to Clim and the others.

"I saw Em the other day."

Daisy grinned. "How is the old witch?"

It wasn't the reaction I'd expected. "Worried."

The flat word had Daisy frowning. "She's not injured herself again, has she? Last time she wouldn't go into clinic. Said she'd heal up just fine if I'd go away and leave her alone. So I did, much against my will. She's too old for some of the things she tries – and those others in the mud berths don't help."

"Well, you won't have to worry about it much longer, will you?"

"Would you mind telling me what the hell you're talking about?"

Daisy didn't lie. If I knew anything about her, I knew that. This was more complicated than I'd thought. But perhaps there was hope for Em and Clim and the others after all.

"You mean they're wrong when they tell me you're going to drag their boats out of the mud berths?"

"I'm *what?*"

I told her about my meeting with them and their certainty they would soon be homeless.

"That's got to be Gus! Damn the man. He hears half a story and immediately thinks he understands and makes a half-arsed battleplan and rides charging in without checking his facts. No, Humility, I am not about to wreck the mud-berths. There has been talk of a second-stage development and, yes, it might affect them. I'm trying to see if the Company will work round them or, failing that, offer an alternate site."

"You might have told them."

"Not before I had anything solid to offer. And I don't want you to say anything. It's not certain yet. They shouldn't even have heard any rumours, though I suppose that was too much to ask."

"You know Em."

"I should."

"And you know Gus."

"And him. I'll tell him to back off. Leave him to me."

"Gladly."

It wasn't much, but Clim and the others would be grateful for even the hint of a reprieve. They were survivors.

I probed a little for her opinion of her own troubles. She was less willing to talk about them.

"Forget sabotage. It was just one of those times when everything seems to go wrong. It's over now."

I wasn't sure if she believed it or was trying to convince herself as much as me. "It can't hurt if I just look around."

"No! Let it be! Meddling never did any good."

"What's bugging you? Don't you at least want to find out how Jon died? He was your employee, after all."

The driver never even turned to look back as Daisy's sudden anger flared. I didn't understand. Daisy *never* lost control. The effort it took now was obvious but when she spoke again her voice at least was steady.

"No. I told you. Besides, you were wrong. It wasn't Jon."

If Tom Lee's files still showed Jon alive I wasn't surprised to discover Daisy had learned the same thing. If she hadn't done the research herself Byron Cody would have told her. I'd been waiting for her to tell me.

She was staring now, my lack of reaction obvious. "You *knew*?"

"That the files show him still alive? Yes."

"So now you can forget whoever it was. It's nothing to do with you or me or the Port any more."

Subject closed. Without proof that was how it would stay. If I wanted to salvage our friendship from this evening, I knew when to shut up. It was only when the car stopped that Daisy brought up the subject again.

"You won't say anything about dead bodies to Sheba."

It wasn't a question. As an order, it was unnecessary. Sheba was not someone you talked corpses with.

23

The contrast between the grey exterior and the inside of Daisy's apartment was almost shocking. Sheba had been watching for us and the door opened as we arrived, so that we stepped without a break from the Company's bleak livery into a home.

It was all Sheba, not Daisy: full of colour and busy with *things*. There were handmade curtains shielding the bomb-proof plex. Matching cushions. Paintings on the walls. Small ornaments on shelves. The home-cooked meal would be served on unchipped plates all from the same service. There was no dust anywhere.

I always felt clumsy here, afraid that my clean boots had picked up dirt somewhere, that I would knock something from a shelf or break one of the fragile figurines. Though there was less space on the *Pig*, it was here I felt stifled. When Sheba handed me a glass of my own wine I held it with care, somehow certain that before the evening was over I would have spilled it on the pale floor covering.

Daisy was sprawled at ease. She should have looked more out of place here than me but this was her home. The comfort Sheba had created was for Daisy and they both knew it. When Daisy's hand touched Sheba's as she accepted her glass I felt as though I was intruding on something private. I offered a toast.

"To you, Sheba. Congratulations."

She smiled. She was as pretty and delicate as her surroundings. If I felt clumsy round her, she was unsure how to take me. She had never really accepted that I had run away from my family for no reason that made sense to her. I was sure she secretly thought I'd been the victim of some abuse too terrible to mention. Today, though, she had a new confidence.

"Thanks, Humility. It's so wonderful I still sometimes think I'm dreaming."

"And then she wakes up sick and we know it's real." Daisy's dry intervention didn't conceal her own delight.

An evening talking babies held little appeal but I had to show at least some interest. "How long now?"

"Just over five months."

That was Daisy. Sheba would probably have given it me in days, down to the last hour. Or second.

"And all's well?"

It wasn't an idle question; I knew Sheba had miscarried once. Daisy's hand tightened on Sheba's.

"Just the one more test."

Sheba laughed, unworried. Pregnancy had given her an assurance she had always lacked. At the moment hers was the strength in the partnership.

"You worry too much. Everything is fine. I *know* it." Her free hand touched her stomach and her smile turned inward.

"It has to be. It's *our* child. It has to be perfect." An intensity of love, passion, possessiveness thickened Daisy's voice and Sheba soothed her.

"It will be. *She* will be."

Yes, of course. They would have insisted on that. Though neither Daisy nor Sheba had any prejudice against men, I couldn't imagine either wishing to parent a boy. Across the room I saw Daisy relax, releasing Sheba's hand, believing her.

My own discomfort grew. This was too private for me and I am not good with even the thought of children. I was glad when Sheba straightened and hurried out towards the cooking alcove.

"Go and sit at the table," she urged. "I'll bring everything in and then Humility can tell us about France and where she found such a good wine."

She wasn't drinking but I was too grateful for the subject's turn to comment.

The table was covered with a cloth edged with lace. Old Portuguese lace. When I had given it to Daisy it had been crumpled and yellow. Now it was as white as when it had been new-made. It looked good. My peculiarity that I preferred the history which the yellowing of age had given it.

The food was great. If she'd had any wish to earn her own living Sheba could have run any one of the vacant food openings at the Port. And probably put all the others out of business. Tom Lee would have taken her on at once if he'd ever had the chance to sample her cooking. The thought of an encounter between the two of them did a lot to restore my humour.

Inevitably, perhaps, conversation turned towards the Port's development, though I was careful to follow Daisy's lead, highlighting the comic upsets and the progress and avoiding any hint of trouble.

"I do have one bit of news."

The table had been cleared and Daisy was leaning back in her chair, nursing a glass of brandy. There was something suspiciously smug in her voice.

"What?" Sheba pounced eagerly when Daisy let her

words hang.

"The Board has decided the project's worth looking at."

"What do you mean?"

Daisy was *definitely* smug. "I mean," she spoke with care, "that I had a message today from the Board saying they want to send a party down to see the progress we're making. Someone must have told the Family it was going well."

Who? Byron? Nothing had changed in the last few days, unless you counted the negative fact that no further damage had been done. But surely Board members – always Family – didn't associate themselves closely with a project they thought might fail. No wonder Daisy was smug.

And now I understood why she wanted no one, including me, making waves and asking awkward questions about things – and people – which might be better off buried. She didn't even want to *think* they might be coming because they'd heard of her problems.

I swallowed the questions before I spoke. "Well done, Daisy. It's a vote of confidence."

Sheba was basking in reflected pride, thrilled with the acknowledgement of her partner's abilities. Daisy's smile turned rueful.

"Of course now I've got to waste valuable time making sure everything's ready for them and laying on the Grand Tour."

"How many coming?"

"About a dozen. Two direct Family and their followers. I don't know anything about them."

Family don't travel without a court.

"Ask Byron. I'm sure he could find out."

She shot me a glance which was distinctly wary. I'm not

sure what she thought she heard in my voice but all she said was, "You may be right."

"So he's finished his audit?"

That was Sheba, anxious that anyone who upset her partner should disappear quickly.

Daisy shrugged. "Who knows? He's still here. I've no authority over him."

And that irritated her. Daisy liked to be in control. Sheba was watching me and I read the unspoken warning. This was her home territory and she did not welcome anything which upset her partner. The subject was closed. I had my own reasons not to want to discuss why Byron might be staying on at the Port and, besides, it was time I left.

I took a cab back. Tom Lee's credits for the wine could stretch that far. And public transport by night demands an alertness which doesn't come easily after a large meal and several glasses of wine.

The streets blurred past. If I'd been Family or rich enough for a private auto I'd have travelled the toll road. Cabs and buses and the occasional biker have to brave the streets. Brief impressions from pools of lamplight surrounded by tunnels of darkness. Yellow light gleamed on a solitary black girl leaning against a street wall, there in body only. Two men walked past, ignoring her. I swung round in my seat in time to see one of them break off and turn back to the girl. Don't think about it, I told myself. Round the next corner the flickering light of an open fire made the shadows dance. Half a dozen huddled round it. Men? Women? Just shapes wearing rags. Only dangerous if you came between them and the warmth which was all they had of value.

Then we were among brighter lights. There were food stalls open here, trading with the people who clustered round the entrance to basement clubs whose dancing signs offered live delights but where they'd probably find no more than two worn-out girls among the jerking holos. Or perhaps they'd be boys. Anything you want if you've got the credits. Everything you fear if you haven't. I preferred the dark streets to this and was glad when I caught a glimpse of the sea to my left. Not far now.

We were only minutes away from Midway; we'd crossed the bridge from which I could imagine I saw the lights of *Wild Goose* glinting off the exposed mud, perhaps even pick out the silhouette of the *Pig* dark against the lights of the Port a little further downstream. Almost home.

Something – perhaps that sense of unfinished business, perhaps the buried irritation with Daisy's refusal to admit anything might be wrong in her world – made me change my mind.

I leaned forward and spoke through the intercom. "Not the Port. Can you take me on to the northshore towers?"

A silence. He didn't turn but I saw the way his eyes sought out my face in his mirror. "You sure? It's not a good place."

It was reassuring to discover that the midtown desert was as disturbing to him as it was to me. He'd rather have dropped me in the streets we'd already passed through. I almost gave in to his concern but the evening had left me wired. I needed space, something to concentrate on. Then I might be able to unwind. And since I'd already managed to discover news which might placate Em and her friends, perhaps my luck was in. *Never quit when you're on a roll.* I doubt if Jack had ever quit before he'd lost every credit he owned, but sometimes I'd hear his voice and take his advice just for old times' sake.

"I'm sure."

"They're your credits."

He'd charge extra, if only because I'd rejected his concern.

24

The silence of the cab journey was less friendly as we swung past Midway and out along the coast road. Then the towers were looming up ahead, two with a scattering of lights showing, the third in ruined darkness.

"Which one you want?"

"Inshore side. Drop me before you reach the entryway."

"Wait for you?"

It was reluctant, but he was honest, unwilling to leave me adrift. Or perhaps he just wanted to be certain he was paid before I got myself killed, raped and robbed. Not necessarily in that order. I hesitated. He seemed to be making up his mind about something.

"Or I could call back. I'm going on into Sutton, could swing by here on my way back. Hour or so."

It was a good offer, worth what I'd have to pay. "Thanks. I'd be grateful."

I hadn't looked forward to making my way home, or staying out here till dawn.

"'Kay. Here's my card. Call me up if you want."

I took the card while he scanned my bracelet and collected his credits. Then he released the door lock.

"Thanks."

I waved and turned towards the towers and tried not to feel a sudden ache of loneliness as his lights faded towards the city.

The emptiness of the place was almost familiar by now. I was wearing a dark tunic and trews and no one looking out from a lit room would have seen me as I walked across the waste ground, pausing for a moment in the shadows where I had watched last night, before slipping round to the inland side of the building. Across the deserted play area, careful not to trip on the remains of the broken swing and the jagged bars of metal which might once have been a climbing frame. Then I was staring up. Counting. Fifth floor. I frowned as I concentrated, remembering the turns in the staircase and that Jon's old room had been on my left when I reached his landing. It was in darkness. I made my way back to the entrance.

Five flights up, stepping quietly. No one was likely to come out to look, especially not at night, but I'd rather they never even thought about it. I'd have to watch for the single vid on Blue Eyes' floor which I knew was live.

If I'd been asked to explain what I was doing, I'm not sure how I'd have answered. The impulse which had driven me here seemed more stupid each time I thought of it but it was safer to loiter inside than out and the cab wouldn't be back for a while yet. I could sit on the landing out of line of sight of that single red tell-tale and hope for Blue Eyes to wake up and answer the door or come back from wherever he was. Perhaps, just perhaps, he could tell me a little more about the packets he left for collection by the blader.

That was what I thought until I reached the landing and saw that the gate on his door was open.

25

Blue Eyes wasn't coming back from where he'd gone. He was lying on the couch and he was staring right at me but he wasn't seeing me. He wasn't seeing anything.

He didn't look surprised. One arm had flopped aside so that the back of his hand brushed the soiled floor. The other was bent at the elbow, its hand palm-up beside his face as though in mild protest at what had been done to him. The dark red stain centred on his chest told its own tale.

I noticed everything, even the caf-mug half-full of scummy liquid and the small rip in the side of one of his worn shoes. The room was no untidier than when I'd last been here. In the corner the monitor flickered in silence. I don't know how long I stood there before I started to shake.

Dead. Because I had interfered?

No. I had wanted to believe I could do something to make Jon's death less insignificant. Why? To show someone cared if a man died? I no longer knew. I had wanted to solve a puzzle. I had not thought Blue Eyes would meet the same fate as Jon.

Not quite. Even as my stomach churned and the small inner voice told me to run, I couldn't stop thinking. They hadn't hurt his head. *His* ID would have sent out its last signal. File closed.

I took a step into the room. Shut my eyes. A remnant of childhood said I'd open them again to find him laughing at me, at the trick he'd played with a bag of fake blood. But Blue Eyes hadn't laughed when he was alive. He'd been too afraid. At least that was over. I opened my eyes. He hadn't moved. His sightless stare was fixed over my shoulder now that I was closer. Close enough to reach out a hand. I have never done anything harder than stretch my fingers across the last fraction of a millimetre between his flesh and mine.

He was cold. Gone beyond anyone's touch. Still, his eyes must ache, unblinking and wide like that. My fingers reached up to close them.

From him that hath not shall be taken even that which he hath.

I still felt the cold wax of his eyelids against my finger-tips when I saw I'd been wrong. The lack of blood had fooled me. They had hit him. The shape of the head against the cushion was wrong. Flat. When I made myself lift him, both hands gentle against his cheeks as though I might still hurt him, the cushion that had soaked up the blood lifted for a moment with him before it fell back. I set him down again with even more care. Then I looked around the room again. Anger was beginning to displace fear. Whoever had done this had come only for that one thing: there were no signs of search or robbery. And the killer was long gone. Everything here was cold: Blue Eyes, the sticky blood, the caf he'd never had the time to finish. Me. I shivered, tried to concentrate.

The knife that had killed him was the only thing missing. The screen in the corner was still there. It would have gone had street thugs done this, so it wasn't a robbery. If this room had held any secrets, they were still here. I touched nothing as I walked over to peer behind the partition.

The state of the sink made me gag. Nothing would have persuaded me to rake through its accumulated filth. He'd been in the room less than two weeks and I doubted if he'd ever washed anything. But it wasn't Blue Eyes' secrets I was after. Jon had hoarded things he didn't understand – whether they were toys or something altogether more serious. After all, he'd passed one on to me, and though I still didn't know whether it was a toy or not I was beginning to have a bad feeling about it. Now I hoped there was something else here for me to find which might make sense of things.

The cabinet in the corner between sink and toilet was the only piece of furniture neither built-in nor so rickety it would fall into splinters in a few months. It was solid. Heavy. It would have been hard to move from the corner where it was jammed, especially since the mover would have had to lean over the stained toilet bowl to work. It had probably been there when Jon was the room's tenant. I swallowed bile and knelt in front of it, muffling my hand in my sleeve to open its door.

Trays of food. Mostly unsealed and festering. A fork. Two spoons. A cloth whose uses I would not guess at. Nothing else. Not inside. I straightened and tried not to breathe in as I did what I had known I would have to: I pulled the cabinet away from the wall.

It wasn't easy and the thick rim of greasy dirt told me it hadn't been done often. Never by Blue Eyes. Once by Jon?

The thin package taped to the back of the cupboard was familiar. I couldn't tell if it was the one I'd put in the mail box or another like it. The latter, I suspected.

Outside a siren wailed.

It probably had nothing to do with the dead man on the

couch, was probably just another routine call to another routine casualty of the night, but it hurried me. Pushing the cupboard back was easier than pulling it out had been and I just hoped no one would decide to take a close look. The scratches in the grease where it had dragged on the floor would tell their own tale. Nothing I could do about them now. I shoved the stiffened envelope deep into my sack and left the apartment. I didn't look over at the couch as I left.

26

Two bodies in less than four days. As I said, I don't deal well with death: now it looked as though I was being forced to face my hang-ups. Even if I wanted out, and I didn't know if I did, I wasn't convinced I had a choice left. It depended whether whoever ordered Blue Eyes' death had descriptions of his visitors.

Outside I took a deep breath of night air. It tasted clean. Whatever stinks drifted across the water from the smoking chimneys on the far bank were pure after the taint that had hung round the fifth-floor room. And I wasn't thinking of the mess in the sink.

We live in a world where it's almost impossible to survive without technology. But some things stay primitive. Absolute. The brutality of murder is one of them. There is no sophistication to a blow on the head or a knife in the chest.

Somewhere towards Sutton the wailing siren died, its urgency gone. Around me silence ballooned. I tapped my chrono. Barely thirty minutes had passed since I'd left the safety of the cab. Another half hour to wait for the driver to return. Somehow it was hard just then to believe he would bother. Trust and safety seemed a long way off.

I was barely under cover of darkness when I heard the whisper of sound.

I was wearing black, deep in shadow. Invisible to the blader. Tonight there was no display in the forecourt, just a quick, graceful dash across to the entry. And then the pause in front of the mail boxes.

"That will likely be your last pick-up here."

The blader whirled when I spoke. A girl. Maybe fifteen. The street sets marks on a child's face which make it older than its years. She was quite still now, just the one flick of her eyes telling her she could not pass me.

"What you mean? I'm OK here. Just blading."

"And picking up the post."

The mail box behind her was ajar. She'd had time to tap its code before I followed her inside. She shrugged.

"Got the codes, got the right. Not so?"

"It's so."

My agreement didn't make her relax. She was waiting for me to make a move so she could get past and clear. Kids like her don't like being penned up inside. The street was her world. Nothing I could do, except warn her.

"Like I said. Last pick-up. Man who uses that box is dead upstairs. Knife."

She wasn't as tough as she wanted me to believe. For a fraction of a second she was unbalanced on her blades. A single frightened glance at the staircase made me revise my estimate of her age down by at least two years. Then she steadied, tried to look bold.

"What's it to me? I never see a man. What's he done?"

A few years from now, if she survived, she'd know better than to ask.

"Nothing. It wasn't his fault. He wasn't good or bad and probably no greedier than the rest of us. He's still dead. Thought you might want to get clear."

"Clear of what? I just take deliveries. Different places each time. I don't ask what. Don't look to see."

Probably couldn't read. Illiterate kids who could

recognise numbers and remember a code made good messengers when discretion counted. The kids didn't last long.

"Might be safer to end it." Another shrug. Indifferent, disbelieving. "Your choice. But if you need help you'll find me at Midway. Name's Humility."

She blinked. "Why tell me?"

I wasn't sure. I couldn't tell her she reminded me of me, when I'd thought I'd known enough to take on the world even though I was dying of fear inside. Couldn't tell her the risks I feared she was running. Why should it matter to me?

Perhaps two bodies were enough. My turn to shrug. "No reason. Forget it or use it. No problem."

Unless of course she chose to use it by selling it to whoever she delivered her pick-ups to. I was a fool to trust her. Angry, with myself this time, I stepped aside and let her blade past, out into the open.

27

She'd gone and I still had twenty minutes to kill before the cab came back. If it did. I shivered, wished I hadn't thought about killing. Without the girl the night was emptier than ever, even though above and around me were little rooms full of people going about their own furtive business, hiding their own terrible fears, finding their own swift pleasures. Except in that one room where business, fear and pleasure were all ended now.

I shivered again. I wanted to be bold, certain that I'd done the right thing, but something inside me was whimpering. Remembering that sense of being watched I'd felt before, here.

Darker shadows loomed against the darkness. I could wait here in the lobby with its dim lighting and at least I would see anyone coming. As long as I could watch the doors and the stairs at the same time. And as long as I didn't mind being visible to anyone who happened to be lurking. Or I could go out into the dark.

There really wasn't any choice. But I did take the precaution of sneaking round the edge of the lobby and down the short passage which led to the small service door I'd seen earlier. It opened with only a token groan.

Outside, the blackness seemed to lift a little. I remembered the concrete bunker and began to drift towards it, glad when the light from the lobby no longer cast my shadow in front of me. I slithered sideways, looking from one anonymous mound of shadow to another, wondering what they hid, and discovering just how hard it is to concentrate on moving silently while listening until my ears ached for sounds that might threaten me.

There! A scuffle in what might have been bushes. Nothing. Rats? A restless bird? Both? More silence. I edged closer to the bunker. Began to see its low walls more clearly. The smelly, fire-blackened structure was looking more like sanctuary with every dragging second.

I was beginning to breathe again, ready to relax, could almost feel the protection of the filthy walls at my back when I saw it. Just a glimpse of movement that might have been yet more vermin, except that something screamed inside me that this vermin had two legs and that my hiding place was already occupied.

I sucked in my breath. Froze and flattened myself as best I could against a scrubby bush. Thought invisible thoughts and cursed. Half-started back towards the lobby and saw a shadow cross its floor. I remembered the room with the vid on the fifth floor and that I hadn't been too careful when I'd left Blue Eyes' room. Had whoever lived there called up reinforcements? I was caught in a pincer, unable to retreat to the lobby which now looked like some sort of spotlit killing ground.

And there was no hope that the man pushing open the door to the flats might be harmless. He was walking with a definite purpose and whatever he held in his hand looked very like the large knife which had disappeared from Blue Eyes' room. I was wondering if I stood a chance of reaching the road and the forlorn hope of rescue from a passing car when the shape moved in the bunker again.

"Humility."

My name, hissed in a voiceless whisper. My killer

knew my name. It was the only thought that reached my paralysed mind before the reasoning circuits, which had been dead from the moment I saw that knife, cut back in again and told me who it was in the bunker.

The blader girl.

I didn't care who she was or what she was doing. All that mattered was that she wasn't the partner of the man looking out into the night with the light behind him turning him into a black silhouette. I scuttled backwards. Ducked into shelter. Remembered how to breathe.

"Thanks." Then, belatedly, "Why are you still here?" She could have bladed away faster than anyone on foot could have followed.

A faint shrug, not much more than a twitch in the gloom. "Curious."

Not a good quality in her line of work. But I wasn't in a position to criticise. Twenty yards away the man was speaking into a small unit. Calling up reinforcements? Then the unit was back in his belt. Now he had something in his left hand which looked like a blunt club but which I recognised just as the strong beam of light spilled out and across the ground. Flashlight. We crouched together behind the frail wall and stopped breathing again.

"What we goin' to do?"

Good question. I looked down at the faint glow from my wrist unit. Took a gamble on the reliability of someone I'd only met that night.

"Lose the blades, then be ready to follow me when I say. *Quietly.*"

Blades are good for speed, not furtive movement. She hesitated a moment, then reached down and fumbled with the latches.

The sweep hand on the chrono crawled round four more times. Enough. The flashlight had swept our bunker once. It couldn't be long before the man with the knife decided to investigate the bit of cover his light couldn't penetrate. If he'd seen me on the vid, he thought he was after one female and I doubted if he expected that to be a problem for him.

I crouched and led my companion back out of the bunker, keeping as low as possible, towards the empty road.

I was hoping it wouldn't remain empty.

We were caught in the torch beam just as we reached the pot-holed tarmac. If he was surprised to see two of us, he didn't hesitate. I could hear the thud of running feet just as headlights swept round the corner and I waved like a mad creature at the oncoming cab.

28

The girl looked at me as though I'd conjured the cab out of the air. The driver looked at her with a hint of scorn, recognising a streetkid. I didn't care because we were behind steel doors and speeding towards home and the man with the knife was far behind.

We dropped her at the main road with enough credit for a fare into the heart of town. As she left she muttered thanks and then in a voice like a scared child, too low for the driver to hear, said, "My name's Luna."

I guessed she'd pocket the credit and blade back through the night, but that was her choice. When we reached Midway I thanked the driver again and overpaid him. It wasn't worth trying to explain.

There was a public phone terminal at the top of the hill. Just what I needed for an anonymous call. I wasn't quite sure why I bothered. It wasn't going to trouble Blue Eyes any if the peeps found him tomorrow or next week. I just didn't like to think of what traffic would pass through that room before anyone reported him dead. Didn't like to think there might be another tenant in there before morning.

I suppose I should have told Byron. Perhaps I would. Later.

The Port was empty. The faint hum of machinery which was masked by activity in daytime was there now, just below the threshold of hearing. Machines somewhere were busy ignoring night and doing whatever tasks they'd been programmed for. My footsteps slapped on the dew-wet asphalt of the forecourt. No one watched me walk across to the dark edge where the Port met the river and I could climb down the rusting ladder to the *Pig*.

Home. Light. Not the harsh orange of the powered lamps but the old lantern with its smell and its yellow glow and its heat. I held my hands out to its living flame and watched their tremor while a small part of my mind replayed what had happened with the unforgiving precision of a vidcast.

I didn't open my sack. Didn't take out the package which lay inside it and which I wasn't ready to face. Instead I took the cards from their pack and began to lay out a game. The automatic motions steadied my hands but when I stared at the cards they were meaningless. They stared back at me and I saw Blue Eyes in their blind gaze.

No point trying to tell myself I was not involved in his death. At best I had made it come sooner rather than later. At worst I had caused it.

Facing truth is something I have been brought up to do. *The truth shall make you free.* Soul-searching and public confession were weekly entertainment in the Community. I had never found it came easily, nor did I ever feel any better once everyone knew what I had done. Once *I* knew what I had done. I felt no better now, either, but the process wasn't easily stopped. It was partly being born a New Puritan. Another part was a liking for logic. Consequences had to have causes and if I was part of the cause I wanted to know who else had been behind the hand which held the knife. And why.

I kept coming back to that *why*. Jon's death and Blue Eyes' had to be linked. And there had to be a reason why Jon still showed alive on everyone's screens. The packages collected from the mail box were part of it, but who they were sent to or from I was no nearer knowing. I should have made Luna hand over what she had collected, or at least tell me where she was taking it. She had clutched it to her in the cab and shaken her head at the couple of questions I'd asked but I was bigger and stronger.

The guy who had chased us wouldn't have hesitated to take it.

And that made me think: had he seen her pick up the packet from the lobby? If his surveillance equipment was more sophisticated than you'd expect from that building – and since nothing else was as it should be, why not? – he might have had a viewer on her, which meant he'd ignored her for two possible reasons. Either it was only me he was interested in and he was ready to ignore what anyone else did. Or he knew exactly what she was doing, which meant they were working on the same project.

Did that mean that she'd never been at risk? Or that it was me talking to her that had put her in jeopardy? Just like Blue Eyes.

And why had she let me have her name?

The cards blurred and I tucked my feet up under me on the padded bench. The smaller problem, that unexpected trust, somehow seemed bigger right then than all the rest. Murder and pursuit included.

29

When I woke it was daylight and rain was drumming on the cabin roof. I was cold and cramped and the cards lay enigmatic and untouched on the table. The last card I'd dealt, the one-eyed jack of spades, sneered up at me. My head ached and I creaked when I straightened. As I stood up the sack slid off the settee and thudded to the floor.

I picked it up. I couldn't go on pretending its contents didn't exist. Without even starting my first caf of the day, I reached in and pulled out the package.

It was unaddressed, rectangular, about thirty centimetres by twenty. I weighed it in one hand. Heavy enough to tell me it contained more than paper but not really weighty. The stiffened wrapping made it impossible to learn any more about the contents without opening it. I hesitated a moment longer. The flap at one of the narrower ends had been unsealed and crudely refastened with tape. By Jon, I guessed. Unlike Luna and Jon, Blue Eyes had known better than to be curious. Not that it had helped him in the end.

I opened the envelope with care and reluctance. Tipped it to spill the contents on to the settee beside me.

A ring. An empty purse. A thin chain necklet, dull metal showing beneath the gilt. And one other item. I picked it up with care, resting it on my palm and wondering whether it was still operating. What it was operating.

It was thin, less than five millis square and only a couple thick. Micro- rather than nano-tech. A chip. I don't know much tech, but even I could see that. It still struck me as ludicrous that something that small and inert could handle so much information. Witchcraft. I shivered and laughed at myself and the heritage which had slid the thought into my mind. Even the Wessex Community hadn't been *that* primitive.

But if the chip mattered, and it must, then I was way out of my depth. I couldn't access its contents or begin to guess its function. But I was beginning to remember my early thoughts that this was about technology, not people. Perhaps I'd been half-right. These days the two can be hard to separate.

For Byron Cody it might be impossible: he was pure 'crat. He would know at a glance what I was holding as though it were a poisonous spider. The question was whether I would be in even worse trouble than I already was if I consulted him. And how much I would have to tell him.

I should tell him about Blue Eyes: he couldn't pretend *that* death was an accident. It might even make him take the idea of Jon's death a little more seriously. Still, I knew I wasn't going to tell him anything yet. We had more or less agreed that I would leave the murder alone and concentrate on the sabotage end of the trouble. But after seeing what had been done to Blue Eyes, something which I might have brought on by my interference, I couldn't stand aside. I looked down at the array of cards. I couldn't see a pattern.

All I had learned from the carefully hidden package was that the contents hadn't belonged to Jon. The cheap jewellery was a woman's. The thought I was trying not to think was that the chip might also be a woman's. The part of her where flesh and technology met. Her ID.

I still think the state could and should have found an alternative way of tracking taxes. The Puritans had resisted the basic ID link for over a decade after its introduction, but it's hard to hold out against something with the inertia of EuroGov. So these days there are very few Outlaws. Only those too old to stand the neural interference, and a few who had their own reasons to stay hidden, didn't have IDs. My grandmother had given in when I was five. I still remember her fury when the Elders – most of them younger than her – insisted.

"I don't want anyone interfering with my head!"

"It will keep the inspectors away."

That was the great lure, I later understood. The illusion that there would be *less* interference.

"It's unnatural!"

"The Community has decided."

There was no appeal against that but exile. I'd been sitting on her lap when they came to her and still remember the way her arms had tightened round me. She had shaken her head again but they had just waited. They'd known she had nowhere to go, too many ties to break.

"To obey is better than sacrifice."

Even at five I could have finished it: *for rebellion is as the sin of witchcraft.* That was why they'd Shunned me when I'd left a little over ten years later. After grandmother had gone. I hadn't had the ties which had made her bend her head in apparent submission, hiding the mutiny in her eyes against my hair.

I shook my head, rejecting the memories. I knew why I was sidetracking: I didn't want to think about the fact that whoever had removed Jon's ID had not bothered with anything as subtle as surgery. I didn't want to think of the damage to Blue Eyes' head. I didn't want to think that the chip I'd just been holding had once been inside someone's head. I didn't want to decide what I had to do next. Then I looked down at the clothes I'd slept in, the ones I'd worn when I'd found Blue Eyes, and altered that to not wanting to decide what to do *after* I'd showered.

It was in the shower that I realised that there were still details of Jon's death that I didn't know about which I could explore without help from Byron or technology. I finished washing more quickly than I'd planned – in Port, with unlimited fresh water paid for in the extortionate mooring fee, I tend to get self-indulgent – and dressed in old clothes and shoes which were stiff with age and sea-water. I just had one call to make before I went out or Daisy would be making oblique comments about manners. Worse than my mother, sometimes.

"Sheba?"

Her face filled the screen. Despite my phone's inadequate equipment I could see that last night's glow was still there. She even looked pleased to see me.

"Humility! How are you?"

"I'm well. Just called to say thanks for last night."

"No trouble. I wanted to thank you for the wine and I know how Daisy enjoys your company. I'm glad she has a friend like you in the Port."

No one working for the Company would be a reliable friend, I guessed. Rivalry did nasty things to friendship.

"No more glad than I am."

I meant it. Daisy was the one person who could convince me it was possible to work for the system and not lose your soul. She didn't know the first thing about compromise but if she made a promise she kept it. And if she offered friendship it was without conditions. I knew, I'd put plenty of pressure on ours.

I smiled at Sheba's image. "When are you due for that test?"

"Not for another three days. I can't wait till it's over. Then we can *both* enjoy this baby." Her sigh was exasperation.

Impatience with Daisy's concern mingled equally with affection. It was a surprise to discover Sheba really did not want to be fussed over. I might have been wrong over the years in taking her softness for weakness. She complemented Daisy but their dependence was mutual. With more warmth than I usually felt for her, except as Daisy's partner, I wished Sheba well and cut the connection.

Then I pulled on a waterproof and went outside to bail out the dinghy.

30

I like to row, even in the rain. I like to feel the pull of the oars tug at my shoulders and I like the way the oar blades cut the water. Something about the rhythm always relaxes me. Even when I'm going to talk to a man about a body.

I had thought of trying to talk to the man I'd seen at the clinic. The one I'd left with a puddle of vomit to clean up. Then I'd realised it was unlikely Daisy would fail to register my presence there and I wanted to postpone telling her that I hadn't yet agreed to forget her problems. Anyway, the medic might not be able to give me the details I wanted. Whoever had taken the body from the spoil-heap could.

The body. Not Jon. If I was going to do this I would have to avoid thinking of the living person I had known.

There wasn't much tide running, so it took only a few minutes to cross the river to the waste ground. I could remember when it had been a marsh: now it was filled with dredged mud and before long it would be landscaped. No one seemed to be doing much work. I couldn't see any active machines except one pump chugging monotonously to itself as it jetted water from the site back into the river.

The ground squelched under my feet. My shoes leaked. I could feel mud, slippery and gritty between my toes as I walked over to where I had seen the body fall from the dredge. Unidentifiable scraps of metal and plasteel garbage jutted out from the sides of the grey-black spoil and water oozed from underneath. I supposed it would all settle eventually; just now it looked unstable and smelled revolting.

"Pretty, eh?"

I had seen him. Sort of. He'd been hanging around on the other side of the site when I beached the dinghy. About fifty or a bit less, grey-haired but looking fit enough and used to rough work. No uniform, but a crudely fastened name-tag told me he was called Pete. Not Company. Not directly, anyway. Casual labour, more like. Someone willing to take on the dirtier jobs which regular staff might balk at. Just the man I was looking for.

"I've seen more promising parks," I acknowledged.

He laughed. "Park! They'll be replanting every night if they don't do something about this stuff first." He scowled at the oozing heaps.

"What do you mean?"

"Couldn't grow boils on a sailor's backside with it. It's solid with salt and God knows what other pollutants. Oil's the least of them. Would *you* like to put down roots in it?"

I had to admit I wouldn't. Even if I didn't have a congenital aversion to roots.

Pete stared sourly back at me. "You came over in the dinghy?"

No point in denying it. I gestured across the river. "Yes. That's my boat, over there."

He looked at the *Pig*. She didn't seem to impress him. Then he looked from my boat to where the number seven dredge had been working, just across from where we stood. He had been chewing on something, now he spat sideways, adding to the pollution of the would-be flowerbeds.

"You the one who spotted the body?"

"You know about that?"

"Be hard not to, the fuss there was when the alarm went off. Me and a couple of others do the chores here. I was still on duty when it happened."

I didn't ask what the 'chores' might be. Round here they'd have to do with tending the spoil heaps and getting rid of the more obvious and unmanageable bits of debris which were dredged up. Their compensation for low pay and a short-term contract would be the right to do what they liked with whatever it was they salvaged. Pete was one of those whose lives were tenuous links between the unbending hierarchy of the Companies and the anarchy of the streets.

"They asked you to deal with it?"

He looked suspicious but decided I had some sort of right to interest. "Yes. Nasty business. I got him free and into the loader they sent as quick as I could. Don't mind muck but I didn't sign on for dead bodies."

None of us did.

"What you reckon happened? Fell in drunk?"

"If he did he took his clothes off first. No. Bastard wasn't that lucky. Don't know if he was drunk but if he'd ever woken up he'd have had a hell of a headache."

I swallowed. I didn't like to remember what I'd seen of the sheeted figure in the mortuary.

"Where do you reckon he went in? There's plenty of places upstream I wouldn't wander round alone."

I still wanted it to be a possibility. It would mean the Port wasn't at the centre of whatever was happening. But Pete was shaking his head.

"No chance. He went in the same place the dredge pulled him out."

"How can you be sure? The tides are fierce enough to shift something heavier than a dead man."

He smiled. People are always pleased to show they know more than you. "Not this one. Didn't get a clear view when you saw it dredged up, did you?"

"No. And it wasn't the kind of thing I stare at for long, either."

"Can understand that." He grimaced. "No, whoever pushed him in didn't want the body found. It was wrapped up in cable heavy enough to hold it till it fell apart."

Or until a dredge designed to wrench up several tonnes at once bit through it. I had to be sure, though.

"Couldn't it just have got tangled in the cable when it came downstream? There's plenty of that sort of junk on the riverbed, especially off the old boatsheds."

"Tell me about it. I've had to sort through most of it and there's precious little worth any credit. No. You soon learn if something's been down there years or days. Easy enough with a body, of course, but that cable hadn't been there any longer. Metal in it was still bright. No corrosion at all. Besides, he wasn't tangled, girl. He was *tied*."

I hoped he enjoyed the effect he was having on me. I didn't. The conversation had gone about as far as I wanted to take it. Pete seemed to have lost interest too; he was kicking around in the sludge as though he was looking for something. Then he straightened, holding something out.

"Here. I thought there was a chunk or two left – nothing long enough to be worth carting away. Have it as a souvenir." He was holding out a mud-encrusted piece of what might be cable, bigger than his meaty fist. It was surprisingly heavy.

"Thanks." I recalled the heaps of stuff waiting for the recycler that Clim had been rummaging through and thought the killer hadn't had to look far for something to weight the body with. It wasn't a souvenir I'd treasure.

Something in my face seemed to make him think maybe he'd been a bit too blunt. "You all right, girl?"

"Yes. I'm fine. Thanks for telling me about it. Perhaps the Company peeps will find out who killed him."

His laugh was for my naivety. "Perhaps the river will run clean and this place will blossom after all. Don't hold your breath, girl. And don't go asking Company security about what they're doing. *I* didn't tell them nothing and if you've any sense you won't talk to them neither."

I opened my mouth to tell him that I hadn't been a *girl* for a dozen years now and then heard what he was saying. "Someone else been asking questions?"

"Didn't I say so? Black guy in fancy shoes."

"Techno?"

Not that I needed to ask. So Byron wasn't just pushing buttons. I rather liked the idea of him squelching round here in those shoes; wished I could believe he'd fallen flat.

Pete was grimacing at his own memories. "Course he was techno. Wanted *data.* Recorded everything."

"You tell him much?"

"Don't like being *data.* Being dumb labour is better." A snort and a spit illustrated his contempt.

I gave him the coins he'd been expecting, a few more than I'd intended, and went back to the dinghy. On the other side of the river, between the *Pig's* mooring and the new marina, was a cluster of figures which included Gus and Daisy but most of whom I'd never seen before.

31

I parked the dinghy back alongside the *Pig* and washed my feet and shoes in the tide. Daisy was still talking with Gus and the others, but I could see even from a distance that she'd watched me row back and knew exactly why I'd been over at the spoil heaps. She would have something to say about the fact that I was ignoring her wish to forget Jon's death. But she'd wait until she could get me alone. Gus would have settled for having me tied up in brand-new and very heavy cable and dumped in the harbour, but that was normal.

I turned my attention to the rest of the party. I knew who they were; after all, Daisy had told me about them last night. Family.

Their head man was tall and bearded, looked humourless. Most of the others had that slightly too-perfect look that body-sculpting gives. Only one of them didn't seem engrossed in whatever their leader was listening to. When he saw me watching, he brightened up and committed the impropriety of leaving the others to come over and peer down at me from the dockside.

Anyone who could get away with that had to be fairly senior Family himself. Almost as senior as the big one with the beard, the one like the jack of spades in my pack. This one was more like the jack of clubs: the young one, the one with no moustache and a round face. Looks a bit sad.

It was disarming.

"Hello. I'm Milo. I like your boat. It has character."

I wasn't as offended as I might have been. He had a good voice and an undercurrent of laughter, which went oddly well with mournful brown eyes, inviting me to share a joke.

I wasn't going to go that far. But I did hear myself say, "So have I. Drop in for a drink one evening."

Gus had overheard and was turning purple again. Daisy looked resigned. The others pretended not to have noticed that a Family member was slumming.

"I'd like that."

He didn't mean it, of course, but I couldn't help enjoying its effect on Gus. He was trying to get his Important Visitors out of the rain and away from my contaminating influence and didn't seem to know which would do more harm. It was the tall guy who saved him.

"Milo, we need to take a look at the mall." It was a barely veiled order. Somehow he managed to look at Milo without seeing me.

Milo shrugged. "Time to go," he told me with a grin and strolled off to join the rest of the obedient flock.

The memory of that grin followed me back inside the *Pig*. I allowed myself to think about it for a couple of minutes before I forced myself to concentrate on what I'd learned. I had the answer I'd been looking for, the one I'd expected and not really wanted: the Port *was* central to Jon's death. There was no real room left for doubt that, dead or alive, he had gone into the water from here.

And that meant one of two things: either someone had been sure the dredger would retrieve the body and wanted to create more trouble for the Port or, more likely, the disposal site had been chosen because it was where Jon had died and his killer knew his way round here well enough to be able to drop the body at a time when he wouldn't be seen. The cable had been to make sure he never was.

Either way the killer had Port access. That wasn't a narrow field. Almost a hundred people worked here and the Port isn't a fortress - I'd proved before now that it was possible to come and go without troubling the barriers. Even so the odds favoured someone who knew the place well. Someone who worked or lived here.

I stared down at the cards on the table. Moved a couple. The sequence was beginning to emerge but that didn't mean I had to like it. I still had no idea *why* all this was happening but it had to tie in with the chip and the cheap jewellery I'd found, and the fact that no one else believed Jon was dead. These days having his carcass wasn't enough.

I stopped fiddling with the cards and decided to talk to Tom Lee again. I had my bargaining counter and the northshore flats were his territory. If he didn't know there was trouble there, he just might be glad to learn about it. I hoped I wasn't wrong to think it wasn't the sort of trouble he organised himself.

I could think about Milo's smile on the bus.

32

Midday at Tom Lee's. Busier now, though the rain still kept most people away from the outdoor tables. One was occupied: an andro with rainbow hair, shaved high over the forehead, long at the back. Hi-maintenance. Looked at me as I walked past. Admiring the way he/she was admired. Eyes matched the hair, swirling colours. Gorgeous.

I felt plain. Went in. Went to the counter and bought a juice. Waited.

The juice was finished before the server came over to me. "Tom Lee's got five minutes. Over there."

Better than I'd hoped. I made my way to the mirrored door beside the bar. It opened without a sound and slid shut behind me.

I was in a sort of air-lock, facing another mirror. Watched myself with resignation while around me unseen cameras checked my ID and ran the contents of my sack through some sort of weapons scan. Tried to look indifferent. I'd been in here once before but that didn't prevent the chill which fingered my spine. I don't like tight spaces and no one but Tom Lee himself was likely to be able to persuade either door to open. He knew I wouldn't be armed and he couldn't be in any doubt about my ID. Keeping me on hold was his way of reminding me who was in control.

I didn't need reminding. Even more, I didn't need to be made to think about IDs. The way my thoughts had already started to develop was too unpleasant.

After a couple of hours, which a chrono would have

registered as around twenty seconds, the mirror turned into a door and opened.

"Humility."

"Tom Lee."

There were no windows in the room. Above the door behind me and to my right, banks of screens showed him every corner of the restaurant and gave a good view of the street outside. I'd have been surprised if there weren't other vids available scanning a far wider segment of town. I didn't sit. There wasn't a second chair.

"You looking for me." Not a question.

"Yes. Got you a contact with the Port if you want it."

"Daisy?" He wasn't impressed.

"Her if you want. Also a man named Steven. Concessions superintendent. Looking for someone good for the food stalls."

No way of knowing if it impressed or even interested him, but he didn't throw me out.

"That all?"

Yes. Go now. If you don't ask, you may never need to know.

"Got something here I'd like you to see."

He nodded when I hitched my bag round to unfasten it. His scanners would have told him it held no threat to him. I fumbled for a moment and then brought out the chip I'd found in Jon's envelope.

He looked at it without moving from his seat. "ID chip."

My guess had been right. Had I wanted it to be? If it hadn't been, I was further than ever from knowing what was going on. I let myself marvel for a second at the perversity of human thinking before I asked the next question. "It still alive?"

He shook his head. "Not likely. ID's not meant to survive without neural link-up. Can go on a few hours but that's all. 'Less you have a lifebox, of course."

"What's that?"

He reached across. Lifted the chip from my hand. The dirty fingernails barely brushed my skin. I tried not to shiver.

"Box to store these things. Has artificial synapses. Medics use them if they've got a long operation for augments and need to lift the ID for a while. Without it…" He shrugged, tossed the chip and caught it, closing his hand. "Dead meat."

So I hadn't been walking round with a dead woman's live ID in my sack. I was glad of that. Perhaps she wasn't dead?

"So a person can live without an ID?"

He opened his hand, looking down at the chip in its palm before he looked up at me. I wondered in what past life he had gained his medical knowledge. His eyes were cold. Dead.

"Depends."

"On what?"

"What you mean by life. Most times you lose your ID it scrambles your mind. Easy enough to insert but then it's too tight into the brain to be pulled permanently. Can bypass for a while but for all time…"

Another shrug. Now I hoped the woman was dead. I held out my hand and, after a moment in which I thought he might not agree, he dropped the chip back into it. I put it in my sack with care. Unlike Tom Lee, I couldn't separate it from the flesh it had once monitored. Tried not to think what was in my own skull. Tried to control the anger. We are all androids, tied to a chip which is nothing more than a miniaturised bureaucrat. The Elders had been wrong: there was more supervision, not less. Tom Lee was watching me and I had no idea at all what went on behind his skull-face.

"Word is out you asking questions all round. What you Linked to, girl?"

It seemed to be everyone's day to call me girl.

"Not sure. Trouble, perhaps." No point denying what he already knew.

"Thought so. I don't want a share. You got more questions, you ask someone else. Tom Lee's not the place for you till you got it sorted, you hear?"

"I hear."

"So why you waiting?"

The door behind me had opened. I didn't move. Something like resignation came and went in his face.

"What now?"

"Girl called Luna. Street kid. Blader. Northshore. Your ground?"

"Maybe. So?"

"Trouble out at those flats. She may be in trouble, too. You might be able to help."

"Why would I want to?"

"No reason."

"That's right. You going now?"

I went. He probably wouldn't do anything about Luna, might not even be able to trace her, but I'd had to try. Tom Lee didn't have a reputation for using kids and I'd half-hoped he might be able to shield one from whatever was going down.

I made my way back between the busy tables. The man

148

at the door nodded as I left. The gesture had a sort of permanent look. That was when I realised what Tom Lee's dismissal also meant: he wouldn't be buying from me. If he wouldn't, nor would anyone else. I'd lost my wine market. Now I'd *have* to find out what was behind Jon's death and do something about it – or else look for a regular job.

I hardly noticed the rough jolting of the bus on my way back to the Port. I was too busy wondering whether the damaged cube which Jon had given me, and at which Byron had looked without expression, had once been what Tom Lee had called a lifebox.

33

I supposed I was making a sort of progress. I had some idea of what was happening, though I still had only a list of possibles for who and no idea at all of why. It was to do with IDs. It had to be; there could be no reason why Jon should still be listed alive unless his missing chip had found its way into a lifebox. Everything else was speculation.

The box. It came back to that. The little cube which let someone kill a person and still be able to prove he was alive. The box which had made Blue Eyes open his door to me. I took it from the drawer in the chart table and looked at it more closely than before. When Jon had left it for me I had assumed it was solid, a toy or token of some sort, or a puzzle. I was guessing now that he'd left me a puzzle – but not a toy.

The damage to one side made the opening hard to find. I pressed every corner and face and tried to slide a finger-nail between them with only a broken nail for my pains. I swore. The more I peered at the cube and tried to twist or pry it open, the less certain I became that it was anything but the token I'd first thought it. I was about ready to give in, or at least to see whether throwing it from one end of the deckhouse to the other would do the trick, when I felt it shift in my hand.

I looked at it. Yes. A crack had appeared on one edge. It had happened when I had squeezed two opposing sides together with more force than I'd thought they'd stand. Whatever had dented it had obviously jammed the opening mechanism but now I could get the tip of a knife-blade in and ease back the surface which had moved.

Nothing. The box was empty. Two narrow slots inside the thickened walls, which must contain some sort of circuitry, told me it was built to hold something. I hardly needed to take out the chip and slide it in to have the answer I'd looked for. It was, or had been, a lifebox. So what did that mean?

The cards on the chart table in front of me had no answers. I ignored them. I was restless but unable to think of what to do next. I needed something to keep my hands busy while what passed for my brain tried to process what I'd learned. I decided to cook.

I don't cook often. My mother worked hours every day preparing meals for my father and brothers to swill down. When I complained at learning to bake and brew, she told me that men built the outside and women built the inside and that both were necessary for a strong home. I didn't believe it. Not when I saw that men could complain about the women's work but a comment from me about what they had done was likely to earn me a beating.

So I had learned to cook and to value the time when I no longer had to. But today there was something soothing about chopping onions and tomatoes and discovering that there were still fresh leaves on some of the herbs which struggled to survive in pots beneath the window of the deckhouse.

As I chopped and tasted and watched the sauce simmer and thicken I let myself think of what I'd learned. Jon was dead. Blue Eyes was dead. Someone else – a woman if the jewellery meant anything – was dead. The Port development was being sabotaged, although Daisy might be right and it had been nothing more than a run of bad luck. But three deaths were more than bad luck.

Three deaths that I knew about. How many others? *Why* had there been no official investigation? Why had Byron needed to be pressured into making the simplest inquiries?

Family business? I hoped not. Then the phone shrilled.

I nearly cut my finger off when I dropped the knife. I wasn't expecting a call. I glared at the screen and then blinked when Milo's face looked back at me.

"I'm in the Harbour Office. Did you mean it when you said I could visit?"

No. I hadn't thought so. But I don't mind when someone accepts a challenge.

"Of course. Come down."

So this was how the wealthy behaved. Was privacy not an issue with them or was it fashionable this season to be impulsive?

Perhaps he just enjoyed slumming, I amended, as I disarmed the system and opened the deckhouse door to watch him negotiate the ladder. The tide was half-full so he had about three metres to descend and the rain didn't make it easy.

"That is not the most friendly of entryways."

I grinned. He was brushing fragments of rust from soft palms with delicate revulsion but his comment had been edged more with laughter than complaint.

"Sorry. You should have waited for high water. Come aboard."

I stood back to let him step up on to the deck from the pontoon and duck into the deckhouse. Rain glinted on his dark hair without spoiling its styling as he looked around.

"Cosy." Then he grinned. "Something smells good."

"I'm cooking."

"And I'm interrupting?"

"No. Your timing's good. I was ready to stop and open a bottle."

If he wasn't used to bottles which bore no labels and all-purpose glasses – solid enough to cope with falling off a table when the seas, or the night, got rough – at least his upbringing had given him the manners not to show it.

"Thanks. That ladder makes a man feel he's earned a drink. I had no idea boats were so hazardous." He took a cautious sip. Didn't quite hide the surprise. "Your wine is good."

I decided he wasn't being patronising, or not deliberately, and refilled my own glass. He pointed to the chart table.

"What's that?"

"Patience."

He blinked, unsure if I was warning him off or advising him to wait and I explained.

"Patience. Solitaire. A card game for one player. Most versions rely entirely on the fall of the cards but this one takes some skill as well as luck."

He was shaking his head, openly laughing.

"Daisy was right about you. You really do come from a different world."

So he'd asked about me. I wasn't quite sure whether I was flattered or annoyed. Depended what else Daisy had said. "Different from yours."

He could hardly have avoided hearing the stiffness in my voice and had the grace to acknowledge it.

"I'm sorry. I didn't mean to offend you." He sounded sincere, appalled at his own tactlessness, and he'd put his glass down as though expecting to be told to leave at once. It was a change from Tom Lee's arrogance or the rough directness of Em and her friends. Even Daisy didn't often apologise for being forthright. I piled the cards together and shovelled them into the drawer. I could stack and shuffle them later. A pity, the spread had looked as though it might work out.

His protesting gesture was half-complete. "You shouldn't have done that."

"I'll need the table if we're going to eat."

"You're inviting me to dinner?"

I hadn't meant to. Another glass of wine would have been enough to show I was used to entertaining the privileged. He didn't need me to justify clearing the cards away. Hell, *I* didn't need to justify it. Keep telling yourself, Humility, you might even get to believe it.

"Why not? I always cook too much for myself and I'd only have to preserve half of it. And now I've made the effort, it'll be good to have company to share the results. Unless you don't like to take risks with someone from a different world?"

He looked hurt. "I said I was sorry, didn't I? And I would consider it a privilege to share your meal."

I hoped he'd still think so after he'd eaten. Normally I'm confident about a skill I've had to practise from childhood, but I was still annoyingly unsettled at dealing with Family.

"It's not what your Estate would supply," I warned.

His turn to be exasperated. "My Estate would probably provide something so exotic it was inedible or else decide I needed to diet and try to tempt me with something that looked like food and had no calorific value whatsoever."

He might be a little soft, but he wasn't overweight. I was fascinated. "You can do that?"

"Eat valueless food? Yes. The Company which patented it shot from seventh to third in the rankings almost overnight."

It wouldn't sell on the streets, where you ate any protein you could catch, but I liked the idea of Families fighting to pay for substantial portions of nothing at all.

"What's it like?"

"Like being cheated." He grimaced. "Like discovering at the critical moment that the girl of your dreams is a holo. VR food. If I'm going to diet, I'd rather suffer."

"Only people who never have to suffer say things like that."

He looked at me. Sighed. "Prejudice showing, Humility?"

"Sorry." I put up both hands in surrender.

"Why don't you top up the glasses, while whatever it is finishes cooking, and we can trade prejudices and preconceptions with a mutual agreement to stop apologising or taking offence?"

It sounded like a fair deal to me. I passed him the bottle.

After that false start we got on better than I'd expected. When he asked about my upbringing I allowed myself to read honest curiosity in his voice, not patronage.

"What do you know about New Puritans?" I asked.

"Very little, except that they're mainly confined to the western peninsula. Don't take much interest in EuroGov and vice versa. Fairly lo-tech. There're only about five or six Communities, aren't there?"

"Five. And 'fairly lo-tech' is an understatement. They let in the ID chips a bit over twenty-five years ago but they still don't allow augments."

He stared, finding it hard to imagine. I wasn't going to tell him that I was still a virgin as far as augments were concerned. And intended to stay that way.

"The movement started back in the twenties," I explained. "At least that's what my grandmother told me. She always said she was a Traveller. Said there'd been small groups of them all over the west when she was a child, never settling anywhere."

"Why not?"

"Partly because that was how they liked it. Partly because no one wanted them around. She told me how they used to get together for the big solstice festivals – music and dancing and whatever anyone could find to smoke."

I'd also heard how the peeps then were as unpopular as they were today, always breaking up the party just as it was getting lively. It had sometimes sounded like fun, sometimes frighteningly uncertain. She'd always looked as though each memory was a treasure.

Milo was frowning. "I always thought Puritans were strictly fundamentalist?"

"No-fun fundamentals?"

He looked small-boy embarrassed. "It's only what I'd heard."

"Don't worry. I've heard it before. It's not far off the truth."

"So what happened to the smoke and music?"

"That was when the fundamentalists moved in. A couple of waves of them left the cities at the time of the food riots. Went to set up new lives in the unpolluted west. According to grandmother, the Travellers took them in when no one else would give them any space, then found themselves taken over inside a decade."

They'd traded fun and uncertainty for absolutism and the Book. My father must have remembered some of the early days but he never spoke of them. All I remember him wanting was to be accepted as an Elder and being certain his mother's outspokenness would cause trouble with the Council. *Let your women keep silence.* He'd have had it engraved on the meeting-house lintel if he could.

I couldn't blame Milo for looking as though he was hearing about an alien planet. It seemed a world away to me and I'd *lived* there. I decided it was time I learned a little about his exotic world. "So why are you slumming down in Midway?"

"It's my brother's pet project," he explained. "Morgan. I came down with him. He was the one talking to the Harbour Master. The one with the beard, remember?"

I remembered. "The one who didn't see me?"

He winced but didn't pretend not to understand. Credit for that.

"Yes. He's crazy about yachts. Fast yachts. He's sailed everywhere he can and tried out every new form of sail and hull he can invent or have invented for him. Now he wants to share the kick. He thinks people will go for challenge and adventure."

"Why doesn't he just try walking the streets without a bodyguard?"

The shudder wasn't all acting. "I said crazy. Not certifiable."

"And what do you think of sailing?"

Another shudder. "As little as possible."

"So why are you here?"

"To make Morgan look even more important. And to

run a check on some of his deals. My contribution to the Family mostly involves checking that my brother doesn't get too carried away by his enthusiasms."

Morgan hadn't looked as though he was ever carried away by anything much. Perhaps Milo's first answer was the right one.

"What will all the new business here mean for you?"

"Either nothing or the loss of this mooring."

He glanced out of the window. Darkness and rain hid the ladder he had climbed down but his thoughts needed little illumination. "Loss?"

"A small thing, but my home."

No need to tell him just how unwilling any port was to take in itinerants like myself. Those problems were mine to deal with. My grandmother's stories about how she and her family had been moved on, or denied access to decent facilities, when she had been a child had sounded exciting to me once. Now I realised I had taken more of my heritage with me than I had ever wanted when I left home.

Milo laughed, not understanding. No reason why he should nor did I feel like explaining. But perhaps I could put in a word for Em and Clim and the others.

"It's not too bad for me. But it would be a pity if the development put others out of their homes, especially if its success isn't guaranteed."

"What do you mean?"

He was wary and I didn't blame him. But at least he listened when I told him about the mud-berths.

"What do you suggest?"

"Do nothing. Leave the development small and exclusive."

"Expensive?" For all his soft looks he wasn't a fool.

"That's right. Double the price and halve the availability."

"You should be in business. I'll take a look at your mud-berths. Talk to Morgan. The old boats might be an asset: part of the return to nature which clients can pay mega-credits to experience."

I should have been pleased but it left a sour taste. "They can keep their homes if they agree to be part of Themepark Midway?"

"Compromise is the name of the game."

"I prefer patience."

He laughed and, after a moment, I joined in.

It was a while since I'd spent an evening like this with a man and as time passed I grew increasingly aware of it. I couldn't tell what Milo thought. He hadn't made a move but I'd caught the glances which lingered from time to time. It might just be because he was as unused to talking to primitives as I was to feeding aristos, but I didn't think so.

I was still trying to make up my mind, and wondering if my cabin was as much of a mess as I remembered, when he stood up.

"It's late and I'd better leave."

You don't have to. I didn't quite say it aloud. "At least it's high water. No problems with the ladder."

We went out on deck together. The rain had stopped. The river ran black past the boat, the fierce ebb-tide just beginning. Milo looked at it with distaste as he stepped out on to the pontoon.

"Are you *sure* you prefer this to the comforts of dry land? That water looks dangerous."

"It is. And yes, I'm quite sure."

He took my hand before I could make up my mind just

how to say goodnight. His lips were astonishingly gentle against its back and then he had released me and was taking the easy single step up on to dockside.

"Sleep well, Humility. Thanks for the drink and the meal – I'll be in touch."

I decided he meant it. I didn't expect his interest in alien lifeforms to outlast his time here at Midway, but I was beginning to like his style. When I went back into the deckhouse I found myself looking at the back of my hand with an expression which would have infuriated me if I had seen it on anyone else. So that was how the aristos did it? I wanted to be annoyed by the extravagant gesture, but found that what annoyed me more was my own reaction to it.

I slammed the door and reset the alarms and poured the last two centimetres of wine from the bottle into my glass.

34

Next morning was soon enough to seek out Daisy. I only did it because I guessed she would be down on me before long and I needed whatever advantage I could get.

When I called she told me I could have ten minutes if I got over to her office. Now. I got. I didn't even take time out to exchange banter with the thug on security.

"So what are you playing at now?"

She sounded resigned, as though a night's sleep had told her that she couldn't stop whatever I was doing. On closer inspection I doubted if she'd slept at all. Either she was worrying about Sheba or more hung up on this Board visit than she wanted to admit.

"Poking around," I admitted. "Seeing if I can find out how or why the guy was killed."

No point in insisting the guy was Jon. She didn't want to hear it and I had no way of proving it. Opposite me she tapped neat fingernails on the grey desk and waited for me to say more. Today's earring was a chain of three gold balls. Discreet. Out of deference to the Board? I was sure Morgan would deplore the usual cascades of colour. Milo might not. That thought short-circuited whatever I had planned to say. Daisy sighed.

"I suppose I should have known you wouldn't give up. Even for a friend. Is it too much to ask that you take some care?"

"Don't worry. I won't drop you in it." Not unless I must.

Daisy's tapping fingers stilled. She looked at me and I

wondered how you balanced the demands of living friends with dead ones.

"I wasn't thinking of me. I was thinking of you. But since you mention it, I would be grateful if you'd keep in mind that the Company may be willing to tolerate one unexplained death but two might be more than they'll stomach."

How about three? I wondered. Aloud I said, "I'll take care. Do you know if Byron's around today?"

"Byron? What on earth do you want to see him for? On second thoughts, I don't want to know. Anyway, I can't help you. He's not in his office at the moment - I still have enough access to know that - but where he is or what he's up to or why he's even still here is something else. He comes and goes as he pleases. I hope he remembers to tell me when he's leaving."

She had my sympathy. I knew how she valued her control over the Port.

"Soon?" I suggested.

"I wish. I'm coming close to praying he doesn't tangle with the rest of the visitors."

I had already wondered whether he was deliberately avoiding them. I didn't know if it had been Morgan or Milo or some other, more senior, Vinci who had called him in.

"Oh yes. The Board. How are you getting on?"

She glared. "More important, how are *you* getting on? What's going on with you and the younger brother?"

"Milo?" I tried to sound indifferent but my colour betrays me every time. She was grinning now. Relaxed. Satisfied that she'd caught me.

"That's the one. Security tells me he didn't get back in

till after one this morning. And the evening vids show him heading from the Port Office towards that rustbucket you call a barge."

"May a virus get your security. It's nosier than neighbours. Besides, nothing happened."

She just sat there.

"All right. He came for a drink and stayed for a meal. We talked. He went home. End of subject. Nothing's going on."

I thought of the hour I'd spent between one and two this morning when the effect of the wine wore off and I cleaned up every trace of our meal before going to bed on my own in my messy cabin.

"Perhaps it should be."

My turn to stare. "What do you mean? He's Company – worse, he's *Family* – and he and his brother won't stay here any longer than they have to."

Daisy was wearing her patient look. "I wasn't suggesting you marry the man."

"This from the woman who used to lecture me about irresponsibility?"

"This from the woman who thinks you can carry independence to extremes. You haven't had a serious relationship since Jack."

"That wasn't…"

"I know what it wasn't. I also know you won't replace it. That doesn't mean you can't relax from time to time."

"I do."

I didn't need to be reminded how disastrous my last bit of relaxation had turned out. He'd thought I had rebelled more completely against my background than I would have dreamed possible. I suppose I could forgive Daisy for thinking Milo an improvement on him. If she'd known he'd kissed my hand when he said goodnight, she'd have been even more smug than she was looking right now.

"Why aren't you out showing them all a good time?" I asked.

"Because I have work to do. I showed them everything yesterday and Gus is panting to do it all over again. If they need me they'll call."

"They'll probably need rescuing from Gus. Where are they now?"

"Why? Want to check up on Milo?"

I gritted my teeth and waited while she tapped in a sequence. Three screens changed channel.

"The one that's showing mostly feet is on Gus's badge."

"If he spends that much time bowing you should have put it on top of his head."

"Thanks for your concern. I'll try it next time. The other two are stationary units."

They showed Morgan at the front of his entourage asking questions and looking serious and superior. Daisy wasn't letting me have sound. I didn't mind. The man just behind Morgan was recording everything. The rest of the group tried to look as though they'd always had a passion for boats while hoping no one suggested they went sailing. Milo was next to Morgan. He looked bored. I tried not to feel pleased.

On the screen in front of me I saw the group turn and move as Gus began to lead them down to the marina. Morgan looked keen. Milo looked resigned. The others followed. I frowned.

Daisy noticed. "What's up?"

"Nothing. Just thought I saw something."

"If you're going to start imagining things, do it some-where else. I've got to do a day's work before that lot get back."

She switched the screens and I stood up.

"Point taken. I'll get on with my own business."

When I left I could tell she was hoping that meant Milo and not whoever killed Jon.

35

I didn't go straight back to the *Pig*. Something about that glimpse of Milo and the rest of the court had unsettled me. Not Milo. It's a long time since a man I've known little more than a day could disturb me that easily. Certainly not when I'm looking at him from the safe side of a vid lens. No, it was someone else in the huddle of sycophants who'd triggered an alarm. Trouble was, I had no idea who. Or why. It hadn't seemed like a good moment to ask Daisy to rerun the shot and the chances of her giving me a copy were nil. But at least it had told me where they all were.

It wasn't that I wanted to see Milo. I wanted to look at the whole party, to know if the nagging sense that I had seen something without knowing it was imagination, frustration or something more substantial. I wasn't hopeful. To myself I could admit I was fishing desperately for anything which might get me further along a path which had become far darker and more complicated than I could have anticipated when I'd looked up and seen a body hanging in the air like a mouse in a cat's jaw.

They were still at the marina. It was half-tide so I was looking down on the pontoons from the harbour wall. I stayed where I was. No point in giving Gus a reason for banning me from the Port. Besides, I wasn't sure what form marina security took and the thought of setting off all the alarms in the place had little appeal. That Milo would be one of those observing any such embarrassment was irrelevant.

There were eleven of them. Slightly foreshortened figures clustered around Gus, who was pointing at something on one of the smart boxes which went with every berth. They had a show boat in there so that all the links could be demonstrated: a sleek twelve-metre self-rigging ketch with a drive which made the sails an affectation.

Apart from Morgan and Milo – who was staring around without any apparent interest – there were five men and three women in the Company group. Daisy said I was good with faces, but I wondered how easy it would be to distinguish these. It wasn't that they wore any sort of uniform, unless you count the sameness of high fashion: fitted to show perfect figures, beaded belts which clipped narrow waists and contained more circuitry than the *Pig*. They weren't flaunting sex, it was power that was on show. The power of the wealth which could afford form-fitted clothes and the body-sculpting which made the clothes wearable. Hair colour and length and style varied but if I was close enough to see faces clearly I wondered if I'd find more of the generic sameness. Family likeness? Surgically achieved? Whatever had nagged at me from the vid was silent now I saw the reality.

Morgan and two of the others had gone on board the yacht with Gus following them. He seemed to be apologising for something, but then he always looked like that when he was with someone who outranked him. The rest of the party stopped looking interested as soon as Morgan was out of sight. Milo, who had never bothered pretending interest, turned to stare shorewards as though wondering when the real entertainment would begin. He saw me.

No reason I shouldn't be there. No reason to feel

embarrassed. I stood my ground and watched him approach, deciding he hadn't had any surgical intervention. He was different enough from his court, *flawed* enough, for me to be certain of it.

I hadn't come here to see him but I wasn't going to avoid him. "Milo. Going sailing?"

His mouth twisted as though he'd tasted something sour. "Never. Morgan already owes me for making me come on this trip and he couldn't begin to afford what it would cost to make me go out on that boat. Any boat."

"So why did you come?"

His smile was crooked, appealing. "I don't know. Boredom, mostly. I owe you for the only bright moment of the trip so far. I was going to call as soon as Morgan decided I was off-duty."

"Just to say thanks?"

My formal manners were obviously inadequate. A message on the phone was as much as I'd expected. And, possibly, a return invitation? Whether that was on his mind I couldn't tell. It wasn't what he said next.

"Partly. I also wanted to tell you I'd spoken to Morgan about your neighbours on the hulks."

Hulks sounded depressingly lifeless. It wasn't a word I liked even though I admitted its accuracy. But I was both surprised and pleased that he'd remembered.

"My turn for thanks. Dare I ask what Morgan said?"

"It wouldn't tell you much. Morgan specialises in inscrutability. We're going to look at them this afternoon."

"Gus taking you?"

He laughed. "Yes. He didn't have much choice. I think it was a bit of the Port he was hoping we'd never discover. No chance. I may be lazy but Morgan's thorough. That's why he's in charge here, of course."

Lack of authority didn't seem to worry him. Another point in his favour. Beyond his shoulder I saw renewed movement beside the show boat.

"Looks like he's decided not to go sailing today."

Milo looked behind him. "Then I'm back on duty. Call you."

This time I decided to believe that was more than courtesy. I watched him saunter back down the pontoon, pausing to speak to someone on his wrist unit before rejoining his brother and the court.

I watched the group for a few moments longer but still saw nothing to tell me what I had seen on the screen in Daisy's office to make my nerves twitch.

They were still twitching. I went back to the *Pig* feeling as though I was the one being watched. Considering the level of security in the Port, this wasn't necessarily paranoia but I wasn't usually so aware of surveillance.

Back at my berth I grabbed the muddy bit of cable I'd tossed into the dinghy the day before. I'd washed it off to reveal bright yellow cladding which confirmed the newness Pete had spoken of. It still weighed heavy, and I had no real doubt where it had come from, but I thought I might as well check out the recycle heaps in case they had more to tell me.

36

The old dockyard is the area between the new mall and the river, which will be levelled and tidied once all the rest of the work is done. Right now it's a junkyard. It's by the water so the waste barges can just ooze alongside and fill up when they're called in. I hadn't been surprised to see Clim there the other day and now it was my turn to forage. The place is a mess but there's a rough sort of order once you get used to it. Most of the metalwork, rusting hull plates, old boilers, empty drums of some nameless – and undoubtedly toxic – waste are in one area; woodwork is piled high where it can be burned; the paint and other liquid cast-offs are under a sort of lean-to. And the bits of wiring, cable and chain are all together just above the shore line where the old dock wall overlooks the tide. Or, at the moment, the mud.

I did find time to wonder whether Morgan had any plans to make mud look more appealing. There was a lot of it when the tide was low.

The newness of the cable might mean it wasn't from here after all. But there was plenty of stuff that hadn't seen much wear – off-cuts and lengths that were of no real use to anyone except scavengers like Clim and me. And killers? It would take no more than three or four metres of metal-cored cable to tangle and weight a body.

I started to rummage through the appropriate heap. It was heavy, sweaty work; my nails were soon torn and my knuckles grazed. But it wasn't hard to find a match for my piece once I'd shifted half a tonne of assorted other gear.

I don't think the killer had tried to hide it. Why should he? It was where he'd found it in the first place. Now I had to decide what to do about it. I may have satisfied my curiosity about the source of the cable but I couldn't see anyone considering it any sort of evidence. Whoever had tied it round Jon's body would have worn gloves – anyone handling heavy cable wears gloves – so there weren't likely to be any prints. And what would prints prove? I'd already convinced myself the killer either worked in the Port or had access. His prints probably had a higher security clearance than mine.

But if the cable was here, perhaps the weapon wouldn't be far away. I began to look more closely at what I'd disturbed. If I'd wanted a blunt instrument there was plenty of choice here. Perhaps one of the iron bars or twisted rigging screws still held traces of blood.

The search seemed endless. Dried blood and old paint could look sickeningly alike. My stomach lurched half a dozen times at false alarms. It was hopeless, but I couldn't just give up. I had to *try.*

I was reaching for a promising-looking length of pipe when a sound behind me caught my attention. I turned. "Clim?" He was the one who spent most time out here. No answer. Probably a passing cat. Or someone coming to dump some stuff. Couldn't see anyone. Turned back to the waste heap. Nerves twitched in my shoulders. I straightened, looked around again.

There was a tall man approaching.

"Hey, you! What are you doing?" Obviously the same mind-set as Gus.

"Nothing."

"Making trouble, that's what."

It was only as he began to speed up that I listened to the alarm bells which had been trying to ring in my head. He wasn't some Port type with a God-complex like Gus. He knew exactly what I was doing and didn't like the idea I might have found something interesting.

Speed and my knowledge of the place were my only advantages. I ran for a corner between the sheds. Turned down it. Heard feet pounding behind me. He'd have seen where I went and I didn't want to get trapped in a dead end. I slithered down the narrow passageway, jinked right and left again to come out behind him.

Mistake. There were two of them. A rougher-looking type had come up behind the first one and was hanging around the entrance to the junkyard, blocking my escape that way. I didn't think either of them had conversation in mind.

They hadn't spotted me yet but once they did they'd have me boxed. I wished I'd thought twice about checking out the cable. Wished I'd told someone where I was going. Wished I had a smart wrist-unit like Milo's so I could summon the cavalry. *If wishes were horses...*

Tough. I'd had long enough to get my wheezing breath back under control and accept that I couldn't stay where I was. They knew I was somewhere behind the sheds and it wouldn't take them long to flush me out. I thought of cornered rats and for the first time in my life felt sorry for the rat.

I couldn't get past the rough guy at the open entrance and I couldn't stay here behind the sheds for much longer. Which left only one way out. The only question was: how to get there?

I risked another glance out the front. The first man was peering up the alley I'd taken. The other guy was still waiting, but he'd taken the time to pick up a metre-long length of wood. I wondered if he was the one who'd seen the opportunity offered by a length of heavy cable and a piece of iron piping.

I toyed with the idea they were just here to frighten me. But they'd done that and they didn't seem about to stop. No. If I was lucky they'd just beat me to a pulp. But I had a nasty feeling that this might become a disposal site again, if I hung around. So I wouldn't.

"Any sign of her?" He was getting impatient, swinging the wooden club lightly as though testing its balance. Wanting to try it out.

"No, but she can't get away." He paused. "Hey, little girl, why don't you come on out of there? We just want to talk."

Calling me "little girl" wasn't only inaccurate: it was a mistake. It made me angry. The surge of rage combined with the frustration and guilt I'd been carrying around and I felt my pulse beginning to race. I wasn't quite mad enough to think I could deal with either of them physically, but when the fight-or-flight mechanism kicks in you've got to go with what you know best.

I fled.

I took the precaution of lobbing a piece of rubble up and over the low shed roof so it clattered down behind the guy who'd been first to give chase. An old trick, but I defy anyone not to turn and look at a sudden noise. And one man distracted left only one to get past.

I used what cover there was to slide out of the alley and behind the paintshed. But the shout behind me – "There she is!" – told me I'd only bought myself a few seconds.

I hoped it would be enough.

It was less than twenty metres across the yard and when I vaulted over the low wall into the exposed mud beneath, the guy with the club was less than half that distance behind me. I slithered and fell on landing and had to fight against the thin mud and rubble beneath to regain my feet. But I was banking on my pursuers being no more sure-footed than me in the conditions. And that they wouldn't want to risk gunfire here.

Logic is one thing, reality another. My back felt as though it had a target painted on it as I pushed my way through the clinging mud. I heard the splatter and curse as someone jumped in behind me and didn't stop to see which of them had chosen to risk his clothes.

I was getting in deeper. There wasn't much bottom beneath the mud just here and I could feel its drag and suck with every move I made. We must have looked like a slow-motion chase. It might have been funny if it weren't for the guy behind me and the knowledge that the mud held risks even nastier than a blow with a piece of wood. It doesn't like letting go of things that land in it, and the tide would be back in soon.

Every step was a heave against the suction of the thin muck. I was hoping that the weight of the man behind me was slowing him, dragging him deeper than me. Hoping that panic would set in for him before it overwhelmed me.

"Stop, you bitch! You'll kill yourself!"

Was suicide an affront if it prevented him murdering me? I didn't stop. I'd just felt the first hint in what felt like hours of something like firm footing. I knew where I was.

It was what I'd been depending on. The uncertain memory of three years ago when Jack and I had hauled the

Pig out on to the old abandoned hard-standing which jutted out of this corner of the yard. We'd had to hose what seemed like half a metre of mud off it before we could do the work on the boat's keel that had been needed, but under the mud the old paving had been almost intact.

The club-wielder didn't know he was a couple of metres from safety and I wasn't about to tell him. When I risked a look back he was wallowing thigh-deep in grey mud. I let myself stumble forward, seeming to scrabble for air and balance while I braced myself, hands and feet, against the old stone slabs. They felt disgusting and wonderful.

"You've almost got her." That was the one who'd stayed ashore.

"This mud's got me. I'm not going any further without a rope." My pursuer seemed to have lost enthusiasm for his work. "Help get me out of this fucking stuff or she's not the only one who's going to drown."

"Oh, I don't think we'll let her drown."

It wasn't as reassuring as it should have sounded. I risked another glance back and started moving again, as fast as I could. He'd reached into his belt and pulled out something that looked like some sort of gun. I'd been wrong about them not risking gunfire.

"Let her go!" The shout came from ahead of me. The voice sounded familiar but I didn't care who it came from if it stopped what was happening behind me.

We were far enough out in the river bed to be visible from the end of the mall. The Family party must have just emerged from their tour. They were all looking over at me with a range of expressions which varied from disgust to amusement. Gus was more purple than ever.

It didn't matter. All that mattered was squelching to my

feet and up the hard standing to the wall. When I looked back the man who'd been following me was levering himself ashore without much help from his friend.

I wasn't getting much help, either. After a closer look, most of the party had backed away from both the smell and the sight of the mud and decided to finish their tour as far as possible away from me. I couldn't blame them.

"What do you think you're playing at?" Gus, of course.

"We weren't playing. They were trying to kill me."

He looked around. Noticed that the family had drifted out of earshot. "You're out of your mind. It looked from here as though that man was trying to rescue you."

"What about the gun?"

"Gun? What gun? You know no weapons are allowed in the Port."

Who needed to bring in a weapon when there was a junkyard full of them? But Gus didn't want to admit that any unauthorised guns had managed to sneak in under his supervision.

I turned away, suddenly weary. All I wanted was to hose the worst of the filth off and go home. When Gus headed officiously off to intercept the two men, who were just about to leave the yard I just sat on the dockside and felt the mud hardening on me.

And wondered: if it had really looked like someone rescuing an idiot woman, just who had shouted out to let me go?

37

I needed to clean up and I needed to spend some time where no one could get at me. That meant the *Pig*.

I also needed to think.

It had been no surprise when Gus had come back to tell me that the men were perfectly innocent, that they had every right to be here, that one of them had ruined his clothes trying to prevent me from getting stuck in the mud and that I should be grateful that they weren't going to ask for me to be charged. With what? I wondered. Being in the wrong place?

I shouldn't have been disappointed but I found myself near to rare tears of frustration at the descent of drama into farce. And what would happen next time I was on my own somewhere? The Port was possibly not the best place to be. I should just sail away.

But I couldn't. Things had gone too far. The morning's events told me I'd hit a nerve really hard. If I didn't want to end up a corpse – with or without an ID – I had to work out what was happening and either stop it myself or find someone who would. It all felt too big. And no one here wanted there to be trouble. Without real evidence they'd bury it, and me if necessary, rather than damage the progress of the development.

I could only think of one person who might be able to give me the backing I needed. It irked me to do it, but I called Byron.

He wasn't available.

When you've nerved yourself to do something you really don't want to do, which feels like an admission of defeat, it's depressing to find yourself thwarted.

The phone I'd just failed to call Byron on rang. Em. I looked at my chrono and discovered most of the afternoon had gone. Scrubbing the mud off and arguing with Gus had taken more time than I'd realised.

"Humility? Where you been?"

"Paddling."

"Ha ha. I owe you one."

So Milo kept his word. "You've met Morgan?"

Her grin was broad. Stained and uneven teeth defied modern dentistry. I could guess what she'd have to say about body-sculpting.

"And the brother. You've made an impression on that one, haven't you?"

"Have I?"

"Coyness don't suit you. He said it was you told him about our problems. Good idea to go to the top. Now it don't matter what happens to Daisy."

It mattered to me. "He was helpful?" I was cautious, unsure if Milo had suggested the sort of deal he'd mentioned last night.

Em was nodding. "Certainly was. Neither of them wants the hulks to move on. Thinks we might even be an attraction." She didn't mind calling *Wild Goose* a hulk.

"And you can live with that?"

The thought of the old boats, which were rotting away with a kind of quiet dignity, being turned into a tourist spectacle revolted me. I'd rather take the *Pig* out and sink her. But it wasn't the *Pig* which was being exploited. And I wasn't Em. She shared none of my doubts.

"You're joking! It's the opportunity we've been waiting for."

For a moment I couldn't see what she meant. Then I had a vision of Clim's scavenging and began to understand. The old manipulator and the rest of them would find their own ways of profiting from whatever the Company planned. They were survivors. And perhaps it wasn't the hulks which would be exploited.

"I'm glad it's worked out all right."

"It couldn't be better. We're having a celebration in two nights' time and want you to be guest of honour. You coming?"

"I'll come."

After Em had rung off I stared at the blank screen with some satisfaction. At least I'd managed to solve one problem. Milo had gone to some trouble to take Morgan down to the mud-berths and, I guessed, suggest how they could use the odd assortment of boats lying there. Em might be right about his interest.

As for my other problems, I'd tried to contact Byron and couldn't think of anyone else who could help. And I certainly didn't want to go out and prowl again today. I decided to let myself be distracted by someone else's difficulties. I reset the screen to catch a local broadcast.

The usual ads. Trailers for the usual games shows. *Win more prizes!* The usual list of bounties for the usual crowd of criminals. The local Missing list. It was mother's birthday in two weeks. I must call her. I almost turned it off when they trailed the result of the most recent demopol. I did shut down the sound.

I don't believe anyone votes. I certainly don't believe the figures which are solemnly announced every week or two when some local issue is put to public vote. Push the right code on your home terminal and your democratic voice will be heard and you can influence the decisions of the local council? Someone has a sense of humour. If I wanted to influence the council, I'd do better to slip Tom Lee a free tankful of wine. He and his friends hold the puppets' strings.

The demopol trail faded to be replaced by local news. A fire. A tall building almost swallowed in black smoke. A flicker of flame. Crowds around pointing and shouting, their faces a mixture of horror and greedy fascination. A fire appliance failing to save anything.

I didn't need the commentary to tell me where it was. I'd spent hours outside that building, trying to work out what Blue Eyes was up to. At least the fire wouldn't matter to him. I turned up the sound.

" … fire was reported earlier this afternoon. There is thought to be little hope of saving the building."

No one was trying. The old towers were no value to anyone; they'd rather pay for the land to be redeveloped. Not for the same class of tenants as Jon or Blue Eyes, of course. They'd want people who could pay. I wondered if everyone had got out and whether anyone would ever know.

"… casualties taken to the General."

A series of shots of faces. Most twisted in pain or spasms of coughing. One or two quite still. They showed them in case someone recognised them and cared enough to pay for somewhere, *anywhere*, other than the General.

And then there was a face I knew.

Luna. Lying so still I thought she was one of those beyond help. But then I saw the terror in her eyes, which had sunk back into her smoke-stained face, and knew it for the stillness of someone afraid to move.

I watched until her face left the screen to be replaced by a man who was shouting at the stretcher bearers. Then I blanked the screen.

I couldn't let her stay in the General.

38

It took me over an hour to get there. I'd put in a call to Tom Lee and been unsurprised when he wasn't available. I'd left a message to say it was Luna, not me, who was in trouble but didn't place much faith in his help. Then I took the bus to Sutton Central and another out to the northside, where the General was the last hope of the poor and friendless. A desperate hope. The hospital looked as sick as the people who crowded inside its open doors. It relied for security on big men with big weapons.

The shoreside fire seemed to be their worst emergency at the moment. Most of the bodies on trolleys smelt of smoke. At least one was beyond any help from the hospital. I pushed my way through clamouring minor injuries to a desk. No one there. I drew a breath and started searching.

The entryhall to the General is big enough to hold two or three hundred people – on their feet or squatting against a wall or lying across a row of seats – as well as a couple of dozen trolleys. The place is so primitive I doubt if it's changed since it opened. There are probably still 20th-century accident victims waiting for attention there, patient skeletons. I peered behind curtains and through starred glass viewports and grew so used to the smell of blood and piss and disinfectant that I stopped noticing it. I'd almost given up when I found her.

Kids like Luna are low priority. One look and anyone could see no rich relative would turn up to sue because she'd not been treated quickly. They hadn't even left her on a trolley: someone else needed it. She was in an alcove formed by two vending machines where at least she was in little danger of being trampled - had she dragged herself there? - and was half-curled, her arms across her belly, her breathing shallow and careful. There was no colour at all in her face. No recognition in her eyes when I knelt beside her. All her concentration was on the next breath.

"Luna?" I touched her cheek. It was almost as cold as Blue Eyes' had been. "It's Humility. I'll get help."

No way to know if she heard or understood.

I didn't want to leave her but there was no safer place to take her. Yet. I pushed my way back through the crowd. Couldn't find anyone who looked like a medic but there were plenty of guards around. I went up to one of them.

"I need help."

He looked down at me. I tried not to stare at the weapon holstered beneath his arm.

"You can still walk. Round here, that's healthy."

"Not for me. A friend. Caught in the fire."

"He'll have to wait."

"She'll be dead if she does."

It was a story he must hear a hundred times a shift. If he'd ever had any sympathy for the people who came here, he'd had to lose it if he wanted to stay sane. He shrugged. He had nothing else to offer.

"I can pay."

That changed things. "Should have said so. There's a half-and-half not far from here."

Half-private, half-public. Underfunded, and not for the rich or choosy, but better than I'd hoped. Far better than here. It might be Luna's only chance. Tom Lee might not be taking my calls but the credit he'd traded for my wine could fund this.

"How do I get there?"

"You said you could pay?"

I showed him my credit. He checked it out, nodded.

"Wait here."

It took another hour. I went back to Luna, checking every few minutes that the shallow breaths were still coming. There were beads of sweat on her forehead and she was shivering. I stole a blanket from a man on a trolley who'd never need it. I don't know if it made any difference to Luna but it was all I could do.

"Told you to wait over there. This her? Looks bad."

He was shouldering me aside as he spoke, making room for a man with a floater. He even bent and helped lift Luna, who moaned as they put her down. It was the first sound I'd heard her make and it frightened me more than her silence. It told me she was losing control.

"You coming with her?"

That was the man from the clinic. He wasn't going without me: I was the one paying. I nodded, turned back to the guard.

"Thanks. I owe you."

I held out my wrist, credit up. No point in haggling at this stage. When he put his scanner away he'd taken far less than I'd expected. He saw my surprise.

"It's enough. The clinic gives me a cut, too."

I guessed it was as small as the slice he'd taken from me. If he did this often I suppose he earned enough to make up whatever they paid him into something he could raise a family on. But he wasn't getting rich doing it.

"Thanks."

"You'd better get going. She doesn't look good."

She didn't. I went with the floater and out into the van. It took ten minutes to reach the clinic and the people in there showed so little reaction to our arrival that I wondered just what percentage of their patients they got this way.

They took Luna away and told me I could wait. Then they took my bracelet and returned it with enough left on it to keep me for a couple of days if I was careful. A good thing I'd stocked up the *Pig*.

39

It was dark before they told me anything. I'd had plenty of time to convince myself the only word I'd hear was of her death. I also had time to discover how hard the chairs were and how inadequate the food dispensers. I paced a little and pestered the attendants for information and watched more local news. The fire had been demoted to minority interest: it was out, there was nothing left to watch, no one important was injured, no one admitted to having seen it start. No surprises. Buildings burned down all the time. Sometimes it was even accidental.

"Person for smoke patient?"

"Me." I stood up.

The medic was tired and impatient to get on with her next case. No time for soothing words. "She'll live. Full recovery if she can rest and get some protein inside her. We'll keep her three days, after that she's out."

"What's the damage?"

"Smoke inhalation, mostly. Not helped by a recent beating: damaged ribs. She doesn't have much protection in that area."

No fat. The beating might have nothing to do with the fire. Kids like her get kicked around all the time. But she had been seen with me at the northshore flats and that might just have been enough for a beating. I thought of the man with the club and thought he might have dealt in punishment, even enjoyed it. I remembered how she had lain there holding her stomach, retreating inside herself, and knew she had lived through pain before.

"Is she conscious?"

"No. We'll keep her out for a while."

"Can I leave a message?"

"Not with me. Try the desk."

She walked away, shouting for someone to bring her a boost before she fell asleep on top of someone's new liver. I went to the desk. The attendant gave me a notepad and I keyed in a vox message for Luna to contact me or Tom Lee.

The energy of fear and guilt and anger which had driven me here and kept me alert drained away. I was tired. It was time to go home.

40

I hardly felt the journey. A bus slowed, I got on it. Another bus took me away from Central. The walk down to the Port. A pause while the gate looked into my eyes and decided to let me in. An endless walk across the empty forecourt, wondering whether someone was watching me, waiting for me. Two rungs down the ladder and then the familiar safe comfort of the *Pig* reached out and took me in and I could fall into my bunk and a sleep untouched by dreams.

When I called the clinic next morning they told me Luna was conscious. They gave her a hook-up so she could talk to me.

"Humility?"

The voice was blurred and smoke-roughened. Her pupils were wide and her eyes didn't focus. I wondered what drugs they'd put her on and just how broad the clinic's definition of consciousness was.

"Me. You OK?"

"OK. I owe you."

"You don't. Just passing on a favour someone did me once."

Her shoulders were thin enough without the sort of weight of debt she was talking about. Anyway, I wasn't lying. She blinked, not taking much in.

A cough. It hurt. Her eyes were half-closed now, concentration fading. "Got something for you."

"Keep it. I'll be in before they discharge you. Tell me

then."

It seemed to be enough, or perhaps she just hadn't the strength to persist. I saw her eyes close the rest of the way before someone else took the handset from her and blanked it.

I wondered what had happened to her blades. She hadn't been wearing them when I'd found her in the General. Probably stolen as payment for the trip there. She wouldn't find it easy to afford another pair and I knew without looking that I didn't have the credit to cover them even if she'd let me buy them.

It seemed a good moment to check for other calls. Didn't want any. Found two. Byron had called first. I hesitated. Spoke his code.

He looked at me from the screen. No greeting. No sign of any thanks for the callback. "Humility. Heard about your mudbath. And about the northshore flats." He didn't mention the call I'd left with him.

For a moment I wondered what concern it was of his, how he knew about Luna. Then I remembered he didn't; I'd told him Jon lived there and he'd said he would check it out.

"So. Arson?"

"Likely. But no one will trace it – too many possible culprits."

The building's owners. A grudge by or against a tenant. Kids having fun. Any link with Jon's killer had to join a list. I nodded.

"Heard about a body in the room you said was Jon's. Anonymous call-in." It wasn't quite a question. I didn't have to answer it. He let the silence grow a little before he went on, "We should talk."

If he'd been around yesterday I'd have agreed and been grateful. But what had happened to Luna had made this very personal. I had no intention of turning everything I knew, *guessed*, over to someone whose interest was in preserving Family stability and tidying away anything which might threaten it.

"I'll try to find some spare time."

He didn't bother to look as though he believed me. "We might also talk about why the sabotage seems to have stopped. You did say you'd look into that side of the trouble, didn't you?"

"I did." He knew quite well I hadn't given it a thought. If it had stopped, that was enough for me. And for Daisy. "We can talk about that, too. Later."

I didn't see a need to be any more formal than he had been. I ended the call without waiting for his reply.

The other caller was Milo. I listened to his message almost indifferently.

"Sorry I missed you. Can I tempt you out for the evening tomorrow? Call me anytime."

I checked the call's timing. Last night. While I had been staring into faces of pain and despair as I searched for Luna. He was talking about tonight. Had probably given up by now or found something better to do. I wasn't sure what he wanted or what I was ready to offer, I wasn't even sure whether I wanted to go out for the evening. My social life was usually simple and I had an idea his was not.

What else you planning to do? Play cards?

What's wrong with that?

Can do it anytime. Afraid to take a chance?

I'd seen what happened to Jack's chances often enough to have reason to be cautious. I entered the return code.

I'd assumed he'd be out with Morgan doing whatever it was they had to do while they were here. I'd been prepared to leave a message, not to see his face and the smile which replaced the frown when he saw who was calling.

"Humility! I was beginning to think you'd sailed away somewhere."

"Not yet. I've been busy. I only picked up your call a minute ago."

"So can you make it tonight? Save me from my serious brother?"

I had been going to turn him down. I'd had my polite but firm message carefully planned. I looked at the rather wistful smile and heard myself answer, "I'd enjoy it."

"I'll call for you. Around twenty?"

"Fine. Thank you."

I was abrupt because I hadn't adjusted to the sort of gallantry he seemed to regard as conventional manners. It kept reminding me how different our backgrounds were. It also reminded me, as I cut the connection, that I didn't have a wardrobe suited to his sort of background.

It took me ten minutes to decide there was no point worrying about something I couldn't change. And he'd seen enough of the way I lived to know he couldn't expect high fashion. If he wasn't embarrassed to be seen out with me, why should I let it worry me?

I did have one smart set of clothes: dark green trews, ruffled shirt which I'd hardly worn, short cape in the same green as the trews. I tried a little face-painting and decided the effect wasn't as bad as I'd feared. I wasn't one of the body-sculpted clones who hung round Family members hoping to be noticed, but he already knew that. Tall, thin red-heads were at least different. If I'd been offered the credit for surgery I'd have taken the money – and spent it on refitting the *Pig*.

I laughed suddenly, the sound bouncing off the cabin walls: Milo probably thought I was exotic.

He was on the dockside just before twenty. No keeping me waiting. When I stepped off the ladder and joined him he smiled with what I chose to take as approval. Then he led me towards the Company accommodation on the far side of the Port.

"We're going to your rooms?"

Perhaps he *was* worried about being seen out in public with me.

"I've a skimmer calling in fifteen minutes. There's a pad on the roof. You don't mind?" He sounded anxious.

"Of course not. Besides, I've never been inside the Company block."

"You haven't? It's the same as all these places. Good enough for a short visit but no home comforts."

His idea of home and mine were different. We stopped briefly at his apartment before going on up to the roof. They'd given him the whole of the second floor. While he went into another room to make a call, I looked around. The Company hadn't employed their grey-minded decorator here. As far as I could tell everything was antique, from the ornately turned and moulded mahogany sideboard to the pedestal tables poised by every chair. Sheba would have liked it. So would Tom Lee.

"Sorry about that, just checking that everything was arranged." Milo was holding open the door leading to the roof.

The skimmer was waiting. I tried to go up the steps and take one of the opulent seats as though this was nothing new to me.

"Ready, sir?" The voice from beyond the panelled partition was polite and not quite subservient.

Milo looked at me and I nodded. The stairs, I saw, had pulled themselves up behind us and the door had closed.

"Ready. You know where to go?"

"Yes, sir."

We were airborne without a tremor and only a faint hum reached us from the engines.

"So I'm the only one who doesn't know where we're going?"

"It's a place I know out in the country. You don't mind, do you?"

I discovered I did. I'd rather be consulted, or at least go to a place from which I can make my own way home. But that was petty. I knew what Daisy would have had to say about my lack of social graces. I'd waited too long to answer; he was looking concerned. Any moment now he'd turn the skimmer round and embarrass us both.

I spread both hands in apology. "I'm sorry. I'm finding it a little hard to adjust."

"You'll give it a chance?"

I'd decided I would when I'd returned his call. It would be cowardice to retreat now. "Of course. I'll probably enjoy myself. You're very well-organised."

"I try to be." I read pleasure and relief in his voice and relaxed. It was only a few more minutes before he pointed out of the window. "We're almost there."

I looked down. For the first few minutes after we'd left the Port I had seen a sprawl of buildings cut by the dark curves of the rivers. Yellow street lights had given a soft glow to the thin smog which lived over the city, blurring details. Now all I saw was darkness. No. Not quite. A cluster of lights. Their clarity was almost shocking. Then another group of lights came on: landing pad. The skimmer circled once and touched down without a jolt.

Milo stood and offered me his hand. "Ready?"

As ready as I'd ever be. I was certainly interested. I took the hand. "Where are we?"

"It's a tavern I use sometimes. It's comfortable and the food is good."

I liked the word *tavern*. It sounded like a dated historical vid, conjuring images of swords and elaborately skirted costumes on women who had little better to do than fall into the sword-wielding hero's arms. Never the other way round, I'd noticed, when they'd been popular a few years ago. The skirts had looked troublesome.

The tavern's owner had watched the same vids.

The place was old, no doubt of that. Though there were naturally no thatched buildings in the city, they had been a commonplace of the New Wessex Community – but any real resemblance to my birthplace ended with the roof. The tavern was long and low and white-painted, its windows apparently old-fashioned glass. Inside, a broad wooden staircase led upwards. I went up, trying not to feel as though I should have been wearing a long skirt. At the top were half a dozen private rooms off a long corridor. Outside each stood a uniformed waiter. One of them saw Milo and opened a door without asking for any sort of ID. I wondered just how often Milo came here, then guessed the staff were implanted with images of all the most important clients.

I didn't want to think about implants. Better to have a closer look at exactly what I'd let myself in for. I surveyed the room. Antiquity had compromised with modern comfort. Though the chairs had an antiqued look, they fitted whoever sat in them with all the adaptability of modern materials. And the discreet screen which offered the menu might have been framed in gilt but its controls were as familiar as the one on board the *Pig*. I was reassured. I liked the atmosphere but wasn't yet ready to sample antique cookery. I looked at the heavy curtains drawn in front of the windows which had seemed so old.

Milo smiled. "Don't worry. I'm told it'd take a fission device to damage that glass."

"I'm relieved. Except that being in a place which takes that sort of precaution makes me wary."

"It's not the place. Some of the customers are paranoid."

I remembered the vids I'd seen of Family funerals, including the recent one for one of his own relatives, and thought perhaps some had reason for paranoia.

"Not you?"

"Of course not. Who'd want to harm me, the Family fool? Now, if Morgan had enough imagination to worry."

He laughed, and I might have imagined that the sound held a hint of bitterness. "A drink? They've the basics in here or I could order."

"I'm a basic sort of person. I'd like to sample their wine. Your choice."

The crystal of the glass was cool and so fine I thought it might shatter in my hand. Through it the honey-gold of the wine glowed. Milo lifted a matching goblet.

"To your health and our future."

I lifted my own glass in silence. I wasn't sure what future he meant and it was still too early to ask. The wine filled my mouth with the flavour of late summer.

"Australasia. They've some interesting vineyards there."

"Too far for *The Flying Pig*."

"That's why I chose it. I thought you might like some-thing from outside your usual range."

Had he called in earlier to be sure it was there? Was that why we'd stopped in his rooms on our way to the skimmer? I was touched.

"You've been there?"

It seemed there were few places he hadn't visited but he claimed to be more interested in my travels. I found myself telling him about the lunacies of sailing a barge in the Channel and Biscay. He was easy to talk with, even in these surroundings.

The surroundings weren't without effect. I was little more than half-way down that first magical glass of wine when I gave up and surrendered to the mood of the place. When Milo asked me what I'd like to order, I didn't even look at the screen.

"I'll trust your choice."

An eyebrow flicked up but when I grinned back at him from the embrace of my chair he laughed, understanding.

"Gets to you, doesn't it?"

"Just for tonight."

We chose not to use the waiter who, presumably, continued to wait outside. Instead we let the table revolve through the wall so that periodically a semicircle of emptied plates disappeared and returned at Milo's summons, laden with new temptations. Everything was served on translucent porcelain painted with elaborate filigrees of fantastic birds and fruiting trees or glowing with dark, jewelled colours.

If I hadn't felt that I was part of the same fantasy as the

painted bowls I might have been repelled by the opulence. But tonight the tavern's tranquillity was unreal and I needed it. Reality had become too brutal recently. I was grateful for Milo's easy companionship. He made me laugh with some of his stories of the boredom of Estate life.

"No thrills in your work?"

His smile was a little off. "Not really. Thrills usually mean something's gone wrong with the planning – and I don't like it when my plans go wrong." It sounded as though he'd been thwarted from time to time. Big brother, I guessed, wasn't always willing to go along with him.

"Sounds great."

I thought of Luna. Boredom would be a luxury in her life. The fantasy shivered around me but did not quite dissolve. Milo refilled my glass.

I wasn't carrying a chrono and there was no way of telling how much time passed in the small room. The meal and the conversation and the wine ended eventually. Milo called back his skimmer and we went outside to wait for it.

You don't see bright stars in the city, only far out at sea. And here, in an invisible parkland which you needed wings to reach.

Then we were on the skimmer and it was hurrying towards the yellow glow of the city and I was shaking my head when Milo offered me something to drink, a tab if I preferred. I didn't want any more stimulation. I didn't want to come down. I could float like this for ever if I wanted. I didn't need a skimmer to fly over the smog and the streets.

I didn't feel the landing but I remember I was quite steady on my feet when we walked back to the elevator, which took us down to Milo's level. Its doors opened. I didn't move. Milo looked at me. We were about the same height and it was no trouble at all to look back at him.

"You'll stay?"

I nearly did. He had every reason to expect me to say yes. *I* expected me to say yes. But I'd remembered that this was all fantasy and I wanted to make decisions like that when I was back in the real world. I moved my head once from side to side and the patterned wall of the elevator swung.

"I don't think so. It's late."

Time didn't matter but I've never yet apologised for saying no. An excuse was as much as I would offer him.

"I'll walk you back."

Moral victory to him. I didn't try to explain it wasn't necessary and we matched steps across to the quayside. I looked down at the long dark shape of the *Pig* below. The tide was just past half-ebb and rushing out at its most vicious. It was later than I'd thought. I turned to begin the climb down.

"You'll be all right?"

"I'm used to it."

He looked at the sheer drop with distaste. Then he put his hands on my shoulders and drew me towards him for a kiss.

It was very persuasive. I was beginning to hope he would ask me again to stay with him when he let his hands fall. I bent to step down on to the ladder with more care than usual. Milo's foreshortened figure watched from above.

One rung. Two. I hoped the rust flaking under my hands wouldn't wreck my only set of good clothes. Wished

I had a second set in case Milo invited me out again. Felt the ladder protest and creak and sway a little under the combined pressures of my weight and the tide below. Another rung.

The crack was explosive. The whole of the vertical support in my right hand ripped away from the wall just as the rung beneath my lower foot buckled and gave. My weight was on my hands for less than a second before I fell.

I hit water. My first coherent thought was that now I really had ruined the clothes. My second: *I'm drowning.*

Cold water closed over me, filling my mouth, choking me as I went down and felt the slimy touch of mud beneath my flailing hands. I closed my fingers in it, seeking anchorage. Nothing. I kicked back towards the surface, fighting the grip of the tide which would keep me under until my struggles stopped. Fighting the numbness which bit into my bones. Impossible to swim for more than a stroke...

More than the two strokes which brought my left hand down hard on the edge of the pontoon.

My fingers closed on a rope's end. I hoped the other end was tied fast to something.

I tried to grab the pontoon with my other hand but couldn't reach it. I was already being swirled away, the rope my only lifeline. I wondered if I would still be holding it when the tide swept me out to sea or into the piers of a jetty or the hull of a moored boat.

The jerk as I pulled up short almost tore the rope from my fingers. Now I had to use it to haul myself to safety. It sounded easy. But it was a huge effort even to bring my right hand far enough forward to find a grip. And all the time the cold, the tide's other ally, was dragging at me.

I didn't know if I could fight them both.

Hand over hand. A handsbreadth at a time. I couldn't see the pontoon and water broke over my face, driving up my nose, making me choke. My shoulders screamed with pain. I couldn't feel my hands. Relax. Just for a moment. Letting go would be easy. It wouldn't hurt any more.

Milo was up there on the dock. He would have seen me fall. I wasn't going to let him see me drown. I forced myself to focus, to release each finger and unclamp a hand to clamp it again beyond the other fist. Clench. Release. Clench. Ignore the water in your mouth, breathe if you can. Release. Clench. Why couldn't I clench?

My knuckles were hard against something. It took me three shuddering breaths to identify the pontoon's padded edge. The *Pig*'s bulk loomed just beyond reaching distance. If my groping hand could reach out, find a cleat, a ringbolt, *anything*. Just to close my fingers on something that wasn't rope was a victory. I began to heave myself, a crippled seal, out of the water.

I nearly didn't make it. My last strength was running out faster than the tide swirling round my legs. One chance. One gasping convulsion. I was lying on something solid. It didn't matter that a bolt was digging into my stomach, that my legs were still in the water. Nothing mattered except that I didn't have to fight any more.

"*Humility!*"

The urgent voice was faint. To lift my head and answer was too much effort.

"*Humility!*"

He wasn't going to stop and let me sleep. I flopped on to my back, staring upwards. I could just see a silhouette on the dock above me. A faint glimmer of reflected light whitened his face. He was bending over, staring down.

"Are you all right?"

It took more deep breaths before I could answer. My throat was raw and my mouth was full of a foul taste which I couldn't clear. I was on my knees now, clutching my stomach with aching hands. I'd vomited: a thin trail of vile stuff. I felt no better.

"Humility?"

"Fine. I like a swim before bed."

"I couldn't get down to you!"

I heard the anger in his voice. Guilt. Without the ladder he'd had no way down. By the time he'd run to the marina and tried to find a dinghy it would have been far too late. Even if he'd sounded an alarm, whoever arrived would have had nothing to do but try to recover my body. I sat up, still gasping but steadier now. "It's all right. I'm not hurt."

"Are you sure? How can I get to you?"

Find a dinghy. Get someone else to drive it. I thought of hours of anxious attention, of reassurances.

"Don't. I'll be fine after a shower and some sleep. Tell Gus to do something about the ladder tomorrow. Then come and see me."

He hesitated, wanting to do something. "I'll wait till you're on board."

It meant I had to move. I didn't think it would matter if I crawled. When I reached the deckhouse door I pulled myself to my feet, fumbled as I palmed the locks and stumbled inside, thumbing the light as I passed. With any luck Milo would take it as a signal to go. If he chose instead to wait there for the rest of the night I found I couldn't care. If I sat down I would sleep.

I went into the shower fully dressed and left the ruins of my clothes on the floor. I'd lost the cape. It didn't seem important. I let the shower run until I'd stopped shivering though I was still cold. Then I drank a litre of water. It removed all but the memory of the foul taste from my mouth. After that I went to bed.

41

When I woke I was comfortable until I moved. Then I felt as though I'd been in a fight with the toughs from the recycling dump. I couldn't lift my arms above my shoulders and every time I turned my head I had to stifle a wince. I ached. I was also alive. It was a reasonable trade.

Someone was shouting from onshore. I tried to ignore it. It didn't go away. Then the phone buzzed. They weren't going to leave me alone.

When I got up into the deck house I saw there were two people waiting for me. Milo and Daisy. The tide was well up. If they wanted to see me they could jump down on to the pontoon. I opened the door.

"Good morning."

"Are you all right?" Daisy, voice sharp with anxiety.

"Never better. Don't fuss."

"Milo told me what happened. You're lucky to be alive."

"As long as I haven't swallowed too many lethal parasites, I'll survive."

Milo didn't like that. "You'll let the medics check you over?"

"Worried I might sue?" I don't know why I was annoyed. It wasn't his fault.

"Of course not. I'm worried about you."

"No need."

They were both just standing there and I gave in. "You'd better come aboard."

Milo would have preferred it if Daisy had found an

urgent reason to return to work, but she wasn't leaving till she'd heard every detail. I let them both settle while I made caf and ate some of yesterday's bread. Daisy was first to show impatience.

"Sit down, Humility. I want to know what happened."

"The ladder broke away from the wall as I was coming down it. I must have eaten even more than I thought last night."

She glanced sideways at Milo. The interrogation about last night would come later when he wasn't there. "How did you get out?"

"Yes. How?" Remembered shock was in Milo's voice. "I couldn't see. I thought you'd been swept away."

I explained about the rope and Daisy shook her head at my luck. Milo found it hard to believe.

"You should be dead! Just think about it…"

"I'd rather not."

I was discovering I didn't want to think about it at all. I didn't want to remember the horror of the fall, the shock of the water, the eternity of fighting the living river and knowing I could not possibly win. My sore hands were shaking. I held them carefully between my knees and hoped neither of my visitors had seen.

Milo had tried to take my hands when he first came in, looking hurt when I wouldn't let him. Then he'd seen that underneath the quick-heal I'd sprayed on they were raw from the rope and torn where the rusty ladder had been ripped from my grasp. He'd winced, tried to conceal his revulsion, and looked away. Now he and Daisy were both watching me. I shook my head.

"It's over. I'm not hurt. It wasn't anyone's fault."

I wasn't sure either of them agreed. Wasn't sure if that

last statement was true. Didn't want to talk about it.

"Haven't either of you got jobs to do?"

Daisy looked at her chrono and swore. "Yes. I do. We'll talk later."

I wished she sounded less threatening. When she left I discovered I'd rather she had stayed. Milo looked serious.

"I want you to come and stay with me."

"Milo…"

"No. Listen. It's not the same question as last night."

"It sounded a bit like an order." It came out cool. I don't like orders.

"I'm sorry. But you must see the sense of it. You can't know how long repairs will take."

"I can use the dinghy to get to another landing."

He didn't know enough about boats to know I couldn't possibly use oars for a couple of days yet.

"Humility, listen…"

"No, Milo. You listen. I won't leave the *Pig* just because I fell in the water…"

"You nearly drowned!"

"*Nearly*. And I still don't want to leave. I'm comfortable here and if I have any aches and pains to nurse I would rather do it in my own home. Alone."

I'd forgotten aristos were seldom direct, and used to getting what they wanted. He looked both hurt and angry, but I was too sore to feel sympathetic. I waited, feeling the stiffness in my face and unable to do anything about it. He let out an exasperated breath.

"Your choice. If you change your mind, call me. I'll put a priority on your name. The call will find me. Take care."

"Thanks."

He didn't kiss me when he left.

Now I'd won I was shaky again. I didn't move from the support of the deckhouse door when I watched him take the high step which was all that was needed to take him ashore.

42

I watched the tide fall. I'd thrown out what was left of my best clothes. I'd made an effort to tidy the deckhouse. I'd set out a spread of Blue Moon patience. Then I'd sat in the deckhouse, where the sun threw a square of warm light through the plex, and watched as the tide fell and the ladder emerged from the water.

The remains of the ladder.

The left upright was the only part of it unchanged. The other upright had torn away from the wall, buckling the rungs as it twisted. Several were broken, jagged ends waiting to tear cloth or flesh. I winced. At least I'd been flung sideways, clear of them and of the boat and the narrow pontoon beside it.

The water was just above the level it had been last night.

Reluctant, needing to know, I uncurled from my warm seat and went out and down on to the pontoon.

At this distance I could touch the broken ironwork if I wanted. I could see the deep pits of rust, the way the metal was compressed and distorted. The bright gleam of a new breakage.

It took me more than a minute to understand. The broken rungs showed old metal rusted to fragile lacework or dull and brittle with the obvious evidence of terminal fatigue. The glinting metal on the upright was wrong. I could see quite clearly the marks where it had been cut almost through, from the side closest to the wall.

Laser-saw. Nothing else was small enough to work in

that limited space. It would have taken only a few seconds, would have seemed to any watcher only as though someone had paused on the way down the ladder. My brain listed the facts even as I tried to deny their meaning.

I had told Milo it wasn't his fault. It *had* been someone's.

"You causing trouble?"

I looked up, squinting, to see Gus staring down at me. Hostile. I was causing *him* trouble. He'd have preferred to hear I'd drowned: it would have given him the chance to get an eyesore like the *Pig* out of his Port. If I could find a motive, I could easily believe he'd been the one to rig the ladder.

"Me, Gus? I'm not in charge of maintenance."

"What's that mean?"

"I paid for safe mooring, remember?"

"And you're responsible for any damage you cause."

It wasn't even a bluff worth arguing with, although if he saw what I had seen he would probably accuse me of sabotaging my own ladder.

"Getting your intimidation in first, Gus? What you going to do about the ladder?"

"Can't do anything till low water. Looks like you're stuck down there."

He liked that. He would also be delighted to stop me making use of the marina to land my dinghy. I'd have to go a klik upstream if I wanted to get ashore.

I hadn't planned to go anywhere until I thought of being trapped down here. I was wondering how long it would take me to get the dinghy's outboard working when a second head looked down from the dockside.

"Byron. Come to see the damage?"

The dark head bowed. The circuitry was still there,

enigmatic.

"Heard you'd been swimming. And mud-bathing." It was an afterthought that seemed to hint at something that might even have been amusement on that enigmatic face.

I suppose everyone in the Port had heard. I was just surprised he had chosen to come in person to look at the ladder's pathetic remains. And he *was* looking at them. Unlike Gus, he had squatted to stare more closely.

"It prevents hangovers. You auditing the outlay on ladders?"

"Of course." He straightened. Bland. Unreadable. "Wouldn't mind a talk with you."

"Gus tells me I'm stuck till the tide rises. You'll have to wait. Unless someone's devised a personal anti-grav I could borrow?"

"No need for that. An old-fashioned jet pack would get you up. Even easier, why don't you shift the boat?"

Gus and I both looked at him.

"There are no other quay moorings."

Gus enjoyed saying that. I suspected any repairs to the ladder would be temporary: he would make sure I had nothing left to return to once I left here.

"The marina is full?"

Byron's question was so polite I expected it to draw blood. Gus needed an extra breath before he could answer.

"It's not even open! And she couldn't pay for it if it was."

"If it's not open, you needn't charge, need you?"

Gus was finding breathing a problem. Byron allowed him another ten seconds to file an objection. It wasn't long enough to reconnect Gus's circuits.

"I'm sure you wouldn't want the Port to be sued for

careless maintenance."

"She couldn't afford it!"

"Nor could the Port."

Silence. Neither intended to back down. Byron waited. Gus swallowed, blustered, shifted responsibility. "I'll need the Port Officer's authority!"

"Get it."

He turned to look back down at the damage, leaving Gus wanting to protest but unsure of Byron's place in the hierarchy. Doubt defeated him. He went off to call Daisy.

I looked up at Byron. "Why?"

The shrug was more of a ripple. "Told you: I want to talk. And I don't like ladders. In any condition."

He was walking away before I could demand to know what was wrong with the phone.

When Gus came back to find him gone, his face was a mixture of relief and fury. Relief that he didn't have to concede defeat in front of his victor, fury at the confidence which hadn't waited to learn what Daisy said. I was beginning to wonder if I'd misjudged Byron Cody. On more than one level.

It took a couple of hours to tidy the pontoon, including the rope which had saved my life. I coiled it with care. Then I fired up the drive, which started without a protest, used a single spring to help swing the *Pig* out into the tide and started the short journey towards the lock gates.

Too much to hope for any help from Gus. No problem. Even in a tideway with sore hands and stiff shoulders I can handle the *Pig* on my own and locks are easy. I'd had a close enough look at the set-up here to know it was standard but I sent the signal in plenty of time for Gus to react. I didn't trust him not to have left the security wards on. He'd like me to make a false approach. The reluctant but definite swing of the gates said he was more eager to avoid another encounter with Byron than to humiliate me. Just.

No sign of Byron as I moored. No sign of Gus, either; just a curt message over the phone directing me to a berth as far from the sight-line of his office as he could contrive. Suited me.

The mooring web held the *Pig* as though she were made of glass, as though the slightest scratch would send an owner clamouring for compensation. My barge had never been better protected.

I hooked up the *Pig's* systems to the bank of controls by the berth. That took three of the dozen outlets available. I speculated about the possibilities offered by the rest. Gus wouldn't tell me about them. A pity. I liked the idea of my own private VR room. Especially today: escapism had its own appeal. But I couldn't spend all day experimenting. Or even an hour. I kept looking around me, unable to forget that glint of clean metal on the rusted ladder.

The marina had facilities better than any I'd ever sampled, with the added benefit of unrivalled opportunities to bait Gus. It also had hectares of unoccupied space. Apart from the showboat, the *Pig* was the only craft moored here. If anyone wanted to find her, or me, I might as well be broadcasting to the whole net. Despite what Gus had claimed about the level of the marina's security, I felt exposed. I would have felt safer back on the old wooden pontoon with a ladder no one could climb.

A ladder which had been deliberately cut.

I called the Harbour Office. "Gus? You cleared me to come and go here?"

He didn't want to, couldn't find a reason not to. I waited while he pulled my file and input whatever was needed to tell the marina I was legit if I went ashore and tried to come back.

"You're cleared. Until your fees run out."

Three days. It wouldn't take that long to replace the ladder but if I hadn't found work of some sort by then, I'd have to go sailing. Luna's bill had changed my plans.

I'd worry about that later. Daisy might help. What mattered was that I was free to go ashore. I picked up my sack, set the *Pig's* systems, all of them, and left.

43

I went to see Luna.

The journey gave me to time to think. To admit what a fool I'd been. I'd known there was a killer around; I knew that asking questions might provoke a dangerous reaction. But knowing wasn't the same as surviving three attempts, one of which had come far too close to working. Outside the flats I'd been afraid of that knife, but I suppose I'd really thought I'd get away with bruises, perhaps a cracked rib or two, and a warning not to stick my nose in things. Even the farce in the mud hadn't seemed that real, when I looked back on it. It's hard to believe someone really does want to wipe you. But what happened last night had at last convinced me that whoever I was chasing really did care enough to kill. It didn't make me feel any better.

But Daisy was going to have to listen to me now.

I was still planning what to say to her when I reached the clinic. They let me into the ward at once when they knew I was the one who'd paid the bill.

She had a bed in the middle of a line of five. An old man coughed next to her on one side, on the other a woman lay silent, a bluish pallor round her mouth, colourless brittle hair loose against the pillow. I thought at first Luna was sleeping then saw she was tuned in to a box she held. Vids.

"Hi."

There was no chair so I stood awkwardly by the bed. She glanced up, pulling off the headset which accessed a world more fun than this one.

"Humility. Good you came."

She looked her age now. A vulnerable child. I wondered what it would cost her to rebuild her defences. Whether she'd be strong enough.

"Had to check they treating you OK."

She looked alarmed, frightened a wrong answer might get her thrown out. "I'm fine. Almost OK now. They say I can go tomorrow."

That was what was worrying me. It didn't seem to concern her.

"Where to?" Not subtle, but how do you ask a kid if she's got a box or a pimp or a corner in a roofless tenement to shelter her? Something older than the rest of her looked out at me.

"Don't worry 'bout me. You done your share. 'Sides, I do have a place. Tom Lee called." She spoke the name as though she still wasn't convinced she should.

"He going to help you? You sure?"

Possibly I didn't sound as impressed as she thought I should. All I felt was relief. Relying on Tom Lee's compassion had seemed a wild bet when I'd made it. It still did. I needed to be convinced.

"Certain sure. He heard about the fire. Heard I was here. Said he'd take me on. Run messages for him. *Personal*. Get me new blades, *good* blades."

Wonder in her voice. She didn't need me now. And I didn't need to decide if I was willing to give up my privacy to offer shelter to a streetkid. I could spare myself the embarrassment of discovering just how limited my generous impulses could be. So I stifled my doubts about the morality of leaving her in the care of someone like Tom Lee. Besides, Luna wouldn't thank me if I tried to stop it.

"If it doesn't work out, call me. If I'm not in the Port they'll keep the message."

"I'll be 'kay."

She reached down beside her, under the sheet. Looked round for watchers. No one showed any interest in any patient and the patients were unconscious or watching vids. Or both.

"Told you I had something for you."

"You don't have to…"

"Do. Know who got me in here. Know who asked Tom Lee to look out for me. It's all I got."

Except her pride. I took the paper from her. It had once been a label on a foodpack, now torn and stained from where she had kept it next to her skin, where it had been through the same beating she had. She was looking at me, urging me to understand. I didn't at first. Then I turned it over. On the back, in letters which were uneven and crooked, as though whoever drew them had been copying without understanding, was an address.

"Whose?"

"Followed the type I took the packet to. He took it on to another. She wrote another label. Stuck it on. When I bladed past she ask me could I read, I say no. She told me to take it to general post. I copied the words."

That was how it was done. Three cutouts and the last a simple errand to the rundown, inefficient, *anonymous* general service. I looked back at the paper. Almost wished she hadn't done it.

"Thanks. I owe you."

"No debt. Neither way."

She needed to be clean. I nodded.

215

"'Kay. Luck with Tom Lee."

I didn't offer to visit her again. Didn't warn her of what she was likely to be involved in. She probably already knew more about it than I did. At least it wouldn't be herself she sold. And I didn't have to worry about finding new blades for her.

I left the clinic with a piece of crumpled paper pushed deep into one pocket and an address I didn't want repeating itself in my head. Like an implant. It hardly left me room to wonder just what Tom Lee was going to make me pay for his generosity.

44

"She's not in the office."

The tekkie thug enjoyed telling me. He seemed to like me less with every visit.

"Out with the Board?" I wouldn't mind seeing Milo again.

"Out."

He wanted me to think he knew and wouldn't tell. I was unconvinced. But that didn't help me. I shrugged indifference and walked away. Irritated. It was uncharacteristic of Daisy to drop out of contact in working hours. It was also inconvenient: it left me to my own thoughts and I wasn't comfortable with them.

It always came back to Midway. This address. The address which Luna had copied with such painful accuracy, which was only the last in a line of markers which began with Jon's body and last night had nearly ended with my own. Daisy would have to be told.

I'd wondered if she already knew. I'm not a fool. She knew the Port better than anyone and her access was complete. She could have been seen on the ladder down to the *Pig* last night and even I wouldn't have thought her out of place...

No. She wasn't involved. When friendship and gut instinct were balanced against reason, reason didn't stand a chance. Besides, nothing I'd come across so far had suggested any motive for Daisy. Loyalty and her own integrity meant that she would not harm the Port. Hadn't

I already told Byron that?

I thought about the general mail, the old post system that hardly anyone used. It wouldn't go to her without being seen by someone else. But she was the only one I could trust to tell me who handled the mail.

I looked around for Morgan and his entourage but saw no sign of them. I had no wish to ask Gus, who would only have enjoyed telling me I wasn't cleared for confidential information. In the end I had no choice but to return to the *Pig*.

She looked alone and faintly embarrassed. The neat white geometry of the marina around her was too tidy. If I wasn't careful, she'd open her own sea-cocks and sink with shame. I took pleasure in tracking as much dirt as possible on to the marina's pristine pseudoplanks.

When I looked back I hadn't left a mark.

I remembered Em's celebrations when I saw the reminder. She'd told my phone to flash me. She knew me too well. Now I couldn't claim I'd forgotten and I'd used the broken phone excuse with her before. Phones didn't break down. I glared at it but it shrugged that off too.

Going out was better than staying here on my own deciding who had tried to kill me.

45

They'd started without me. At a guess they'd started shortly after they'd spoken with Morgan and had continued with only occasional pauses for sleep or caf ever since. *Wild Goose* looked more decadent than I had ever seen her: the brass was tarnished, the lamps were burning low and there were cups, glasses and empty bottles on every vacant surface. When she sobered, Em would have to spend days cleaning the sticky rings from the woodwork. It was one way to work off a hangover.

At the moment no one was thinking morning after. They were enjoying an indefinite and glorious present. They made me feel old.

I'd waited a couple of hours before I'd come over. I'd wanted to wash the smell of the clinic away and do some hard thinking before I'd faced them. Eventually I'd put the dirty scrap of paper which Luna had given me in the chart-table drawer with the useless lifebox and chip and wasted another half hour on the equally useless spread of cards on top of the table. It told me nothing. In Blue Moon you can re-lay the cards three times before you give up. I'd scrapped most of the first layout but the second made as little sense. In the end I'd just left it there. No hurry.

Then I fitted the outboard to the dinghy and came up-river. It had seemed preferable to walking alone through the unlit reaches of the Port. Besides, I was still stiff. The dinghy was more comfortable than walking.

"You're not drinking!"

Em sounded insulted. Rusty nodded carefully.

"Have to drink. Celebrate."

All things considered, his pronunciation was excellent.

"You like Morgan's idea, then?"

"Like anything that keeps us here. Might even persuade them to lay on a decent water-supply. Can't have visitors seeing us carrying slops, can we?"

They'd obviously given the matter some thought. Between drinks. I almost felt sorry for Morgan. I took a mouthful from the glass I'd been given and tried not to flinch. They must have finished the decent stuff yesterday.

Clim was talking about some scrap tools he'd found which he could easily renovate. "Nothing wrong that a couple of hours in a workshop won't cure."

Em had her own plans: "We can show them what real yachts were once like. In the great days of sail." Days long over before she was even conceived.

Rusty was working on the drinks. No one was concerned with food. Something about their euphoria kept me sober. I smiled and laughed with my friends and held an almost full glass and watched them perform their pantomime of release and relief. Em's wild white hair was a bright aura round her flushed face; Clim was rubbing the swollen knuckles of one hand with the rough palm of the other as he planned what he would do with his liberated tools. Rusty filled glasses. The others talked or laughed, agreeing with themselves and each other. Freed from the fear of homelessness.

I felt as if I was in VR. If I lifted my hands to my eyes, would I touch a headset? Lift the headset and be back in the deckhouse of the *Pig* staring at a set of cards which made no sense? I thought of a move I hadn't completed, saw that it made more sense than I'd understood. Then I came back to the saloon of the *Wild Goose* and understood what I was seeing here.

When I'd faced Daisy in her office after I'd seen the body in the dredge she'd been near despair. Because of sabotage. She'd assumed the corpse was part of it. So had I. It had been a stupid mistake: two things happening together aren't necessarily related. The sabotage had been aimed at the Port and property. No one had been hurt. And, as Byron had pointed out, it had stopped.

But the violence which had been dredged into the light with Jon's body had escalated. And though it was based in the Port, it had been aimed at individuals. Jon. Blue Eyes. An unknown woman. Perhaps Luna. Me. And it was still going on.

I had thought it didn't make sense. Look at it a little differently and it did.

I looked at my friends. Em had called me guest of honour. Now I saw what else was mixed with their gratitude: guilt.

"Here's to Morgan and his Family." That was Rusty. Any excuse to drain and refill.

I didn't drink. Looked down into the cloudy liquor swirling in my own glass. Wondered what new stim he'd found to spice it. Looked up.

"And to Daisy?"

I wasn't certain I imagined the pause before Em nodded vigorously. "Of course. To Daisy. To the Port."

They'd drink to anything anyone suggested tonight.

"She's got her own reason to celebrate," I pointed out.

"What's that?" someone asked. I'd forgotten his name. He was drunker than the others, who were suddenly paying attention.

"An end to the sabotage which nearly ended her job. It is over, isn't it?"

Silence like the one which follows breaking glass. Clim put his drink aside with deliberate care. They were all looking at me now. Only Clim met my eyes, though. The others were glancing sideways, then looking down. Away. None of them protested. I wondered if that was why I was here: they'd wanted me to know. To pass the news to Daisy.

It was Em who found the courage to speak. "Yes. It's over. We never meant…"

"To end her career? With Sheba pregnant? After the way she's looked after your interests since she's been here? Of course not."

"She wasn't going to stop them throwing us out."

I couldn't see who that muttered defiance came from. A shuffling around me suggested one or two others agreed.

"Did you ask her?"

I knew they hadn't. It didn't take the renewed silence to tell me. They'd waited until they could give the job to me. That was also when the sabotage had stopped.

"What did you think would happen when she'd gone? Someone else would have replaced her. Someone with less sympathy for you than she's shown."

"We didn't want her to lose her job. It was just the development…"

They had wanted to stop the development and been naive enough to think the delays they could cause would do it. That they could somehow turn back the clock. They had no idea how far a Family member would go to complete a job he wanted done. I shook my head, wondering.

"What are you going to do?"

If they weren't sobering, they were at least approaching that state when melancholy could easily swamp triumph. My disapproval seemed likely to swing the balance. No one was looking at me now. No one wanted to look at anyone else as far as I could see.

Suddenly I was finding it hard not to laugh. Seven people, all older than my grandmother, were looking like crestfallen children caught out in a prank which they'd thought clever but which now seemed silly even to them.

"You'll swear there'll be no more sabotage?"

I was looking at Clim. I didn't need to be told that he'd done most of it any more than they had to tell me the ideas had been Em's. It had been the memory of him scavenging round the old worksheds which reminded me just how good he was at improvising with anything mechanical. I'd remembered Daisy's descriptions of what had gone wrong and realised that there had been nothing beyond the intelligence and skilled fingers of a clever mechanic. Hi-tech hadn't been needed. And Clim was the best mechanic I'd ever met. He'd kept the *Pig* working for years.

He nodded once. "No more." Then the shadow of the grin which turned him from old man into mischievous kid. "No need."

I didn't smile. Just. "I'll make sure Daisy knows it's over."

"You won't tell her..?"

"That the development was nearly wrecked by a bunch of geriatric adolescents? No. You can find your own way of making it up to her."

I didn't tell them I was fairly sure she'd guess the truth, once I told her I'd tracked the source of the sabotage. I looked forward to laughing with her about it, since I didn't think Em and the others would forgive me if I laughed now. Embarrassment and remorse were showing in about equal quantities. It was probably time I left. What was left of the party would go better without me. They'd cleared their consciences, their futures were secured. They didn't need me.

46

The trip back to the *Pig* was quiet. So was the empty marina. Though there was a light in the Harbour Master's office, Gus wouldn't be there. He might breathe Port and eat Company, but he didn't live on the job. Some caretaker was dozing in his chair, letting the machinery run the Port.

It wasn't late and I wasn't tired. I thought of the party I'd left and decided I had to share it with someone. I'd tell Byron later that the sabotage had been so lo-tech he'd never had a hope of solving it. Tonight I wanted to talk to a friend. Daisy would still be awake. As long as I'd known her she'd never needed more than a few hours' sleep in a night. Sheba grumbled about it. I keyed in their home number.

No reply. I was puzzled. She'd not been in work earlier either. But if she'd been called out of town, Sheba should be in. Sheba never travelled. I let the phone ring on for another minute, then decided Daisy must be away and Sheba asleep with some knockout. I was reaching for the cut-off when I got an answer.

"Yes?"

The screen stayed blanked. Perhaps she'd answered by remote and forgotten to open the screen. It wasn't Sheba's voice and it didn't sound like Daisy's. But it was.

"Daisy? Humility. What's wrong?"

Dragging silence. Still no face on the screen. She was going to cut me off, I felt it.

"*Daisy*? Do you want me to come over?"

More silence. A sound like a breath taken with massive effort.

"Yes. Come over."

"Now?"

"Yes. Humility, *please*."

The connection died. I didn't try again.

47

The cab driver was surly, and I wasn't sure she spoke English, but she knew the streets and drove fast. It was all I wanted. I didn't even haggle on the fare. I tried not to think what I would find when the journey ended. Tried not to hear Daisy's *Please* in a voice I'd never heard before.

Security didn't want to let me in. They didn't believe Daisy wanted to see me. She hadn't told them. When she took minutes to respond to their call I could see they believed me even less. They checked every detail of my ID and warned me not to disturb anyone when I went up.

I didn't want to disturb anyone.

The grey door opened when I pushed it. Inside, the hallway was empty. So was the main room. I couldn't go any further. Daisy and Sheba's jewelbox of a home suddenly had the same smell as a filthy room in the northshore flats.

"Daisy?" I had to try twice. The first time it was little more than a cracked whisper.

"Here."

Flat word. No expression at all. I turned towards the door I didn't want to open.

Daisy was sitting on the bed. Its pale green cover had a floral design. Beside it were the phone and group of small ornaments. A clutter of facepaint tubes and sprays were the intimate debris on the dresser. The small rug in front of it was dog-eared at one corner. I wanted to straighten it. I did not want to look at Daisy and the way she was holding Sheba. Rocking her.

"Daisy? Let me see."

She let me reach a hand to Sheba's cold throat. Then she brushed the hair back from the white face and went on rocking her.

"What happened?"

She shook her head. The rhythm of her rocking never faltered. I could see Sheba's profile. She looked peaceful, asleep. I didn't want to see the other side of her face. The blood matting the back of her head told me more than I ever wanted to know.

"You've called security? The peeps?"

No response, just that steady rocking.

I called downstairs.

48

It was a long night. Security took a single look and called in the local peeps as I'd known they'd have to. They didn't like me being there. If they could have blamed me for what had happened they'd have done it, but even they could see that Sheba had been dead for several hours.

Daisy wouldn't let her go. I had to unfold her cramped hands finger by finger before she would set her down on the rose-printed bedcover. After that it was easier to coax her away into the other room.

"Can you tell us what happened?"

The man wasn't unsympathetic, just bored. He wanted to be done with it. This was just routine. File and forget. Daisy shook her head. I knelt beside her.

"You weren't at work this afternoon. Did you find her?"

A nod. Her mouth worked. "She'd had her last test."

"Pregnancy," I explained to the peep before he could ask. "She'd want to be home to share the result."

Another nod from Daisy. "Yes. She was…"

She couldn't go on. I couldn't tell Daisy or this bored peep that she must have been killed because of her connection with the Port. Her partnership with Daisy. But I didn't understand how, or why, it could be linked to the other deaths. Jon and Blue Eyes had had their IDs taken, but Sheba's was untouched. Perhaps Daisy had arrived in time to stop the killer taking that last step and he'd escaped while she was taking in the shock of seeing Sheba's body.

But why Sheba? Could they have meant to get Daisy herself, and been interrupted by Sheba on her return from the test? But why go to the trouble of invading a home that had better security than most, when Daisy was around Midway all day?

I had questions, but no answers. And as I watched the peeps wave their scanners over the room and collect their samples, I didn't think they would find any soon. I tried not to think of what was happening behind the closed bedroom door. Wanted to tell Daisy that it was my fault. Tell her I shouldn't have nosed around. Tell her to shout at me. Couldn't. Fed caf to the peeps and tried to make Daisy drink something or take a knockout. Failed.

"No. I don't want to sleep."

She was more coherent now, answering questions politely, but able to tell them nothing beyond the fact that she had found Sheba. All in the same dead tone. I wished she'd break down. Scream. Throw something. I wanted to throw things: smash all Sheba's treasures against the smooth pastel walls.

"Ready to go."

The indifferent voice belonged to a young medic who'd seen things far worse than this. He wanted only to finish tidying and go on back to whatever vid or bed he'd been dragged from.

Daisy looked up. Understanding. "*No!* You can't take her away."

"We have to. It's routine."

"*No!*"

"Sorry."

"She never went out at night!"

Its simplicity silenced even the peeps. Into the void I

said, "Can't you leave her? Send someone round in the morning? I'll stay till then."

Then the next shift could deal with it. They looked at each other, shrugged. A few hours would make little difference. They could pass the night grilling security, who were explaining how no intruder could break through their system while trying to refuse permission to wake the other occupants of the building. The peeps were enjoying their embarrassment. I wondered how long these two forces had been rivals. Different owners, of course.

"'Kay. We'll wait. But we have to take her in the morning."

Security would rather Sheba's body left under the discreet cover of darkness but weren't in a strong enough position to insist.

In the end they all left and I sat with Daisy in the bedroom, not saying anything. I don't think she knew I was there. The only time she spoke it wasn't to me.

"I'm sorry, love."

She was kneeling by the bed, her head resting on the cover by Sheba's shoulder. She wasn't looking at the closed eyes but her right hand was holding Sheba's left, her thumb rubbing ceaselessly against the plain ring on the third finger.

Let me alone that I may take comfort awhile.

49

I left in a monochrome dawn. Daisy still wouldn't leave Sheba's body and wouldn't talk about what had happened. About an hour before it was light, she'd frowned as though trying to recall something and then asked why I'd called her.

I remembered I'd wanted to share the bathos of Clim's attempts to undermine the development. I shook my head. "It doesn't matter."

Something she might have meant for a smile moved her lips. "Still chasing ghosts?"

I was the one who shivered. She seemed unaware that my persistence might be the reason Sheba had become one of the ghosts. Now wasn't the time to tell her what I'd learned and guessed. I bent to smooth the rug at my feet. The corner curled again as soon as I let it go.

"Just looking for answers to a couple of questions."

"Such as?"

She wanted to be able to answer my questions because she could not ask the only one which mattered to her: *Why me?*

I shrugged. She wouldn't let it go. Insisted. Half-embarrassed, because it felt like I was tricking her, I asked, because I *did* want to know: "Such as: Who handles the Port's general post?"

She didn't think it odd. Everything was so badly dislocated that nothing was strange.

"One of the security teks sorts it. There isn't much, so

it's one of those nothing jobs. No one special taken on for it."

I thought she was wrong. But then the apartment's surly security buzzed up from below and the men with the unmistakable box, which was meant to be so discreet, came up and took Sheba away.

They wouldn't let Daisy go with them. She wouldn't let me stay. She asked for a knockout and when I got back from the bathroom with a drink and the tab she was lying on the bed, where Sheba had lain. I put the tab in her hand and the drink beside her and left. She didn't see me go.

50

I'd taken a boost when I found the knockout for Daisy. I don't use them except during long watches at sea when I can't stay awake and don't dare sleep. But today I had no wish to learn what my dreams might hold, so I'd gladly put them off for a few more hours. I don't know if it was the drug combined with the remnants of whatever stim Rusty had laced my drink with, but the buzz was worse than usual.

I fidgeted in the back of the cab, trying to harness thoughts which raced and wouldn't settle, though I knew they had something important to tell me if only I could work it out. When the cab stopped outside the Port and I walked down the hill to the barrier, the muscles in my legs twitched with suppressed energy. My eyes were gritty, aching. I rubbed them but it did no good. I was hyper.

Milo and Morgan and their entourage were walking away from me toward the Port offices. I wondered if anyone had told them what had happened. Wondered how Gus would cope if he had to take charge for a while. One of the women was talking to Morgan, gesturing, insisting on whatever she was saying with more emphasis than I'd seen in any of the courtiers. I watched. Couldn't see her face, but something in the way she moved set up the vibes I'd felt in Daisy's office when we'd watched the security vid covering the visiting Family party.

I hadn't been able to pin them down then but now I understood. Knew what, *who*, I had seen. Knew why it had been a vid image, not a real person, which had triggered it until adrenaline hype made it impossible for me to tell reality from a screen.

I'd been about to go over to them, wanting to talk to Milo. Now I didn't. I understood too much.

Feeling sick, wishing now that sleep was an option, I headed for the *Pig*.

Byron was waiting in the deckhouse.

I saw him there as I walked down the marina. It didn't seem worth asking how he'd got through my security system. More surprising if he'd had any difficulty at all. And he had said he wanted to talk to me. I wondered how long he'd been waiting.

"Couple of hours. Since I heard about Daisy's partner."

I yawned, shivering slightly. A mix of morning air and adrenaline surge.

"Make you caf?" I hadn't noticed till then that he'd already made a brew for himself. Now I could smell it. I shuddered. Too tired to summon annoyance at his making himself at home.

"Thanks. No. I'll have water."

He got it for me. He didn't know boats but he'd found out where everything was stored. Just how thoroughly had he searched? I hoped he'd tried to look through my cabin. I still hadn't done any tidying.

"Boost?"

I nodded, drank thirstily. My mouth tasted foul.

"Can you concentrate?"

I had an idea that if I nodded again I'd not be able to stop. I thought of Daisy relentlessly rocking Sheba and held myself quite still. "Yes."

"What can you tell me about what's going on?"

"Why should I tell you anything?"

"Because we had an agreement?" He saw I wasn't going to answer. "Because someone tried to kill you?"

He *had* understood what he saw on the ladder. I tried a shrug. Controlled the dizziness. "Happens."

"Lot of death round you lately."

Too much. He was watching me with the sort of patience I imagined a snake might watch a small rodent. I had to be careful. It's hard to edit your thoughts when you're wired. Easy to talk too much.

"Death happens. This is the city."

"Happens on Estates too."

Did he already know what I'd only just discovered?

He considered me. He had no obvious recorder. Wouldn't need one. He probably had an eidetic augment, recall valid in all EuroGov courts. I wondered who else he was in contact with while he sat there in the *Pig's* deckhouse deciding how much to tell me. His employer? If I talked while the boost was making the patterns on his skull squirm with life, I would be even more disadvantaged. It cost me, but I let the silence stretch.

He broke it at last. "You know why the sabotage ended?"

I thought about not telling him. Somehow it wasn't funny anymore. Then I couldn't think why I wasn't going to tell him. Better to talk about Em and Clim than think about Jon and Blue Eyes. And Sheba. Told him.

He stared for a while. I wondered if he was offended to discover he'd been baffled by something so *small*. Then he leaned back, laughing. I waited.

"Sorry," he managed eventually. "I was just imagining how my employer would react when I told him he'd employed the most expensive investigator in the trade to look for a bunch of amateurs with barely a terminal between them."

I managed to focus my thoughts. Recalled who employed him. "You're not going to tell!"

"Why not?"

"Because if your employer realises he's just offered a new deal to the same people who've come close to making a fool of him, he just might reconsider."

"Would you blame him?"

"Of course I would. Besides, I wouldn't like to think what it might tempt Clim to try next."

"You might be right. My employer probably only wants a guarantee the trouble's over. It is, isn't it?"

"The sabotage? Yes."

Unless they decided there was some other concession they could blackmail from the Family. I didn't want to think about it. Byron had stopped smiling, was looking at me.

"And the killing?"

My chance to ask what he'd found out about the flats. To tell him what I'd learned and guessed. But I wasn't going to. It was more personal than ever now. I knew most of the truth. I didn't need whatever his files had told him about the burned-out northshore tower. I shook my head.

"I'm sorry, Byron. I'm tired. I'm high. My friend's partner's dead. I don't want to play games."

"Pity. This one looks interesting."

I assumed he was talking about what was happening in the Port. Would have yelled at him in another second if I hadn't seen he was looking at the cards. I remembered Milo's response. Right now I didn't feel inclined to embarrassment or explanations. I did object when he moved a card.

"Leave it alone!"

"Sorry. I like games with developing patterns."

He probably invented his own fractals. In his head. I wasn't going to have him interfering with my cards. "Get your own pack."

"I might. You sure you've nothing else to tell?"

"Sure."

"Then I'll see if anyone else wants to talk. Quiet types in the city."

"Prudent."

I watched him walk towards the deckhouse door, wondering why he'd given up so easily. Refusing to ask. He turned with his hand on the latch.

"Can't see why you'd want title to a relic like this. State would put it in a museum. Or sink it."

He'd gone, hard shoes clicking on the planks, before I could ask where I would live in either case. And I had too much buzzing in my ears to shout after him down the marina. I doubted if he'd have answered anyway. I took another dose of water and tried to decide whether the comment had been a threat.

51

The boost made me get on with the clean-up I'd avoided since my return to Midway. I threw cushions and mattresses on to the dock to air, ignoring Gus's shouts of "*Gypsy!*" I discovered that the spare outlets included a vac which actually worked. I polished the small brass lamp and the old-fashioned gyro mounts until they gleamed. I set the autowash going in the head and I even scrubbed out the galley. I also cleaned round the game of Patience spread out on the chart table.

By midday I was beginning to slow. I yawned more and drank less. I no longer jumped every time something brushed against my skin. Thoughts began to settle into the silt which passed for a brain. Now I could sieve them.

Byron had only moved one card, as far as I could see, but the move changed the possibilities. What I had seen when I came back this morning had also changed everything. The woman talking to Morgan.

I didn't know her name, though I knew what she had once been called. I hadn't recognised her face: I'd never seen it before. Daisy said I was good at faces but that wasn't what she really meant. She'd meant I looked at people. Not just faces. And though the woman's face had changed, she hadn't altered her gestures or the way she walked or the way she confronted Morgan. Like Family, not courtier.

People look different on screen. And that's where I'd first seen her: on the newsvid I'd watched ten days ago. When they'd run an obit I was too tired to switch off, and shown a retro of her life. Camille Vinci. Morgan's cousin. Milo's cousin. Not dead. Just a new face.

I called Tom Lee. Byron could have answered my question faster, but it would have led to explanations I didn't want to give, pointed him down a road I wanted to explore first. I wanted to be the one to find out who'd killed Jon and Blue Eyes and Sheba.

"Tom Lee's."

Advertising screen. Voiceover. One of the servers. Couldn't tell who.

"Humility. Will he take a call?"

I waited. Three minutes. Better than I'd hoped. His face came on-screen. Background blank. He could be any-where in the city.

"You more trouble than the peeps."

He didn't sound angry but then I'd never seen him show much emotion of any sort.

"Thanks for listening. Two things. One: I owe you for Luna."

"It's on your account. She'll do. What's the other thing?"

"Check your files for me? Vinci Family type, name of Camille?"

"Why? She died." No need for him to look up anything about a Family with local connections. That information was always on-line.

"You sure?"

A twitch which might have been the start of a frown narrowed his eyes. I didn't see the movement which called up the file but I saw his glance slide down as though reading from the foot of his screen.

"Yeah. Dead."

"Thanks. That's what I thought."

No one ever said Tom Lee was a fool. "Your place got Family trouble?"

"Maybe. Did Steven make contact?"

"Yeah. Sounded a good deal. You saying it's not?"

"I'm saying keep it on hold. Did you hear about Sheba?"

"I heard. Sorry for Daisy. And you. The killing connected?"

I didn't doubt his regret was real. It didn't cost him. What mattered, though, was the question. "Looks like it may be."

"Thanks. We're even for Luna."

The screen blanked.

I stared at it for a while, reflecting that it might be a while yet before I had Tom Lee's cooking on my doorstep. Then I thought about what he'd confirmed.

Camille, who was alive, showed up dead. Jon, who was dead, showed alive. I'd been wrong when I'd thought Jon and Blue Eyes had been killed and butchered to conceal their IDs. I'd been looking at it from the wrong end. Now I had to turn it round.

Camille wasn't wearing Jon's ID, but someone was. And she was wearing the ID of some woman who didn't matter enough for anyone to report her Missing or check if her head-injured body was ever found. Some woman who wore a cheap gold necklace.

I was beginning to understand the why, now, as well as the how. From time to time some Family member would do something that made them a liability: an indiscretion, a drug habit that went too far, a weakness someone had learned how to exploit. That would normally be enough simply to ensure an expensive funeral and a poignant obituary.

But what if the person concerned also had skills – financial, technical, physical – that the Family still needed? It would be so convenient if they could arrange a change of ID that was far more than skin deep. That even the EuroGov and its central computer system would accept.

It wasn't the down following the boost which nauseated me: it was wondering how many nameless, head-injured corpses would never be found or identified.

Jon had handled the general post at the port. He'd have been a major link in the chain for the packages, sending them on to wherever, *whoever*, their final destination was. He must have opened one. Dropped it and damaged the contents, perhaps, and been afraid to send it on in that condition. Given me the lifebox to hide it. Known it was important, thought he could assure his future with black-mail. Well, he'd done that. Fool. I'd liked him but he'd always been more optimistic than the world justified.

I wondered how they'd contacted Blue Eyes. I doubted if I'd ever know. I guessed someone had recognised in him a man whose file could disappear without anyone asking questions and who would never question his luck in being offered a room with no rent to pay except checking a mail-drop and passing on a package from time to time. He'd also been scared enough for me to know he'd had some idea what the penalty might be for not doing what they asked.

I'd thought at first the Port contact had to be Gus. I'd *wanted* it to be Gus. There would have been a sort of symmetry in finding that Gus was the one who might bring down the whole project. It wasn't simply prejudice: no one would have questioned seeing him at any time in any part of the Port. He'd have enjoyed cutting through my ladder. Even if he'd been found with a dead body, he could have covered it with some story of a threat to Port security. And he was so keen to kiss the arse of anyone who ranked him that he'd have done whatever someone in the Family asked without a nanosecond's debate.

Because there had to be Family involvement. Morgan knew who Camille was, despite her new face, or he'd never have let her speak like she had. Milo must know, too. And although knowing she'd changed identity didn't mean they knew who had organised it or how, it did mean they knew an ID programme was running. Maybe they'd even used it more than once.

If it was a Family product, they could name their own price to anyone in any Family who needed to disappear but didn't particularly want to be wiped.

It was a pity, but I really didn't think it was Gus who did their dirty work here. I couldn't even convict him of cutting my ladder, not even of ordering the cutting. Gus didn't stoop to jobs like sorting the post.

The phone buzzed.

"Yes?" I hoped it was Daisy. Wanting to talk. Wanting not to be alone.

"Milo."

I turned from the window where I'd been looking across to the corner of Gus's office. Milo was grave, concerned. For once there was no laughter ready to lift his mouth into a smile. A single vertical line between his brows was the closest I'd seen to a frown on his face.

"Hi."

"Heard about the Port Officer's partner. She was a friend of yours?"

"Still is."

Daisy, not Sheba. I wouldn't insult a dead woman's memory by claiming a friendship she would never have given.

The frown deepened for a second, then cleared. "Of course. You've had a rough time lately. I'm sorry."

"Not your fault."

"No. But I feel involved."

I wasn't sure how I felt about that. *Involvement* was something to handle carefully. It wasn't the same as friendship. At least, not if I read him right.

I don't know how he read my silence. He hesitated before going on, "I called to ask you to come over here. Thought you might like company."

"Now?"

"Is that a no?"

I shook my head, confusing him even more. "No. Sorry. It's just I don't feel very social."

His smile understood. "I know. But I don't like to think of you being alone. And…"

"And?"

I'd reacted automatically to the hint of protection in his voice but I hate unfinished sentences.

He sighed. Admitting what he hadn't known how to say. "And we're going home tomorrow. The project's under control. Morgan's seen everything he wants and there's no reason to stay."

Of course I wasn't a reason. I wasn't the sort of fool who'd expect Milo to stay behind when his brother left. He probably had business of his own to deal with. *Plans.*

He frowned some more. "We should talk."

"We are talking."

"Not on the phone. Come over."

"Morgan there?"

"No. Everyone's out."

He was going to keep pestering. And what else did I have to do? Besides, Milo and I had unfinished business. I gave in.

"'Kay. Be over in twenty."

"I'll leave word to let you up."

52

He didn't leave word. He was waiting at the entryway.

"Humility."

Both my hands were in his, held with a care which said he remembered their condition, and he was searching my face, concern in his eyes. Then he let me go. His smile was gentle.

"Thank you for coming."

He escorted me inside without even pausing for the usual scans. We didn't speak as we rode up in the elevator until its doors opened at the floor which was his apartment. He'd told me Morgan had the floor above. I wondered whether Camille had special accommodation or if she roughed it with only a couple of rooms to herself like the other courtiers. I couldn't bring myself to feel much concern.

"Sit down. I'll get you a drink."

"Thanks."

It was something to hold, though there was still enough boost buzzing in my system to make me cautious. I cupped the fragile glass in both hands – it was cool against still-sore palms – but didn't drink.

"How's Daisy?"

"I don't know. How do you feel when someone's killed your partner and your unborn child?"

"It was a killing, then? Not an accident?"

I was almost surprised. Forgetting he didn't know about the other deaths. I shook my head. "No. Not an accident."

At least he didn't offer platitudes about the peeps finding the killer soon. They had no leads, no suspects. If Daisy knew anything she wouldn't confide in the peeps anyway. She'd prefer to deal direct rather than trust a company which could always be bought. And what she would want to do to the perp wasn't in any lawtext. I'd help her if I could. I shook my head, stared down into the pale gold liquid in my glass. Looked back up.

"Let's not talk about it. Tell me about going back to your Estate."

He grimaced. "Morgan's decided he's seen enough. That means we all follow him back to base."

"Even you?"

"Even me. I'm on his staff. Even if I don't do anything. That's what I wanted to talk to you about."

"Me? I'm not in a position to offer you a job."

He looked startled. Laughed. Knew I had to be joking to suggest he might have any wish to stay here. "No. But you could come with me."

My turn for shock. "*Me?*"

He laughed again. Then came and crouched in front of where I was sitting. His eyes were a soft brown. His lashes were long and thick. His skin was clear. If he'd ever had a hangover or a high it hadn't left any marks on him. I wondered how old he was. He didn't touch me. Except with his voice.

"You. Why not? We could be good together."

It would have been easier if he had touched me.

"But what would I do?"

"Whatever you wanted." Now he did reach out, a hand gentle on my cheek. "You'll come?"

It was a question. Just.

"What about the *Pig*?"

He hadn't thought about it. Had to concentrate to remember what I was talking about. Spread his hands as though problems like that were trivial to Family. They probably were.

"Keep the boat here. You could come down whenever you wanted. Or I'm sure Morgan would love to share one of his racers with you."

"I'm not."

He straightened, his smile rueful. "You may be right. I'd just have to give you your own."

"Milo…"

"Don't say anything yet. Finish your drink. Think about it. I'll be back in a couple of minutes."

He went through a door into a room I'd not seen, which I guessed was some sort of office or comcentre, since there were no obvious screens in here. Though what the cabinets disguised was impossible to tell. I stood up, went over to look more closely at a heavy antique bureau.

I didn't really see the ornate carving which garlanded it though my fingers traced its outline. I was thinking of what Milo offered. I guessed it was the difference which drew him: he'd developed a taste for something which seemed exotic but was only unusual. He wasn't suggesting a partnership or any sort of contract, but what did I have to lose? I could turn over all I knew or suspected about the ID scam to Byron and disappear with Milo. If I could just forget that he had a cousin called Camille.

Roll the dice, girl.

And take a chance. Jack had died taking a chance. The chance that his worn-out heart would keep going long enough for him to win enough money to buy another.

I turned back to the room. Picked up and put down again the litter of ornaments on a small table. Most were silver; one was a box, wood inlaid with shell. The nacre gleamed with shifting subtlety.

The box had no obvious opening. Intrigued enough to let the smaller puzzle displace the larger, I put my glass down on the table and turned the box in both hands, seeking its catch. It was old. Far too early to have a digital or sonic key. There must be a trick to it.

A bar of inlay shifted. Another. Yes, they had to be moved in sequence, I saw, then one of the ends, not the more obvious top, slid free to expose a small drawer. I pulled on the tiny turned handle.

Inside: a lifebox. Like mine. And unlike. This one was whole, undamaged. With an ID chip inside, gleaming in its secret nest.

When I could bring myself to touch it with one finger, I imagined I could feel the pulse of a life inside it.

Whose?

"It's not your friend's partner."

I turned. Still holding the inlaid box. "No. I checked. She was still …"

"Intact?"

"Yes."

Milo walked over. Took the box from me. Closed it. Set it back on the polished table. Saw my full glass there and gave it back to me.

"You haven't tasted the wine. You should."

"Why? What have you put in it?"

Give strong drink unto him that is ready to perish.

He hadn't changed. He hadn't gone into the other room and come out a monster. He still looked at me with what I had to believe was affection. The thread of amusement was still in his voice, inviting me to share a joke against the system, his eyes were still gentle, warm. Perhaps there was a trace of regret in his face but I might have been imagining things. There was none in his voice.

"Nothing much. Just a relaxant."

"I'm relaxed."

"I don't think so."

"So tell me a relaxing story. Like how you got involved in all this."

"Involved?" He was hurt. "I *devised* it."

I should have known. In a way I had known. I just hadn't wanted to know. The mind's not a machine – though Byron's might be. It can believe two contradictory things at once. It can know a man is a killer, however indirectly, yet believe the opposite. I'm not fool enough to believe that love, or any of its near-neighbours, is an absolute, but it makes me willing to offer the benefit of the doubt. Until proved wrong.

"You devised the scam? Or the technology to do it?"

"Both. I suppose you want me to tell you all about it?"

"It's the tradition, isn't it?"

I tried to look around without being obvious. I didn't give a damn about tradition but I didn't fancy my chances unless I could get to the door without his intercept. There had to be an emergency exit which didn't involve a tech device. Those, I was sure, he could control.

"By all means let us comply with tradition. But first…"

I didn't see what signal he gave, but the door slid open to allow me to see the tekkie. The one who worked block security. The one who had taken Jon's job, which had handled the general post. What else had I expected? He said nothing, but his eyes gloated. On his hip was a sheath: the knife's handle was black This tekkie had handled more than packages. Milo nodded at him.

"Wait outside."

The tekkie stepped back. Let the door slide shut. Milo's message was delivered. Any violence he considered necessary wouldn't come directly from him.

He was watching me with mild curiosity. "How did you know it was me?"

"I didn't. Not until just now when I found that box. I'd thought it might be someone else not even here, or possibly Morgan."

"*Morgan.*" It was a sneer. "He doesn't know about anything except boats. He doesn't even know why Camille had her face changed. Do you know about Camille?"

I wished it had been Morgan who had smiled at me and taken me out for a luxury meal. At least we had something in common.

"I saw her obit on a vidcast. Saw her arguing with Morgan this morning."

"You *recognised* her? I wondered if you were cleverer than you look. She had to disappear because she was caught up in a messy affair with a member of a Family which didn't like the association. But we couldn't afford to lose her business acumen. She's been running the Family's finances since she was seventeen. A mind like a computer with the sexual discrimination of a rabbit and no discretion at all."

"So you arranged a new ID."

"That's it. There's no risk in it. Once I've got the new ID it doesn't have to be reimplanted. The trick is to lift the old codes from the one you want wiped and retune it. That's the technology I developed."

I was working it out. Trying to understand the implications. A part of me was also wondering if there'd ever been any feeling for me but contempt beneath the easy charm.

"But if you can do that, no one need die! Surely you could just make a copy?"

He looked pleased by my quickness. "Of course. But that would leave two people with the same ID. And the anomaly would be bound to show up sooner or later. Logical to delete the donor."

I'd been wrong: it was Milo, not Byron, who thought like a machine. Logic translated into Jon's bound and disfigured corpse. Blue Eyes' sightless eyes staring at me. I swallowed. Tried to equal his indifference.

"That why you chose people like Jon?"

"Which Jon? Doesn't matter. Donors are people no one would miss. Nothings. The IDs will achieve more in their new hosts than the originals could ever have imagined."

Except that ID chips weren't sentient. The *donors* had been.

"How many IDs have you transplanted?"

"Not many yet. Half a dozen. It's important to stay exclusive, and I charge megacredits for the service. Nor am I easy to locate. Even my Family don't know just who they paid for Camille's new name."

He liked that. The secret pleasure of knowing more than anyone else. He'd said he liked planning. I remembered thinking on Em's boat that they'd no idea how far a Family member would go to complete a job. I should have listened to myself. Had he also liked the killings, the vicarious thrill of dealing random death to people who would never know he existed? Or why they died? I remembered what he'd said about the boredom of a safe Estate life. Had Jon died because Milo was bored?

"And now you're going to get rid of me. What made you decide?"

He took a sip from his own glass. "I saw the lifebox on your boat. In the drawer, when you put the cards away. I'd already heard you were asking questions about the dead man, had been over to where he lived. Knew you might put it all together eventually."

Might. Not would.

"There was a chip in there too. A woman's, if the jewellery with it is a clue. Do you know whose?"

He smiled as though I'd given him the solution to a small but irritating puzzle.

"It must have been Camille's. It took me two months to find another. The one you have would be the first one I requisitioned. The contact here claimed it had never reached him, been misfiled somewhere. I realised he was lying, of course, and knew it when he threatened me. He'd guessed some of what was happening. And now you have it."

He was pleased.

He'd answered the question I hadn't thought to ask: who was the chip *for*? I'd meant: who was it *from*? But for him that was a meaningless question. *Donors* had no independent existence. I wondered again if he'd felt as little for me. Something, conceit probably, still made it hard to accept.

"So you took me out to dinner and arranged for an accident when we got back?" He hadn't been ordering wine when we'd stopped here. He'd been ordering my death. *You should be dead,* he'd said the morning after I'd gone into the water. He'd meant it. I'd taken the horror and revulsion to be at his own helplessness to prevent my near-drowning. But it had been fury at the failure of his plan.

And not for the first time: now I knew who Milo had been calling on his wrist link, whose voice I had heard telling someone to "Let her go!" as I scrabbled through the mud. He hadn't want the enquiries a gunshot would have brought down on the Port. "So who cut the ladder?"

"You've met him." Of course. The tekkie who was standing outside the door. He had others to help him out when there was a chance I might see his face, like down at the scrapyards, but he was the main muscle here. And at the flats? I'd only ever seen that man in the dark – but he'd had the knife.

Milo still had that reasonable smile on his face. "I gave you the chance to stay here."

Which I'd almost taken.

"Are you going to recycle *my* ID?"

He pursed his lips, shook his head. "I'd like to, but you know too many people. Someone would notice when you showed up alive in the records but no one could trace you. A pity."

It wasn't going to stop him killing me. Or ordering in his thug to do it. I jerked my thumb at the door. "Did he kill the man whose job he took?"

The soft smile congratulated me. "That's it. I told you, the other one asked questions. Besides, he didn't want to do the wet work. When I insisted he tried to threaten the Family. *Me*. He had to be replaced. This one likes his work."

I believed him. It was probably the thug who'd found Blue Eyes: middleman and potential donor in one.

I imagined they'd once moved in the same circles.

"What about the northshore flats? Did he set the fire?"

An expression which might have been irritation chased itself across his face. "He was going to clean out the room, but the peeps got there first. It was the only way to be sure no one got too curious. Inconvenient."

"And the girl?"

"What girl?"

"A blader. Ran a few messages for you. Got beat up, nearly got burned."

He shrugged. "We weren't using the flats any more. She was redundant, might be getting close to you. He warned her off. Didn't kill her."

He sounded as though he expected congratulations. If he'd needed a female ID just then, I wouldn't have given odds on Luna's survival chances.

"Nearly did. He enjoys his work too much." I swallowed. "So what happens next?"

"I invite him in." He gestured towards the door. "And he takes you away. As you said, he enjoys his work."

I wondered where, *if*, my body would be found. That hint of regret was still in his face. He didn't hate me for my interference. I doubted if he felt anything strongly. I understood the thug better than I understood Milo. At least the thug got real pleasure from his work. Milo's pleasures were all in his mind. He would pore over his secrets like a miser with his gold, intent only on accumulating more.

I needed time. Time to find a way out. Time to think of some way past the security thug. Not the window. The room was climate-controlled, the windows armoured and sealed. Get past and into his office and send a signal? Who did I think I was? I couldn't break into his system if he gave me all day and all night to try. He'd just lock the door and gas the room.

I wished I'd told Byron what I'd seen. Wished he was here, wished *anyone* was here. Knew no one was coming. *Keep him talking.* Jack's advice. Pathetic. I couldn't think of anything better.

"They'll know I was last seen up here. And that you were the only one in the building. The vids will show you meeting me."

He laughed. Pleased with himself. "Why do you think I came to meet you? Walked you through without a scan? The vids were looping. They'll show an empty hall for all that time. I wasn't there. You weren't there. You were never here. Go on, drink your wine. It'll make it much easier."

"Who for?"

"Everyone."

I watched the pleased smile begin to touch his mouth as I lifted the glass. Then I threw it at him.

Evil communications corrupt good manners.

It shattered in his face. For a moment he was blind. He lifted a hand in shock, wiping his mouth and eyes, staring when he saw his fingers stained red. He hadn't felt the cuts till then. Now he did. Something lit his eyes - fear? rage? disbelief?

"You hurt me!"

"Good."

I was backing from him, towards the door. He still stared. No one had ever hurt him before. I wondered if he had ever seen real blood, drawn in violence. Then his face twisted and he reached for me.

I ducked. Slid away. Hoped I was right to think the door would be unlocked so his thug could get in. It was my only way out. Past the thug. He had the knife and he would be stronger than me but with that belly he couldn't be faster. And he lacked my motivation.

"You're going to die!"

Milo was looking forward to it. He'd stopped trying to grab me himself and was laughing as the door slid open before I could reach it. I dived low to get under the thug's reach. Hitting him before his hand even reached the sheath.

His belly was soft and I took him by surprise. His breath left him in sort of *woof*!

Of course I hadn't done more than set him back a little. He outweighed me and his reach was longer. If he'd got hold of me I wouldn't have had a chance. But I didn't give him time to regroup, and life at sea has made me stronger than I look. Besides, he wasn't used to victims who fought back.

Perhaps it was the memory of some of those victims which lent power and accuracy to the kick I aimed just below his gut. That and the thought that any moment Milo could get me from behind. When the thug doubled up with a high-pitched squeal of agony, I was past him and heading for the stairs.

53

I ran into them as I reached the outer door: Byron and Morgan, with Gus just behind.

"Where is he?"

I registered that it was the first time Morgan had bothered to speak to me while I drew two necessary breaths and pointed to the stairs. "In his rooms."

He brushed past me, making for the elevator, followed by Gus. Byron paused.

"You all right?"

"Fine. You'd better go with them. The thug's there, too."

He didn't ask who the thug was. He went. I followed more slowly.

It was over before I was back outside the apartment. Good. The thug was still curled up from my kick, now also cuffed and tranked and on the floor, heavy-eyed and silent. I wondered if he'd been grateful for the trank-shot. Stepped carefully round him. Gus stared down at the captive and then up at me, his face a mix of incomprehension and anger – and fear brought on by finding himself in the middle of a Family dispute. He turned on me. Naturally.

"You've some explaining to do!"

"Not to you."

I let him gobble incoherently and looked over at Byron who had just come out of the room I had no intention of re-entering. "Is he in there?"

Byron moved aside so I could look past him.

Milo was standing alone in the centre of the room. His

hands hung limp at his sides, his face was streaked with blood from three or four superficial cuts which he no longer bothered trying to wipe away. He looked as though someone had disconnected his power supply. Morgan had gone past him into the far room where, I assumed without much interest, Milo had kept his records and equipment. I stepped away, back into the corridor. Waited until the brother came back out.

Morgan forced himself to look at me. "I regret what has happened. Please call on my Family for anything you may need."

He hated saying it. But he meant it.

Gus said nothing. I watched Morgan walk away towards the elevator, watched Gus follow him, cringing and apologising. I doubt if Morgan heard a word. Byron waited till they had gone. Waited till silent security teks had arrived to take Milo and the thug.

"You OK?"

He meant it differently this time. He was the only one who'd asked. I saw no point in lying.

"No."

He thought about it. Nodded. May even have understood.

"I'll give you a hand back to your boat."

I didn't need a hand. Didn't want to be touched. But I didn't want to be alone either so I let him walk with me.

We'd taken a couple of steps before I remembered.

"There's an inlaid box in there. There's someone else in it. I don't know who."

"We'll find out."

He left me long enough to go back in and pick it up.

54

"What happens now?"

We were back on the *Pig*. The box was on the chart table.

"We have a drink?"

I thought of the golden liquid I'd thrown in Milo's face. The pink smears which had run down his cheeks. Shook my head.

"There's a bottle open if you want some, nothing for me."

"Caf?"

I let him make it.

The night wasn't cold but I pulled a blanket round my shoulders and cupped the mug in both hands and breathed in its steam. Looked up at last to find him watching me.

"Well?"

"You still want to know what we do now?"

"It might help."

"Morgan will have to tell the rest of the Family. The tekkie will probably disappear."

That didn't disturb me. "And Milo?"

A half-shrug. "They can't cover it. Too many people know. Camille's retina prints will confirm the ID exchange and the rest of the Family will fall over themselves to guarantee Milo's custody. What they do then will be their problem."

It tasted sour but what else had I expected? He was right about Morgan. I recalled his expression of sick horror, just before he'd left, when he'd looked back into the room at the man who'd been his charming and ineffectual little brother. He hadn't been able to speak to him.

When I didn't comment, Byron went on, "I doubt if Morgan will have any wish to cover things once he knows everything - which I assume *you* will eventually tell me."

"How much do you already know?" I asked.

A wry expression touched his mouth. "Not as much as I should, obviously. When you claimed to recognise Jon, I thought you were wrong but refusing to admit it, despite the evidence."

"You shouldn't always believe what you see on the screen," I told him with some satisfaction.

"Clearly. So when you began to produce more inconsistencies, I began to believe there really was something going on besides the sabotage. It had to be Family…"

"Why?" It had taken me long enough to work that out.

"No one else really profited. And anyone else would have stopped once Family visited – the sort of security they carry around tends to discourage petty crime."

"True enough. So what did you do?"

"Talked to Morgan."

"Why him? If it was Family trouble he could have been behind it."

He nodded. "Possibly. But, since he was the one who sent me down here to look into things originally, I thought it unlikely."

"And what did Morgan have to tell you? I don't imagine Family members are in any hurry to cast suspicion on each other. Not to outsiders, at least." All my cynicism about Family had come back in the last few hours.

"As little as possible at first. What would you expect?" So I wasn't the only cynic here. "I had to do some hard digging." And he wasn't used to that sort of labour.

"Like you did with Pete over on the spoil heaps?"

He grimaced. Didn't ask how I'd known. "Easier on my shoes. I had to throw that pair out. I assume you got more from him than I did?"

"Perhaps."

"You didn't think it worth telling me?" He didn't quite remind me that we'd had an agreement.

"You were out." And then it became too personal. But I didn't feel like defending myself. "So what else did you do?"

"Checked the records of the northshore apartments and discovered that not only had an unknown man been killed in the apartment registered to Jon, but that another Company employee had a room on the same floor. The one you emasculated tonight."

The red light on the vid above the door opposite. The figure watching from a window. The man with the knife he'd lent Blue Eyes, knowing he could take it back any time without breaking sweat. The strength of Milo's suspicions, the attack on me, made more sense. So did the tekkie's growing hostility. It even explained where Jon's furniture had gone and how someone had known Jon wouldn't be coming back to use his room. Perhaps I should have talked with Byron earlier.

"You learn anything else?"

"I ran a few checks on his income. No surprise to find he had a second source. I *was* surprised when I found its size – and how difficult it was to trace."

"But you managed."

It wasn't a question, but he still looked offended. "Of course. That was when I knew I had to talk to Morgan again. If Milo was paying off someone in the Port, he could be behind the sabotage and might be involved in something worse. And then there was the ID."

"Which ID?" There were far too many around.

"The one I found in your drawer while I was waiting for you. Since you'd already shown me a lifebox, I was naturally interested. Morgan eventually admitted that his Family had Camille's ID changed. Didn't know how it had been done – didn't *want* to know, I'd guess. But he agreed we needed to talk to Milo. We didn't know you'd got there first."

"Intuition works as fast as technology sometimes." No reason to tell him I hadn't known about Milo when I'd gone to his room.

"No wonder you and tech don't get on. Your logic is irrational to most systems."

And to him.

"I suppose you think in binary?"

"Near enough. But Daisy was right about you reading people. Look at the way you sorted the sabotage."

"I didn't do so well with Milo." It wasn't a misjudgement I'd easily forget.

"A slip. You won't do it again."

"Don't rely on it. I'm not a machine. I go on making mistakes."

"At least you solved the puzzle." Was that what it had been to him: a puzzle to be solved? Not for me. It wasn't a game of cards. He was watching me. *Reading* me. "Think of the lives you've saved."

"The technology exists. How long before someone else works it out and the whole filthy business starts up again? How long before anyone notices?"

"It won't happen quickly. Whatever his personality

defects, Milo's work was brilliant. But there's no reason I can't let a little gossip circulate as backup. Convenient deaths of prominent citizens won't be accepted so easily in future."

"How can anyone check?"

"The Families are devious enough. They'll find a way. And it might be helpful to feed a little deterrent into the system by creating rumours that ID retuning has some nasty long-term side-effects."

Families weren't the only devious ones.

"So that's it? Case closed?"

Anti-climax. Where was the shoot-out? Where was the retribution? Where was the justice? Jon was still dead and so were the others.

Byron's mouth twisted. "That's it. All you have to do is decide what reward you want from the Vincis."

"Reward? For nearly getting killed by one of them?" For being tempted to feel something real for one of them?

"They'll want to do something. They'll probably insist. Families hate debts. Why not take whatever they offer? They can afford it."

But could I afford to take it? Perhaps it was the only way to free myself completely from them. "I'll think about it."

I'd take enough to give Luna a safety net. Enough to restore my credit to what it had been when I'd done the deal with Tom Lee. No more. Except…

"They might offer you a job."

I nearly laughed, and felt better. Yes, they would expect me to want a secure job, be grateful for one. I thought of the courtiers hovering round Morgan and shuddered.

"I'd rather sign on with the Flying Dutchman. But I'd take a permanent berth for the *Pig* if they offered it." Gus would hate that. I was beginning to feel better.

"I'm sure it can be arranged."

So was I. I straightened, shrugged off the blanket, asked what his plans were.

"Another talk with Morgan. Bed. Home."

"Away from boats?"

"As far as I can get."

Somewhere where all the corruption was in the matrix, where fights were cerebral, not physical.

"Good luck."

"Thanks." A pause. He stood then, reluctantly, added: "I owe you for what you did here."

"Most of it wasn't the sort of thing which shows up on screens." The screens which had lied about Jon, about Camille, about the others.

"I suppose not. By the way, I've left a note on yours. You can call me if you find more trouble."

"You expect me to?"

"As sparks fly upward."

He was better educated than I'd guessed.

"Just don't expect me to solve *your* problems again. I'm going to finish cleaning up the *Pig* and then go sailing. Or possibly just go sailing."

I could see him trying not to look appalled. Grinned. Lifted a hand as he left, taking the inlaid box with him. For a 'crat he wasn't as inhuman as I'd thought.

He'd left the marina before I checked the note on my monitor. He'd given me a contact number for him. I didn't think I'd be using it. Then, as an afterthought, I called up the boat's title record.

Vessel: *The Flying Pig*

L.o.a.: 20 metres

Built : 1985

Last Owner: Jack Fane. Deceased.

I was listed as the current owner. As from today's date. It seemed Morgan wasn't the only one who liked to pay his debts. I had no intention of asking how he'd done it.

55

Solving the problem of Jon's death, outguessing Byron and gaining title to my own home, all at the same time, made a heady fix. For some time after Byron had gone I sat with my feet up and a growing sense of satisfaction inside. Through luck and coincidence and pig-headedness I had unearthed and untangled something he had barely begun to touch. I was entitled to congratulate myself. I was entitled to a drink and perhaps some sort of celebration.

Then dissatisfaction crept in.

I was angry with myself for not having asked Milo about Sheba when he was in the explaining mood. Perhaps Byron could find out for me. The only person I wanted to celebrate with, the only one to whom I could tell the whole story, was Daisy. And that was hardly possible at the moment. Or was it? She'd want to know the killer was caught.

I was restless but reluctant to call her. When I did there was no answer. Unsurprising. I didn't like to go over without an invite. She'd made it clear enough she wanted to be alone and however unwise that seemed to me I had to respect her wishes. And I did not really want to go back to those bright little rooms where Sheba was still present in every carefully worked cushion, every carefully placed ornament.

I called Tom Lee. Left a message that Jon's file was deleted. That Camille's might be updated.

Then I went over to the unfinished card game, began

fiddling.

The card Byron had moved was the jack of clubs. With that out of place, or rather slotted into its right place, I could see the remaining pattern more clearly. I moved a card. Thinking.

With the remote clarity of sleeplessness I stared down at the game. Not many possible moves left. It was going to work out. I moved the last card. Looked down at the flawless sequence.

Then I went to see Daisy.

56

Security recognised me from that morning and let me up with only a token argument. He didn't call ahead. But then I didn't give him much time, walking past him with only a minimal pause at the scanner and heading for the elevator.

I pressed the button beside the grey door. The one which would call Daisy, would show her who was waiting outside to remind her of a world which went on without Sheba in it. I expected her to ignore its summons but discovered I wasn't surprised when I heard the locks begin their sequence. No one invited me, she'd used her remote, but I pushed the door and walked in.

A thin film seemed to have settled on the rooms. Not dust. Not yet. It was too soon for neglect to show. It was more that something had dulled, as though the colours had begun to fade. I didn't see Daisy.

She came out of the bedroom behind me. I turned.

"Daisy."

"Humility."

Her voice sounded the same as it always had. She didn't look different. But there was something missing, an indefinable absence. I thought that whatever had held her together from the inside had gone and only a deliberate care kept her intact. She was wearing Company greys as though she had dressed for work and then not known what to do. No earring.

"Sit down. I'll get you caf."

I sat down. "No. Nothing to drink thanks. How are you

doing?"

She shook her head. "I don't know. I feel…"

Numb. Nothing. Afraid of the time when feeling would come back and she would know the pain of the amputation. She sat in the chair Sheba had always used.

"Have the peeps been in touch? Told you what they're doing?"

A glint of the familiar Daisy showed. "What do you think?"

"Sorry. Stupid question. Is there anything I can do for you? Contact anyone? Make arrangements?"

I knew less than she did about what had to be done. Could only guess they would not let her bury Sheba until the file was closed. It was just the usual reaction of wanting something concrete to do, of hating to feel helpless. Daisy's half-smile made me feel worse. It was too understanding.

"No. There's nothing anyone can do. But I'm glad you came." Meaningless politeness was unlike her. It left me unsure if I was talking to Daisy or Sheba. I was glad when the front cracked for a second. "I just wish it was over!"

"It is."

She stared. "What are you talking about? It's not over. It'll never be over."

The last words were spoken to herself. I went to her, knelt by her chair. Put a hand on hers. She stiffened. Didn't want to be touched. Withdrew her hand from mine. I stayed where I was if only because there I didn't have to look into her face.

"The killer's found. Jon's killer."

A flicker of interest. "I thought it wasn't him? Isn't he still alive?"

I began to explain the ID copying. At first she was barely interested but by the time I reached the point where Milo had invited me back to his room she was really listening.

"You and Milo? Just what have you got yourself into, Humility?"

"A mess. But it's sorted now. Even your sabotage."

"That was Milo? Why would he want to do that?"

"He didn't. The last thing he wanted was Family attention on the Port. He'd been using Midway as a source of supply just *because* it was such a minor holding. He was relying on no one in the Family giving the place any thought. When it started losing money, looking as though the development might fold and Morgan was taking a personal interest, he had to come down with him to see how far his own pet project was at risk. He didn't know Morgan had already sent Byron in."

"So there was no sabotage?"

"Not exactly. I said I wouldn't tell you but I can't see what harm it will do now. Em and Clim and the others were your problem."

As I explained, the ghost of old laughter touched her face and she leaned back in the chair, letting a few of the muscles she had held so rigid begin to relax.

"So it's all over now? Finished?"

She looked sleepy. I wanted to say yes. Leave it there.

"Not quite. There's still Sheba."

Her reaction was just a fraction slow. "Sheba? But surely, Milo…"

I shook my head. "It's what the peeps will put in their files. It'll go down as the official story. But it's not true, is it?"

"What do you mean?"

It was as though we had to go through the ritual denial before she could let the truth be told. I didn't mind. I still wanted to be wrong. I may even have wanted to go through it again for myself. Find the flaw in my own reasoning. *Hope deferred maketh the heart sick.*

"At first I assumed the tekkie had killed her, like he had killed the others, and that something had stopped him before he could take the ID."

"And then?"

"And then I remembered talking to him that afternoon. About the time she must have died. He told me you weren't in the office."

She ignored that. "What about Milo himself? Couldn't he have done it?"

"When did you ever know a Family member go off on his own with no one even noticing his absence? Besides, Milo isn't that sort of killer."

He thought of his victims as donors whose chips were more alive than they were. When he'd seen the reality of my near-death in the river, he'd been horrified as well as excited. And he couldn't take the sight of blood.

Daisy didn't argue. Didn't try to convince me my reasoning was wrong. I hadn't expected her to but that hadn't stopped me hoping.

"Will you tell me about it? Tell me what happened to make you do it? It was something to do with that last test she took, wasn't it?"

For the first time since I had begun to speak, she met my eyes and I looked into hell. It took her three tries before she could shape the words.

"I went home early. It wasn't enough to hear her news on the vid; I wanted to be *with* her. To celebrate."

I heard the irony in her voice. Winced. Knowing wasn't the same as hearing the words which made it true. She took a breath. Went on.

"I was waiting for her when she came in. I knew at once something wasn't right. She insisted on making a meal, giving me a drink. It took me almost an hour to make her tell me."

"Tell you what?"

"That the child, our *daughter*, wasn't perfect after all. There was a DNA flaw. She would never be more than a child, however long she lived. No! Don't touch me, Humility, or I won't be able to say it. Sheba told me that the … the *baby* … could still be ours, we would still love her, no one could make us terminate."

In the Community they would have done. I tried to keep my voice as soft as possible.

"What did you say?"

"What could I say? I reminded her of the plans we'd made. Of how irresponsible it was to replicate faulty genes. How we might be able to try again. How impossible it was to let the pregnancy go on. How *wrong*."

"She didn't want to terminate?"

"She said she wouldn't." She stared at me with eyes so dry they looked scorched. "Did she think I *wanted* it to end like that? Did she think I didn't care?"

"Of course not. She loved you."

"And I loved her! I didn't mean her any harm. I only meant … I don't know what I meant. I remember shaking her because she wouldn't *listen*. Then she fell…"

"She hit her head?"

"I think so. I don't think I hit her. I wouldn't have hit her, Humility, would I? Not Sheba?"

Neither of us would ever know.

"Of course you wouldn't." I had her hands in mine now. I don't think she noticed.

"But I'm still a killer. Like Milo. Like that tekkie."

"*No!* Perhaps you killed, perhaps you did no more than cause an accident, but you're not a killer. No one else is going to die because of what happened here. Sheba's not hurting any more: you're the only one who's still suffering because of what you did."

Her hands were cold and still in mine. "So what happens now?"

It was a child's question in a voice I'd never heard her use. The same question I had asked Byron. I had no easy answer for her.

"Life goes on. You bury Sheba, you take a while away from work, then you come back to the Port and run our lives again and think of a way of getting even with Em and Clim and the others and another of stopping Tom Lee setting up shop in the new facility."

I'd hoped for a flicker of anger. Nothing.

"I'm sorry. None of it seems real any more."

"Of course it doesn't. You should eat something. Sleep if you can."

She let me prepare a meal and pushed it around her plate. She let me urge her into a bath and then into bed. I'd changed the bedding. Wished there was a spare bed so that she need not lie where Sheba had lain. Tried to make her come back with me to the *Pig*. Failed.

"Don't worry about me. I'll be all right."

Neither of us believed it. I waited there all night, unsleeping in the too-soft chair, and in the morning she insisted that I leave her. She said she had things to organise.

Things she wanted to do on her own. So I left her. I went home and when I saw the cards on the table I was sick. Then I swept them on to the deck and cried.

And then I got drunk.

57

I was wrong. There was another death.

Byron disturbed my hangover midway through the next morning. He came on board without permission, still wearing his unsuitable shoes, took one look at me and brought me water and a tab I didn't even try to identify. It didn't bring me the oblivion I wanted but it dulled the pain enough for me to speak.

"What do you want?"

I hadn't given him any thought since I'd come back from seeing Daisy. I'd assumed he'd left.

"I'm sorry." He wasn't apologising for anything he had done. It was for what he was about to do. I sat up. Knew what he was going to say. "It's your friend, the Port Officer. Daisy."

"What's happened?"

"She left a time-delayed call with security. When they went up it was already far too late."

"She killed herself?" I don't know why I was asking, why I hadn't known it would happen.

"Yes. No note. But there's no doubt either. Not with what happened to her partner."

So she'd taken the truth with her. Or left it to me to tell. But I wouldn't. It didn't matter much if the tekkie got the blame: he was accountable enough for other killings which might never be exposed. Byron was watching me. To see if I would cry? I wouldn't.

"Did you know the partner well?"

"Sheba? No. Not well. I doubt if many did. She was a martha."

I hadn't meant to puzzle him but if I could have felt anything I might have enjoyed the frown which wrinkled the smooth forehead – if only for a couple of nanoseconds, while he recalled my background and processed the word. I could almost see the circuits burning.

"A fem?"

"Yes." Fem/martha. Someone so dedicated to her role as homemaker that she seldom went outside. Needed no one but her partner. In joining her, Daisy had done the only thing she could to make amends.

"At least she knew you'd discovered the killer."

I just looked at him.

"You did go over there yesterday?"

"Yes."

"So she knew?"

"Yes. She knew."

He didn't say anything else. Didn't try to offer any comfort. And when he left I still didn't know exactly what he'd meant.

I sat there for a long time and thought of my friend. Wondered if she'd still be alive if I hadn't faced her with what I'd guessed. Cursed myself for not staying longer. Not stopping her. Not stopping someone whose honesty had made her face herself as judge, who'd come to her own verdict and accepted her own penalty: a life for a life.

Like I'd always said: a better Puritan than me.

58

Five weeks later

I was on my way downriver listening with half an ear to the end of a vidcast:

The funeral took place today of Vinci Family member Milo whose sudden death was announced last week. In a trend-setting innovation the burial in the Family mausoleum was preceded by a ceremony in which representatives of all the Families paid their last respects, in person or via holoscan, before the open coffin.

It was a triumph of old-fashioned ceremonial over modern technology. Byron had been right: they'd found a way to check that reported deaths were accurate.

I blanked the screen and turned the wheel and pointed the *Pig* in the direction of the vineyards across the water.

Working Girls   Maureen Carter
ISBN: 0-9547634-0-8

Dumped in a park … throat slashed…. schoolgirl prostitute Michelle Lucas died in agony and terror.

The sight breaks the heart of Detective Sergeant Bev Morriss of West Midlands Police. She thought she was hardened, inured, but gazing at Michelle's pale, broken body she is consumed by a cold fury.

She knows this case is different – this is the one that will push her to the edge.

Plunging herself into the seedy heart of Birmingham's vice-land she struggles to infiltrate the deadly jungle of hookers, evil pimps and violent johns. But no one will co-operate, no one will break the wall of silence…

When a second victim dies, Bev knows time is running out. If she is to win the trust of the working girls – she has to take the biggest, most dangerous, gamble of her life – *out on the streets…*

No Peace for the Wicked   Adrian Magson
ISBN: 0-9547634-2-4

Old gangsters never die … they simply get rubbed out! But WHO is ordering the hits? And WHY?

Hard-nosed female investigative reporter Riley Gavin is tasked to find out. It's an assignment that follows a bloody trail from a windswept south coast seafront to the balmy intrigues of Spain's Costa Del Crime – and sparks off a chain of grisly murders.

As she digs, Riley uncovers a deadly web of vendettas, double crosses and hatred in an underworld that's at war with itself. The prize? Control of a faltering criminal empire.

But this is one story that soon gets too personal – as Riley discovers dark forces that will stop at nothing to silence her. Dodging bullets, attack dogs and psychotic thugs, she fights to unravel the threads of an evil conspiracy.

And suddenly facing a *deadline* takes on a whole new chilling meaning…

23/12/04